Jonas Wainwright Davenport was spying on her!

There was no other valid reason Carla could think of for his being parked on Main Street in Bedloe Falls on an icy December night.

The man's gall was monumental.

She shifted gears, slowly drove down to the corner, turned, then midway along the next block glanced into the rearview mirror again. She'd begun to think maybe she was imagining things, but she saw the burgundy car turning the corner, then carefully following her.

It just didn't make sense.

As she drove, Carla tried to conjure up a logical reason for Jonas Davenport to be behaving this way. Could it be the first time in his entire born-wealthy life that someone had ever denied him a request?

If so, she could only say that by now he had it coming.

Dear Reader,

This month Silhouette **Special Edition** brings you the third (though not necessarily the last) volume of Lindsay McKenna's powerful **LOVE AND GLORY** miniseries, and we'd love to know if the *Return of a Hero* moves you as much as it did our Silhouette editors. Many of you write in requesting sequels or tie-in books—now we'd like to hear how you enjoyed our response!

Many of you also urge us to publish more books by your favorite Silhouette authors, and with this month's lively selection of novels by Jo Ann Algermissen, Carole Halston, Bevlyn Marshall, Natalie Bishop and Maggi Charles, we hope we've satisfied that craving, as well.

Each and every month our Silhouette **Special Edition** authors and editors strive to bring you the ultimate in satisfying romance reading. Although we cannot answer your every letter, we do take your comments and requests to heart. So, many thanks for your help—we hope you'll keep coming back to Silhouette **Special Edition** to savor the results!

From all the authors and editors of Silhouette **Special Edition**,

Warmest wishes,

Leslie Kazanjian, Senior Editor
Silhouette Books
300 East 42nd Street
New York, N.Y. 10017

MAGGI CHARLES
The Snow Image

Silhouette Special Edition

Published by Silhouette Books New York

America's Publisher of Contemporary Romance

For Alison,
whom I, of course,
think is the most beautiful, charming,
terrific seven-year-old girl
in the whole world

SILHOUETTE BOOKS
300 East 42nd St., New York, N.Y. 10017

Copyright © 1989 by Koehler Associates, Ltd.

ISBN: 0-373-09546-5

First Silhouette Books printing August 1989

Books by Maggi Charles

Silhouette Romance

Magic Crescendo #134

Silhouette Intimate Moments

Love's Other Language #90

Silhouette Special Edition

Love's Golden Shadow #23
Love's Tender Trial #45
The Mirror Image #158
That Special Sunday #258
Autumn Reckoning #269
Focus on Love #305
Yesterday's Tomorrow #336
Shadow on the Sun #362
The Star Seeker #381
Army Daughter #429
A Different Drummer #459
It Must Be Magic #479
Diamond Moods #497
A Man of Mystery #520
The Snow Image #546

MAGGI CHARLES

has had a varied writing career, contributing to government reports, public-relations releases, newspapers and magazines. Her nonfiction topics include gourmet food, travel, antiques and history. Primarily, however, she concentrates on her true love—romance fiction and mystery novels. Born and raised in New York City, she has lived for the past twenty years on Cape Cod with her writer husband. They have two sons and two grandchildren.

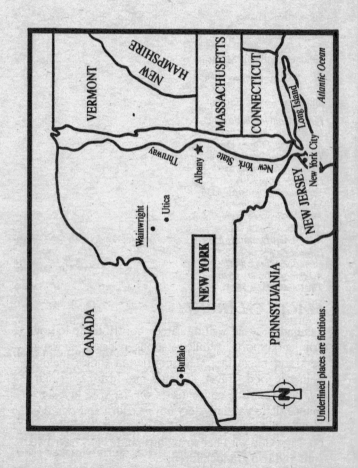

CANADA

Buffalo

NEW YORK

PENNSYLVANIA

Wainwright
Utica

VERMONT

NEW HAMPSHIRE

Thruway
Albany
New York State

MASSACHUSETTS

CONNECTICUT

NEW JERSEY
New York City
Long Island

Atlantic Ocean

Underlined places are fictitious.

Chapter One

Hot pursuit. In the middle of a snowstorm. The man was insane!

Carla risked diverting her attention from the treacherous road for a second and scowled into the rearview mirror. She saw giant headlights zooming in on her—two enormous evil eyes, magnified by the swirling snow, probed relentlessly.

Definitely, her pursuer was dangerous. But not a fool. He was staying far enough back for safety, though he was still much too close as far as her personal comfort was concerned.

She tried to concentrate on her driving and not to think about either her aching knee or the impossible individual following her along a deserted, storm-wracked road. But attempting to block Jonas Davenport out of her mind was like fighting a losing battle.

She knew he must be holding his powerful car down to a minimum in order to keep pace with her tired old jalopy. His was a magnificent car. One of those super vehicles that cost considerably more than she made in a year. She'd watched him climb into it earlier today, peering through a slit in the curtains at the windows of the Bedloe Falls Public Library. They'd made quite a picture, man and car. He was the definition of tall, dark and handsome. The car was sleek and painted a rich burgundy that complemented its owner's coloring.

She'd had mixed feelings as she watched him drive off. Relief, yes. But also...a measure of regret. She had to admit he was extremely attractive. It was too bad they had to be on opposing sides of an issue. Especially since the issue in question was *her* business, and he was butting in. And that was something she couldn't tolerate.

He'd appeared at the library in the middle of the afternoon—stalked into the library would be a better description—just as she was coming out of the Children's Room. She heard him ask for her at the desk, which was a surprise. Though she knew who he was the moment he told her his name, she hadn't recognized him.

The desk librarian spoke, then pointed, and Jonas Davenport swung around. Their eyes met across a distance of a dozen feet, and Carla's first impression was that he seemed shocked by the sight of her.

He actually hesitated before approaching her, and there was an odd expression on his face as he asked, "Mrs. Logan?"

Puzzled by his attitude, she answered, "Yes."

"I'm Jonas Davenport," he said, at which point quite a few things clicked into place. Small-town gossips had found a choice subject in the man before her.

Nevertheless, she was unprepared when he said without preamble, "I understand you're auctioning off the contents of your house in Wainwright this coming Saturday."

"The house is my stepmother's as well as mine," Carla answered, even more puzzled. "And, yes, we're selling the contents at an auction on Saturday."

"Your grandfather's book collection?" he persisted.

"Yes."

"I'm prepared to buy the book collection," he stated, and Carla had the impression he was about to produce a checkbook and finalize a deal without wasting any more time on it.

"The collection isn't for sale," she said, aware that the two of them were drawing curious glances from the desk librarians as well as the patrons milling around. "That's to say, the books have already been listed as part of the auction contents."

"I can assure you," Jonas Davenport informed her, "I'll be willing to meet whatever price you think you may get at auction."

"It doesn't matter," Carla said firmly. "As I just told you, the books have already been committed to the auction."

"You're refusing to sell the collection separately?"

"I can't sell the collection separately, Mr. Davenport."

"No action is irreversible, Mrs. Logan."

"This one is." Carla was glancing at the clock over the main desk as she spoke. Miss Bobbins, the head librarian, was at a meeting of the Library Friends being held in the room usually used by the trustees for their sessions. At any moment the meeting would break up and Miss Bobbins would appear. And Miss Bobbins did not take kindly to personal business being transacted on the library premises.

"I'm sorry," Carla said, "but I really do have to get back to work."

Jonas Davenport looked down at her from his superior height as if he doubted his own hearing. "You are making a serious mistake," he informed her. Then he nodded a brisk farewell, turned his back and walked out. And, watching him drive away, she'd thought that was the end of the matter.

But half an hour or so later, he returned. Carla was shelving some books, and he strode right into the stack area, a frown creasing his forehead as he surveyed her.

"Look," he snapped impatiently, not bothering to lower his voice despite the library's well-publicized "Quiet Please" dictum, "I just spoke with your stepmother on the phone, and she says the decision is yours. To my mind, that puts a different complexion on things."

Carla returned the frown. "Shush!" she admonished, pressing a warning finger to her lips.

"What?"

The word rang out, and she flinched. Miss Bobbins was now presiding at the central checkout desk because the woman who usually handled that post in the afternoons was out sick. Carla saw Miss Bobbins's head swerve in the direction of the stacks, her thin lips pursed in a tight line of disapproval as Jonas Davenport's utterance resounded.

"Please," Carla admonished in a whisper, "keep your voice down, will you?"

His mouth tightened . . . but even so, it had nothing at all in common with Miss Bobbins's mouth. His lips were naturally full, beautifully shaped. They looked soft and inviting. Carla had a sudden vision of what it would be like to be kissed by those lips. The vision got mixed up with reminiscences of all things warm and wonderful, like hot fudge sundaes . . . for which she had a weakness she usually managed to suppress. She also usually managed to suppress errant thoughts about being kissed by handsome strangers. Distracted by her out-of-character behavior, she realized Jonas Davenport had just asked her something, and she didn't have the faintest idea what it was.

He posed the question again. "Where can we talk?" he asked abruptly.

"The Quiet Room," Carla decided.

Those wonderful lips twitched with amusement. "You're saying we can *talk* in the Quiet Room?" he asked her.

"Yes."

He chuckled. "Doesn't make sense. I suppose you know that?"

She didn't bother to answer him. She put the books she'd been about to shelve in a neat pile on the floor and motioned him to follow her.

Jonas Wainwright Davenport. Classic autocrat, Carla thought, somewhat resentfully as she led the way down a short corridor into the large room that people doing research sometimes used and where a variety of local meetings were held from time to time.

She closed the door behind her and faced her adversary across a wide, oak library table. "Why did you call my stepmother?" she demanded, matching him for abruptness. "There was no cause for that."

"I called your stepmother because I wanted to get my facts straight," he retorted. "You let me think this auction was as much her idea as it is yours."

"She's saying it wasn't?"

"She is saying," Jonas Davenport reported, "that the decision was yours. Is yours."

"Jewel's made all the arrangements."

"Because you wanted her to."

"I still want her to. And, I can't see what concern it is of yours, Mr. Davenport."

"You stand to lose a lot of money," he muttered.

"That *certainly* isn't any concern of yours."

His irritated gaze raked her, and she held her breath. Annoyed, angry, bemused, whatever, she had to admit he was the best-looking man she'd seen in a long time. He was also way out of her league, she warned herself.

Tall, he towered over her. He was broad shouldered, excellently proportioned—yes, everything about Jonas Davenport was packaged in as perfect a way as possible. She supposed one would call his face movie-star handsome, except that he was better looking than at least nine out of ten movie stars. His hair was so dark it was almost black, and it was thick, with only the hint of a wave. His features were classical. High forehead, straight nose, firm chin. His eyes were a very light shade of blue, arresting against a skin that was well tanned for early December. She imagined he'd just come back from a jaunt to the Caribbean, or some other equally exotic area. Money, she knew, was no object to him.

Well, money wasn't much of an object to her, either, though for quite a different reason. She'd long since learned that when the chips were down, one couldn't buy what mattered the most with any amount of money.

She deliberately reverted her thoughts to Jonas Wainwright Davenport. His family, at least on his mother's side, were early settlers of Wainwright—Carla's hometown—but it was a long time since any of them had lived there. Then, late in the summer just past, Jonas had suddenly appeared on the scene, moving into the long-empty, huge old family homestead on a hill overlooking the Silver River. Since then, Carla had been fed considerable information about the Davenport scion from her stepmother, as well as from friends in the Wainwright area with whom she still kept up. He'd had considerable work done on the old house—the old mansion, she corrected herself—and evidently planned to make it his primary residence. And to live there alone, from what the local gossips were gathering. He was grist for their mills. Rumors flourished, but the educated guess was that Jonas Davenport—who was the sole inheritor of substantial fortunes from both sides of his family, as well as of a successful pharmaceutical firm—was about to retire at the age of thirty-six.

"And," Carla's stepmother had written succinctly, "he's a bachelor, darling. I can't imagine how many women must be after him, but they say he generally turns a cold shoulder to them. Maybe you'd better come visit more often. Who knows what might happen? You might even decide to emerge from your shell."

Carla had been both amused and annoyed by that statement. Jewel was an incurable romantic, which at times could be trying. She saw things as she wished to see them, often through a rather rose-colored haze. Carla had never been able to convince her that she really wasn't in a shell. The problem, if there was one, was simply that she'd stopped being a romantic herself a long time ago. She'd loved and lost at an early age. Brian had been twenty-three when he died, and she'd been twenty-two, and they'd been married two years.

She'd stepped off the world for a while, after Brian's death, leading a nun's life in the small Santa Monica,

California apartment she'd rented. But then she'd climbed back to earth again, impelled in part because she'd known that's what Brian would have wanted her to do. And she was determined to do it on her own. Brian's family had welcomed her into their circle too late. Strange, but at that most difficult period of her life, she hadn't seemed to need anyone. Though she'd refused financial help from his family—who were probably even richer than Jonas Davenport, she thought with a kind of wry satisfaction—she had been the recipient of Brian's insurance. She'd used a chunk of the money to go back to college, then had gone on to graduate school for a degree in library science. The choice was a natural. She'd always been a book lover.

Right after graduation, she'd gotten a job in a Los Angeles area library and had settled into the kind of niche she still occupied. Then, after her father's death two years ago, she'd applied for the job in the Bedloe Falls Library because it would bring her back to the East Coast where she'd be nearer Jewel... yet not so near she'd be in danger of losing the independence she cherished so dearly.

Jewel wasn't domineering. She cared, that's all. And she was enough older than Carla so that, though she was accepting widowhood for herself, she wasn't ready to accept it for her stepdaughter. Jewel couldn't quite believe that Carla, at twenty-eight, should truly be comfortable with her solitary life and low-profile image.

She deliberately kept that image understated, most of the time, dressing simply, using a minimum amount of makeup and dispensing with the contact lenses Jewel had insisted on giving her for her birthday the previous July. If she wore the lenses too long, they made her eyes uncomfortable. She stuck with her glasses, with their copper-shaded rims that almost matched her wavy, shoulder-length hair.

She was barely five foot three, and she had a nicely curved figure. In fact, she knew it could easily become a shade *too* curved, if she didn't watch her diet, so she was cautious about indulging too often in things like hot-fudge sundaes.

She got along well with people of all ages, of both sexes. She'd had a couple of relationships with men since Brian's death, but both had faded out in time because inevitably the point came when more commitment was demanded of her than she wanted to make. She was not looking for a man in her life. She had the memory of two wonderful years with Brian, and that was enough.

Having the Davenport heir descend on her not once but twice today had not given her any misguided illusions, either. She knew she might as well be a cardboard-covered book, as far as Jonas was concerned. In fact, he obviously was a lot more interested in Carla Logan, the book collector, than in Carla Logan, the woman. It was books he was after. And that was quite all right.

Good as he was to look at, Jonas Davenport was not her type and wouldn't be even if she *didn't* have the sense to realize the two of them moved in entirely different worlds. There was an aggressiveness about him she found abrasive. His attitude, in their two encounters, had telegraphed clearly that he was a person accustomed both to doing things—and having things done—his way.

There in the library's Quiet Room she'd soon come to suspect that Jonas Davenport was a man who couldn't bear to take no for an answer and, for that matter, wasn't accustomed to being refused very often. With his looks and his money, that wasn't too surprising. Also, he knew how to argue persuasively. Nevertheless, Carla wasn't about to change her mind. And, after about ten minutes of fruitless discussion, she knew he knew it.

"So," he said finally, "you refuse to either postpone the auction until you've had time to consider my offer or to call it off altogether?"

She glared at him, by then thoroughly exasperated. "You don't simply call off auctions at the last minute," she informed him icily. "Not when dates have been set, there's been extensive advertising, an appraisal by the auctioneer of the items to be auctioned and considerable other details finalized, as well."

"I disagree," he informed her calmly. "In my opinion, a person can generally manage to do whatever he or she wishes to do. There's always a way out."

"If you want a way out," Carla agreed, then added succinctly, "I don't. I'm quite satisfied with matters as they stand."

He impaled her with a look that made her feel as though she'd been glued to a microscope slide. She'd been giving thought to telling him *why* she was satisfied with the arrangements she'd made for an auction, but she bit back the words. Why let him know her rationale? In his world there was probably no such thing as loyalty to one's old friends.

In the midst of the silence that fell between them, Carla drew a long breath and tried to regroup.

She said politely, but firmly, "Sorry, but there's no way I'd consider withdrawing my grandfather's book collection from the auction just because you want to buy it. It would be a breach of contract."

As she spoke, she knew she was dissembling, at least slightly. It was unlikely she'd be held to an agreement, because the auctioneer was Skip Heggerty, on whom she'd had an enormous crush when he was a senior in high school and she a sophomore. Light-years ago. Way before she'd crossed the country to go to college in Southern California, where she'd met and married Brian.

Skip's sister, Gwen, had been her best friend. She'd spent a great deal of time during her growing-up years in the Heggertys' home. Mrs. Heggerty, plump and prematurely white-haired, had treated Carla like another daughter. She'd never cared much for Mr. Heggerty, a big man who was a shade too hearty, outwardly, yet had a certain sly coldness in his pale gray eyes that was off-putting to Carla. She doubted if Skip had even known she was around most of the time. She'd not been the most enchanting of creatures, already wearing glasses and with braces on her teeth. But, in those days, she'd been quite content to worship Skip from afar.

She smiled at the memory, and Jonas Davenport seemed to take personal affront at the smile. He gritted his teeth and muttered, "You're being penny wise and pound foolish."

Miss Bobbins chose that moment to first knock at the door of the Quiet Room then, without waiting for a response, to open the door and peer around it. She was tall and thin and made up of varying shades of gray. At the moment her eyes—behind their rimless glasses—were like twin icebergs.

"Mrs. Logan, you are needed at the front desk," she informed Carla sternly, then favored Jonas Davenport with her most disapproving expression. The kind of male attributes that would rock most women to their core had no effect whatsoever on Miss Bobbins, Carla noted with an inward giggle. Then, her humor faded. Had Miss Bobbins always been like that? Or maybe, once upon a time, might the sight of Jonas have elevated her blood pressure?

It was a loaded question, because Carla was bent on following in Miss Bobbins's footsteps. Miss Bobbins was close to retirement age, a fact Carla had known when she took the assistant librarian job. Just recently, one of the members of the library's board of trustees had hinted broadly that before long Carla was apt to be finding herself occupying the front office, which was presently Miss Bobbins's domain. Although she wasn't trying to push Miss Bobbins into obscurity, that word had been good to hear. Situated in the Hudson River Valley, Bedloe Falls was an ideal location for her. It was a scant two hundred miles to the east of Wainwright where she'd been born and raised and where Jewel now lived in the old Hendricks family home, which was soon to be sold.

Carla fought back a mental picture of herself twenty years hence, having inherited Miss Bobbins's job long since. She was developing a dry taste in her mouth as Jonas asked, with suspicious mildness, "Are you driving to Wainwright for the auction Saturday?"

"Yes," Carla answered absently, only to see a disconcerting flash of triumph light his eyes.

"Look," she suggested none too pleasantly, "if you're so interested in the books, why don't you come to the auction and bid on them?"

"I'd like to, but I doubt it's going to be possible," he retorted tantalizingly. Then, only confusing her further, he added, "However, you may rest assured I'll be at the auction Saturday. I'll see you then," he finished. He left the Quiet Room without a backward glance.

Carla quickly finished her shelving and went on to other chores. But it was impossible to concentrate for the balance of the afternoon.

There was no doubt in her mind that Jonas was determined to acquire her grandfather's book collection—

which encompassed hundreds of volumes dealing with an extremely wide variety of subjects—by whatever means.

Her grandfather had died while she was in California, at the time when Brian was so ill. There'd been no chance of her going back East, even for the funeral. The book collection she'd inherited had been packed in cartons and stored in the attic of the old Hendricks house.

Jewel had urged Carla more than once, since she'd moved back East, to come home and catalog the books personally so she would know what she had. But, so far, there just hadn't been time for that. She'd been in Bedloe Falls only six months—not long enough to ask for an extended leave of absence. And cataloging a collection like her grandfather's was not a weekend job.

She'd spoken to Skip Heggerty about that on the phone, and he'd assured her he'd have one of his employees list all the titles for her. "Think there's anything of special value?" Skip had asked her.

"I don't know," Carla admitted honestly. "I was a teenager last time I really looked at any of those books..."

"Well, now that you're a trained librarian you'll know how to judge, once you see the list," Skip pointed out, which was true.

Nevertheless, and especially with Jonas Davenport's sudden interest in the collection, Carla now wished she had managed to take the time to evaluate the books carefully. She knew some of them were very old, which didn't necessarily mean they were valuable. Still, memory prodded that there'd been a few interesting first editions. She remembered her grandfather pointing out the first editions in the process of giving her some basic lessons in how to go about *telling* books by their covers.

Carla was still musing as she locked up the library for the day, after Miss Bobbins had departed. And the conviction that, somehow, Jonas Davenport must know more about her grandfather's books than she did herself surfaced. With that surfacing came the sudden, strong feeling that it might be an excellent idea to get back to Wainwright before he did. Maybe Jewel would have some ideas about why the books and the impending auction seemed to matter so much to him.

It was Thursday. Carla had planned, originally, to drive to Wainwright after work on Friday, go over the book list Skip would have ready for her, get a good night's sleep and then be ready for the auction on Saturday. So this really wasn't such a great divergence. She was merely giving herself a twenty-four-hour head start.

She drove past the Haven Motor Inn on the way home. It was the best place in town to stay, and, as she'd expected it might be, Jonas Davenport's beautiful burgundy automobile was parked out in front. Lamplight made it glow as rich a red as vintage wine.

The sight of the car cemented her feeling that she needed to hurry. She parked outside the building further down Main Street in which she'd rented a small second-floor apartment and was speeding up the stairs when, turning sharply on the landing, she felt a wrenching, all too familiar pain.

She stopped, grabbed the banister and forced herself to remain stock-still and to take a few long, deep breaths until the pain began to grind down to a deep-seated ache. But she was cursing her trick knee all the while, a part of her anatomy that always seemed to let her down just when she needed mobility the most.

She'd had the unpredictable knee for over eleven years, ever since she'd taken a tumble in a field hockey game in high school, lost her glasses in the process and then, upon getting to her feet, had promptly stumbled over a small tree stump that had eluded her faulty vision.

Usually the latent injury didn't bother her or impede her activities. Only at vital times like this did it become perverse, she thought resentfully as, still clutching the banister, she limped up the remaining few steps.

It would have been nice to be able to slip into a hot bath, to soak for a while and let the knee relax. But she couldn't risk snatching that kind of time.

A priority was to call Miss Bobbins to tell her that a family emergency had arisen—which was close enough to the truth—and so she had to leave for Wainwright immediately and wouldn't be in to work tomorrow.

Miss Bobbins was not pleased.

Carla sighed as she hung up the phone, then quickly tossed some clothes into a suitcase and left the apartment without pausing for anything to eat.

It was frigid out. There had been dark clouds messing up the sky all day. Some of the people coming into the library had mentioned snow being on the way, but Carla hadn't paid too much attention to them. She'd discovered in the course of her work that half the people in the world considered themselves amateur meteorologists, and most of the time their calculations were wrong.

Nevertheless, she shivered as she limped out to her car, hefted her suitcase into the back seat, then slid behind the wheel.

It took a while for her old jalopy to warm up in weather like this, and if not sufficiently warm, the car—known affectionately as Jenny—tended to balk and stall. Carla sat back and let the old engine ward off automotive arthritis. She was about to switch on a Sting cassette she'd bought with her last paycheck when she glanced into her rearview mirror for the first of what was to be many, many times during the course of her sojourn.

She drew in her breath sharply as she saw a car parked across the street, several doors down but close enough to a streetlight so that the color was clearly visible. Deep, rich burgundy.

Jonas Wainwright Davenport was *spying* on her. There was no other valid reason she could think of for his being parked on Main Street in Bedloe Falls on an icy December night.

The man's gall was monumental. Muttering under her breath, Carla informed Jenny, "Ready or not, we're taking off, old girl."

She shifted gears. Jenny obediently moved forward. Carla slowly drove down to the corner, turned, then, midway along the next block, glanced into the rearview mirror again. She'd begun to think maybe she was imagining things, but she saw the burgundy car turning the corner then carefully following along behind her.

It just didn't make sense.

As she drove along the state road that led to the nearest access to the New York State Thruway, Carla tried to conjure up a logical reason why Jonas Davenport was behaving like this. Could it be the first time in his entire, born-wealthy life that someone had ever denied him a request? If so, she could only say that by now he had it coming.

She pulled up to the tollbooth at the Thruway entrance and took her ticket. Traffic was very light. Carla drove down the ramp and onto the highway, then glanced in the mirror again.

The burgundy car was following at a discreet distance.

At that exact moment, it began to snow.

The snow started slowly. Big flakes melted quickly on the engine's warm hood and yielded easily to displacement by the windshield wiper. Jenny, despite her age, held the road fairly well under most circumstances, and Carla had bought a new set of tires just before setting forth on her cross-country drive from California to Bedloe Falls. So she had no qualms about her safety as she drove along.

It was about a two-hour drive to Utica, where she left the Thruway for State 12, the route that led north through a series of smaller communities to Wainwright. By the time Carla reached the Utica turnoff, the snow was coming down heavily, and she began to have her first doubts.

Had circumstances been otherwise, she would have pulled off in Utica, found a motel, had something hot to eat, gotten a good night's sleep, then made the balance of her trip in daylight.

As it was, the presence of the burgundy car right behind her made her keep going. And the snow kept falling. And she began to feel as if the car pursuing her was first cousin to an extraterrestrial spaceship that could overtake her any time it wanted to and literally suck her up into its maw.

The concept made her shudder. The shudder was enough to cause her to momentarily lose control of the steering wheel. The car hit a patch of ice under the snow and started to skid. Carla forgot everything except working her way out of the skid without going off the road.

The snow was no longer melting off the engine hood. It was coming down so heavily, so fast, that the whole car was enveloped in a thick white blanket, and the windshield wiper was working overtime. Carla glanced at the rearview mirror again and found that there was so much snow on the back window she could only dimly see the gleam of Jonas Davenport's headlights.

This wasn't just anybody's old snowstorm. This was a blizzard!

Chapter Two

Carla, out of necessity, slowed to a snail's pace. She had a sudden, horrible feeling that any second now Jenny was going to develop galloping car pneumonia, start coughing and then conk out on her altogether.

"Come on, old girl," she urged softly. "We can make it."

As if talking back to her—it was unclear whether in agreement or disagreement—Jenny groaned, then groaned again. But kept on.

Even the snowplows weren't out yet on this section of the road. Carla couldn't remember when another car had passed, going in the opposite direction. And, on her side, there were only Jenny and the gorgeous, burgundy vehicle in steady pursuit.

Jenny spoke again. A strangled sound Carla couldn't identify . . . but then she'd never pretended to have much knowledge about what went on under her car's hood.

The internal mechanical details, she'd always felt, were best left to mechanics.

Nevertheless, she had the uneasy feeling her car was giving her the warning it couldn't keep on going like this much longer. Nor could she blame it. She wasn't sure she could keep on going much longer herself.

The visibility was getting worse and worse. A chill was edging into the car's warm interior, and it wasn't hard to fathom that something was going wrong with the heater. Well, it stood to reason that if anything was going to go wrong with *anything* in a car, it would do so under weather conditions like these.

It was too late to turn back to Utica. Matter of fact, Carla wasn't sure she could manage a complete turn. To add to her problems, the rims of her glasses felt frozen to her nose. If her glasses started to fog up, she was in real trouble. There was no way she could see well enough to drive without them.

Then, ahead, a blue-and-red sign glimmered. The letters, distorted by the snow, shimmered like Fourth-of-July streamers.

MOTEL.

Paradise, Carla breathed. Any refuge from this storm would be an oasis.

Peering ahead, she saw an arrow that pointed to the right. The motel driveway?

Carla did some rapid thinking. If she swung off, took refuge in the motel, would Jonas Davenport follow suit?

She doubted it. Obviously his objective was to get back to Wainwright, the sooner the better. By stopping, she conceded, she'd be giving him an advantage. With his newer, heavier car, he *could* keep going. Jenny couldn't.

Carla switched on her turn signal. Then slowly, braking as little as possible, she turned just short of the arrow. There was no driveway, per se, to be seen. Snow covered everything. But, after a moment, she saw a building ahead, its roof edges lighted by blue and red bulbs that looked lovelier, right now, than the most beautifully decorated Christmas tree in the world.

She pulled up in front of the building, turned Jenny's ignition switch, then slumped back and tried to let some of the tension ease out of her body. Finally she opened the car door, and was appalled at the depth of the snow, as yet untouched by human hand or shovel. She took a tentative step, favoring her knee, and immediately plunged in well over her shoe tops. But there was no alternative. Resolutely, she scuffed her way through the thick, white stuff, pushed open the door to the motel office and was met by a blast of warm air that immediately steamed her glasses so she couldn't see a thing.

"Ah, madam," a deep, pleasant voice greeted her. "I'm glad you found us. It's a bad night for travel."

Carla nodded agreement to the understatement, fished a handkerchief out of her coat pocket and hastily wiped off her lenses. Her vision was fuzzy without the glasses, but she did note that the man behind the reception desk was big and wore a bright red shirt. At that moment, he looked better to her than Santa Claus.

With her glasses on again, she determined that he was probably in his late sixties. He had snow-white hair, deep blue eyes and a ruddy complexion. Yes, a perfect Santa Claus.

"We're all filled up, my dear," he said. And her heart sank until he added quickly, "In the main section, that is. But, suspecting what might be coming, I had the heat turned on in our new annex."

"New annex?" Carla asked blankly.

"Less than fifty feet away," he assured her. "I'd suggest you drive over," he added, as he reached for a key dangling from a pegboard behind him. "You'll be in unit 6, right at the end. Pull up as close as you can. And don't worry. I have a private contractor who'll be coming along to plow shortly, so there should be no problems."

Carla nodded, accepted the key, and was about to ask to be pointed in the direction of the annex when she heard a familiar voice behind her.

"I hope you have another unit available," the voice suggested pleasantly.

Carla swung around and faced Jonas Davenport. He was wearing a heavy blue wool parka. He'd thrown back the hood, and his dark hair was faintly mussed. He was wearing high boots, and she had no doubt that, inside them, his legs and feet were snug and warm, whereas hers were freezing.

He arched an eyebrow and smiled ever so slightly. "Well," he said, "so we meet again."

She nodded, gritted, "So it would seem," then mustered up all the dignity she could manage and beat a somewhat halting but still reasonably hasty retreat.

She prayed that Jenny would start up without balking. Jenny obliged. The snow seemed to be letting up a little, but the wind was rising. Minigales puffed the white stuff, making it swirl like masses of pulverized confetti let loose. Nevertheless, the annex was plainly visible. And it was floodlighted. The motel keeper evidently had thought of everything.

The new annex appeared to have been built in the dead center of the motel property. There were wide open spaces all around it. Probably it was quite attractive . . . at other times. Right now, it could have doubled as a Siberian prison, and Carla felt uncomfortably separated from the main section as she drove as close to the end unit as she could and parked her car.

The annex had been built atop a terrace. A raised walkway bordered by planters, presently filled with snow, encircled the terrace. A series of short steps spaced at regular intervals led down to ground level.

Again, Carla plunged into snow whirled by the wind so that it came up to her calves, and she wished she had dug out her storm boots before leaving Bedloe Falls. Investigation showed that the hinges on the back door of her car apparently had frozen into place. It took all her strength to budge the door and creak it open enough so she could retrieve her suitcase.

"Jenny, Jenny," she murmured sadly. "A few more excursions like this and you'll really have had it."

She started for the steps, the wind buffeting her. Holding her suitcase's handle with her right hand, she grasped for the stair railing with her left. Her gloves had interfered with her getting the car door open, so she'd taken them off. Now, the stair railing was so icy cold to her bare hand she felt, paradoxically, as if she'd been burned.

Just behind her, that familiar voice suggested, "Why don't you let me help you with that?"

Carla turned to see Jonas Davenport reaching for her suitcase. Instinctively she drew back, and her knee played another trick on her. She felt herself falling and desperately tried to avert the fall, this only resulting in tensed muscles, which made things all the worse. Searing pain bolted through her knee with such speed she didn't have time to hold back an anguished yelp. Then she felt Jonas Davenport's arms grabbing her, and before she could tell him to let her go, he swept her off her feet and strode with her to the top of the steps like a conquering hero in a vintage black-and-white movie.

"Number 6, isn't it?" he asked.

Carla had to admit he didn't miss much.

"Where's your key?" he demanded.

"In my coat pocket," she managed.

"Can you reach it?"

She tried and immediately brushed his hand. He wasn't wearing gloves, either, but his skin felt incredibly warm, and just touching him was disconcertingly... heady. She silently chided herself for letting such a brief contact rattle her, groped for the key again and this time came up with it and held it out to him.

Jonas took the key and announced, "I'm going to put you down." Then he commanded, "Lean on your good leg and prop yourself against the wall while I get the door open."

Carla bristled. There were few things she hated so much as being *ordered* to do something. Still, since there really was no other viable course of action, she obeyed.

Swiftly, Jonas opened the door. Pocketing her key, he turned and picked her up again as if she were just another piece of baggage, carried her into the motel unit and placed her in the middle of a large double bed. And before her snow-covered ankle boots had time to start melting onto the bedspread, he quickly and efficiently slipped them off.

Again, coming from the cold night into a warm room caused her glasses to fog. She wrenched them off impatiently and stared up at Jonas Davenport. He looked fuzzy... but fit. She marveled that after all his recent exertion he wasn't even out of breath. So much for the alleged decadence of the rich. This member of that class was—physically at least—in top shape.

Suddenly he leaned over the bed, close enough so she could see him clearly without her glasses, and said accusingly, "I *thought* you were limping, back in the motel office," as if the limp made her guilty of something.

"I wrenched my knee before I left my apartment," Carla said rather stiffly, not about to go into the peculiarities of that particular knee with him.

"Hmm," Jonas murmured, watching her so intently she moved involuntarily and couldn't help but wince.

The intentness changed to solicitude. "Hang on a minute while I get your suitcase," he instructed. "Do you have anything in it like brandy or whiskey, incidentally?"

"No."

"Then I'd better get my own stuff," he decided. "Stay put. I'll be right back."

Carla made no response to that admonition, and the minute he was out the door she slid over to the side of the bed and very carefully put both feet on the floor. Exercising extreme caution, she slowly stood up. Then, mustering an entire army of inner forces, she took a tentative step... and promptly sprawled into a heap on the motel's green-and-blue tweed-patterned rug.

Tears of pain and frustration filled her eyes and trickled down her cheeks. Furious with herself and her ill-timed helplessness, she literally howled aloud. Just as Jonas opened the door.

He stood on the threshold, surveying her. Then, without a word, he walked over to the combination sideboard-chest that ran along one wall of the motel unit and put down whatever it was he was carrying. All of which, at the moment, was little more than a blur to Carla.

Next, he swooped her up as if she were a featherweight and plunked her back into the center of the bed again. Only this time he sat down on the edge of the bed himself and a second later was carefully drying her eyes with a crisp, white handkerchief.

Carla summoned enough fortitude to take the handkerchief away from him, then to finish her own mopping-up job.

He sat back and waited until she was through and had put her glasses back on again. At that point she didn't want to look at him, but he was so near that she couldn't seem to resist.

She saw that he was frowning slightly. He looked like a man who'd taken a wrong fork in the road only to come to a dead end. She could imagine that he well might be regretting having gotten into this situation because of an attempt to buy out a book collection he'd never even seen. But that, she reminded herself, was his problem.

He said quietly, "Look, I don't even have so much as aspirin with me or I'd give you something for that knee. As it is, I'm going to pack it with snow, since the ice machine is back in the main building. Snow will do as well. And then later on I'll tape it. Meantime, how about a painkiller first?"

He stood, and Carla watched him cross over to the sideboard. He moved smoothly, with assurance, shoulders squared, head held high. But then, of course, he would. He'd been trained to lead.

He came back with a glass in which there was an inch or so of amber fluid. Handing it to her, he said, "Here. Drink this down."

"What is it?" she asked suspiciously.

"Poison," he said, and then grinned. Despite herself, she caught the full impact of the grin, and she reacted. She felt something inside her grate, like a rusty hinge suddenly put to use again. The grin lighted Jonas's eyes, making his whole face look younger, also making him much too desirable. Carla suddenly felt warm all over, even though her wet clothes were actually making her shiver.

Jonas laughed and said, "Hey, it's only brandy. Come on. Down it."

"I don't usually drink anything stronger than wine," she protested. "And not much of that."

"Well, this isn't 'usually.'"

That was true enough. Carla took the glass, downed its contents as he'd instructed and tried not to sputter.

"Fire," she said, after a moment.

"Maybe it'll burn away some of the pain." He hesitated. "Look . . . we have to get those wet panty hose off you."

"No," she protested instinctively.

"Yes," he corrected. "I think it'll hurt less if you'll let me help you."

"No," she said quickly. "I can do it myself."

"Don't be silly," he admonished. "Look, lift up and I'll reach under."

"No," she said, a bit more forcibly.

He sat back and surveyed her. "Carla," he said patiently, "this isn't a time for false modesty. Pretend I'm your doctor."

There had been a lot of doctors in Brian's young life, but there'd been only two in hers, thus far, one in Wainwright and the other in Bedloe Falls. Picturing them, Carla nearly laughed aloud. They were both on the other side of sixty, one was bald, one gray-haired, one too fat, the other too thin. Both of them were dears and experts in their profession. But the thought of having either of them help her off with her panty hose just didn't fall into the same category as having Jonas Davenport perform the same chore.

Jonas, his face inscrutable, his tone all business, ordered, "Lift up a little."

Carla obeyed because she was reasonably sure that if she didn't do as he said, he'd take matters in his own hands anyway. And though she felt herself a match for him in every other way, she had to admit she was not his equal physically.

She raised her hips ever so slightly and felt his strong hands move swiftly under her skirt to her waistline. Then he carefully began to pull her panty hose down, sliding the sheer nylon over her buttocks, her thighs and along the length of her legs.

His fingers moved with dexterous efficiency... but he left a trail of fire behind, every inch of the way. Those adroit fingers became sensual messengers, telegraphing all sorts of tantalizing vibes that pushed Carla into a supercharged body awareness. The tremor that shook her had little to do with the fact that even the smallest movement made her knee hurt even more.

She watched Jonas Davenport casually toss aside her panty hose. Then he got up and headed in the direction of the bathroom, to return a moment later with an armful of towels he dumped on the foot of the bed. Next, he crossed the room, opened the door and stalked out into the snowy night.

A moment later he was back again, the plastic ice bucket provided by the motel full to the top with snow. He layered the towels thickly then carefully lifted her leg, positioning her injured knee against the towel layers. His touch was so gentle Carla didn't even wince. She was more concerned about the fluttery feeling inside her and told herself that her reactions were becoming crazy, utterly crazy.

"Carla?" Jonas asked.

Carla blinked. Forced herself to take a mental step toward reality. "Yes?"

"I'm going to pack snow around your knee, and it may hurt like hell at first. So, if you want to scream, scream. Okay?"

"Okay." She nodded.

The initial impact of the snow around her knee *was* excruciating. She flinched away from the biting cold and easily could have screamed but managed to hold back. Light, very light blue eyes watched her expression.

"Good girl," Jonas said approvingly...and fought an insane impulse to reach over and kiss her. Stretched out on the bed with her left knee encased in snow and every bit of toweling he'd been able to find in the bathroom, including the bath mat, she looked like a wounded, lost kitten right now. She had gorgeous eyes. He'd noticed that even with the glasses on, and they seemed bigger, even more beautiful, without the glasses. Right now, they looked like drenched violets, and her lovely, coppery hair—still damp at the edges—was drying out and curling around her shoulders. Jonas fought another insane impulse. He wanted to reach out and twirl a tendril of her hair around his fingers. Around and around and around.

As he'd taken off her panty hose, Jonas had fought back some impulses that simply had no place in the present situation. But it hadn't been easy. The smooth roundness of Carla's hips, the silkiness of her skin had unleashed some pretty erotic feelings. She was so soft to the touch, so sweet scented as he bent over her. A floral scent, not too heavy. He wanted to keep breathing it and breathing it and breathing it. And touching her and touching her and touching her.

His thoughts were leading him totally astray, and he forced himself to keep very busy, hoping Carla wouldn't start glancing in wrong directions and notice that he was anything but as cool as he was pretending to be.

She, herself, was *extremely* cool, he thought ruefully. When he'd walked into the Bedloe Falls Library today and introduced himself to her, she'd admittedly recognized his name but had given absolutely no indication of having recognized *him*. Which, maybe, was her way of administering an ego put-down.

He had nearly said something to her, then had thought better of it. If she didn't want to admit she'd noticed him at the Wainwright Country Club over the previous Columbus Day holiday, he'd let it go at that.

He, on the other hand, was more than willing to own up to remembering *her* distinctly. A couple of friends from the city had come up for the weekend. He'd needed to take them someplace to dinner Saturday night and had opted for the country club because he couldn't think of any other place to go. Carla was across the dining room when he entered it, and she happened to look up at exactly that moment. She had smiled as their gazes meshed. And Jonas had felt himself drowning in violets. It had been all he could do not to stare at her continuously from then on.

She'd been dining with an older woman—whom he now suspected was probably her stepmother, Jewel Hendricks—and a middle-aged couple whom he'd not identified. Many times over the course of the evening, she'd looked up when Jonas was watching her. Most of those times their eyes had met again, and again she'd smiled.

To him, she had stood out in the room full of people. Evidently, the same hadn't been true for her where he was concerned. Which was, he supposed, okay, if disappointing. The reason she'd caught his attention was because she'd looked so different from most of the women he knew. She had been wearing a pretty, light green dress, she didn't use much makeup, and she did her hair in a casual, natural way. That was the key word. *Natural.* She had looked delightfully natural to him, in contrast to most of the ultra-sophisticated women he knew who wore glitzy clothes, glitzy jewels and several coatings of veneer.

Later, Jonas had gone back to the country club a couple of times, hoping he might see her again. The club occupied a big Victorian structure outside of town and had been established by his great-grandfather, Jonas Wainwright, for whom he'd been named. The small cough-medicine company that was later to become a major pharmaceutical firm was founded in Wainwright an era ago. Old Jonas had wanted to "do something" for his employees, according to family legend, and so he'd bought a summer hotel on the town outskirts, had it renovated and winterized and had established the first country club of the area, membership nominal for Wainwright company employees.

The present Jonas wasn't much for country clubs. For most of his adult life, he'd sidestepped the opulent society world into which he had an open invitation because it represented a type of glitter that didn't appeal to him.

Would Carla understand that? he wondered suddenly. And he also wondered what she must think of him. He couldn't blame her if, so far, she'd found him an arrogant snob. After the initial shock of recognition, he knew he'd come on strong when he shouldn't have. He'd used the wrong approach, and, unfortunately, it was now too late to retract. He'd considered buying the Hendricks book collection a business deal, nothing more than that, and it had never occurred to him that she would be unwilling to sell when he was ready to meet any price she stated—within reason, of course.

It was Martha Daniels, the town librarian in Wainwright, who had told him about the impending auction, knowing of his interest in old books. Miss Daniels had been acquainted with Carla's grandfather, once had done an informal cataloging of his books for him and remembered that there were some pretty good volumes in the collection.

At that, Jonas's interests had quickened. Old books were his hobby and had been for years—especially rare old books. He'd expanded the hobby into a sideline business venture, a while back, becoming a silent partner in a bookstore his friend, Fred Morris, had opened a couple of years earlier in Utica. The store was already gaining an excellent reputation in the world of bibliophiles, and Jonas got a certain secret satisfaction out of being part of the business.

When he had learned from Miss Daniels that Carla Hendricks Logan was going to dispose of her grandfather's book collection at auction, he'd decided to go to the auction or—if he couldn't because of the pressure of other business—to persuade Fred to go or to send a representative to bid on anything interesting.

Then, the more he thought about it, and the more he talked to Martha Daniels about it, the more Jonas became convinced that he should buy the entire collection himself, in advance of the auction. He could keep what he wanted, let Fred take whatever he wished for the shop and donate the remaining volumes to the library or—if

Miss Daniels didn't want all of them—to some charitable organization for a future book sale.

His conviction took a new turn when he learned that the auction at the Hendricks house was to be conducted by the firm of William Heggerty and Son.

Jonas's business connections were widespread, and he'd used them to launch what he termed a "classified" investigation of the auctioneering firm. He was motivated by things he'd heard about the Heggertys, and by information that had come from Fred. Several times one or the other of the Heggertys had trekked into Fred's Utica bookstore with a couple of first editions or other rare books. Though Fred had bought the books, he'd been curious about where the Heggertys might have obtained them.

Checking, Jonas learned that usually the Heggertys had brought the books into Fred not long after conducting an auction in the general Wainwright area, which included quite a bit of rural terrain and a number of villages with old homes that conceivably could have attics full of hidden treasure.

Maybe the Heggertys had come by the volumes legitimately, Fred conceded. He wondered, that was all. And Jonas had come to wonder about the Heggertys, too, as rumors about the father-and-son team floated back to him during this period, when he was having a great deal of work done by local craftsmen on the family homestead he intended to make his residence.

The Heggertys' business tactics weren't really what had been on his mind, though, when he'd driven to Bedloe Falls to try to work out a business deal of his own with Carla Logan. Because, then, he hadn't known that Carla was *Carla*. The woman who'd made such an impact on him several weeks ago at the Wainwright Country Club.

Now he knew in his bones that the Heggertys were the last people in the world she should be trusting to handle her auction for her. He felt, keenly, that the odds were ninety-nine to one that they were going to cheat her, and cheat her badly. And the urge to protect her, to keep her from being badly cheated, surged.

She looked so young, so small, so cuddly, so vulnerable. Martha had volunteered the information that Carla Logan was a widow. Glancing at her hands, he saw that she'd removed any wedding band from her ring finger, and he wondered how long ago her husband had died? He wondered a lot of things about her. He pushed them to the back of his mind and, looking down at her, saw that her eyes were closed.

He leaned over her, hating to wake her if she were asleep, but it had to be done. "Carla?" he asked softly.

Her eyes flew open. "Yes?"

Jonas didn't immediately answer her, and Carla took a second look at him. She blinked when she saw the expression on his face. At the moment, he was displaying none of the domineering characteristics she'd decided were an integral part of his personality. Rather, he was looking at her with a tenderness that could have melted a glacier. But the question he posed was about as mundane as a question could be.

"Do you have a warm nightgown with you?" he asked.

"No. Why?"

"The heat in here's working fine, but it's electric heat. That's to say, if we lose the power, we lose the heat. And that wind's howling out there."

Carla listened, heard the wind and instinctively shivered.

"You can borrow my pajamas," Jonas decided.

"I'll be plenty warm enough in my own pajamas," Carla informed him.

"Pajamas, eh?" he queried.

"Silk pajamas."

"Well," he allowed, "I suppose silk pajamas can be sexy... but not terribly warm."

There was a teasing light in his eyes as he spoke. Carla, who almost never blushed, suddenly felt as if she were running a fever and was sure her cheeks must have turned scarlet. "Hey," Jonas protested, "there's no cause for alarm." He spoke mildly, but his eyes were dancing with mischief.

Carla had been picturing him as such a cool sophisticate that this glimpse at yet another side of his character was disturbing. Most of the things about him were disturbing, she was discovering, and she fought the impulse to turn her head into the pillows so he couldn't see her discomfiture.

"I'll be back in a jiffy," he promised, and bolted out the door again. A moment later, instead of returning the same way, he walked through the door that connected their two rooms.

Carla jerked upright. Her knee swiftly reminded her it had been the wrong move to make. She winced as she blurted, "How did you..."

"No problem," Jonas explained easily. "I unlocked the door from your side with your key. Just now, I unlocked my door with my key. Simple, when you know how."

"Listen..."

"What am I supposed to hear?"

"I want the doors between our rooms locked again, Jonas," Carla warned.

He chuckled. "Sweetheart, I wouldn't say you're exactly in shape to be seduced just now," he pointed out amiably.

Before she could think of a suitable retort, Jonas continued cheerfully, "Time to get you snuggled down."

Carla's thoughts began wandering toward some rather deep waters. She was remembering Jonas running his hands over her hips and the unexpectedness of the feelings he'd evoked in her. She'd thought that feelings like that had been washed out of her life more than six years ago. It was a shock to discover that they were extremely alive, in fact in danger of thriving.

She said quickly, "I'm fine."

"I wanted the snow to act as a swelling deterrent, but I don't intend to freeze your knee," Jonas told her. As he spoke, he was nearing the bed again, sitting down on the side of it, and those terrific hands of his were beginning to do things with the towels he'd wrapped around her leg.

Carla started to quiver all over, like a high-tension wire vibrating in the wind. She wondered that her skin didn't actually hum as he touched it. She tried to steady herself, to concentrate on his gentleness as he worked.

"You should have been a doctor," she said. The remark was impromptu.

He looked up, and she saw a strange expression in his light blue eyes. She thought he was about to say something, but he didn't. Instead, he concentrated on the task at hand, carefully unwrapping the towels and dropping them on the rug while disturbing her leg as little as possible. Finally he removed the last wet towel and then carefully mopped her leg with a dry one.

He still had that odd expression on his face, and now there was something guarded about him. Carla felt he'd suddenly thrust up some solid defenses, though she couldn't imagine why he would have felt that necessary.

She wanted to say something to him. She didn't know what to say. And, before she could say anything, Jonas announced brusquely, "Now, to get you out of your clothes and into my pajamas."

Chapter Three

It was a relief to Jonas to escape into the bathroom, where he dumped the damp towels into the tub.

He'd been closer than he would have believed possible to spilling out a lot of information to Carla—personal, intimate details of his life he never talked about with anyone. He'd actually *wanted* to blurt out the story of his thwarted ambitions, his frustrations and a lot of other painful facts to her.

Jonas closed his eyes, got a grip on himself and then, recharged, went back into Carla's room. He had brought a pillowcase over from his unit. Now he sat down on the edge of the bed and meticulously began to tear it into strips.

She stared at him, wide-eyed. "Why are you doing that?" she demanded. "You're destroying someone else's property."

"Uh-huh," he agreed. "But we need this more than the motel does. Before I tuck you into bed, I have to bind up that knee."

"That's not necessary," she protested.

"You know it is."

"Look . . . it's a trick knee."

He stared at the knee in question with renewed interest. "Is it, indeed?"

Carla sighed. She had *not* intended to get into this, and she said reluctantly, "I'm serious, Jonas. I did a job on my knee playing field hockey, way back when I was in high school. My glasses got knocked off, and I couldn't see where I was going, and I went head over heels over a tree stump. . . ."

He frowned slightly. "You're that dependent on your glasses?"

"Well . . . I'm sort of nearsighted," Carla admitted.

"Sort of?"

"Very," she conceded.

"Have you ever thought of contacts?"

"Yes, I have some. But I can only wear them for a certain length of time without discomfort. So I save them mostly for special occasions."

The question exploded, and Jonas couldn't keep himself from letting it out. "Carla, when you were having dinner at the Wainwright Country Club over the Columbus Day weekend, did you have your contacts on?"

Jonas couldn't blame her for looking at him as if he'd lost his mind. "What?" she queried.

"Do you remember having dinner at the club that weekend?"

"Yes, of course, I do."

"Do you remember if you were wearing your contacts?"

"I must have been or else I would have had my glasses on," she said. She pondered, then added, "Wait a minute..."

"Forever, if I have to."

"Seriously..."

"I'm serious."

"Please," she chided, for the moment looking not so much like a proper librarian as like someone trying to play the part of a proper librarian. Then she said slowly, "Last Columbus Day weekend at the country club..."

"Yes?" Jonas prodded.

"It's coming back to me. I felt like I had something in my eye. So I went to the rest room and took out the contacts. Frankly, it felt so good without them, I didn't put them back in again. But I'd changed handbags before I left home, and like an idiot I hadn't put my glasses in the other bag. So I just blundered my way through. It didn't matter too much. It doesn't require good distant vision to eat."

But it did require good distant vision to see a person clearly all the way across a very large room.

Jonas murmured softly, "You didn't see me. That's why you didn't recognize me."

She stared at him. "What are you saying?"

"It doesn't matter," he said quickly. He lined up the torn pillowcase strips neatly, then commanded, "Now, straighten your leg out."

"Honestly, Jonas, this isn't necessary. I told you, my knee plays tricks on me sometimes, that's all. It'll be fine by morning. There's nothing wrong with my leg."

Once again Jonas grinned that mischievous grin of his. "I couldn't agree more," he said. "I wouldn't change a thing about your legs, Carla. However, that's beside the point. Right now, if I don't tape that knee you're apt to wake up in the morning with a balloon you can't set free. So don't resist me, okay?''

Reluctantly, Carla sank back against the pillows and tried to keep her pulse rate down as Jonas began to gently but firmly wrap the cloth strips around her knee.

"Okay, now the pajamas," he said after finishing the taping to his satisfaction.

He produced a pair of deep blue, heavy flannel pajamas. "Sit up," he instructed, "and we'll deal with the top first."

Carla could feel her cheeks flaming again. "No," she said.

"Sit up, Carla," Jonas persisted.

"No," Carla said again. "That's one thing I can do myself. Please . . . just give me your pajama top and go somewhere, will you?"

"Okay," he said. "If you insist."

He didn't go anywhere, though, except to the opposite side of the room, where he made an elaborate show of taking up a stance in front of the window, his back carefully turned to her as he stared out into the winter darkness.

Carla nearly chuckled aloud, watching him. Then she went into action, divesting herself of her sweater and bra and slipping on his pajama top. The top was huge and wonderfully warm and fleecy. Carla huddled into it and said, "All right. You may turn around again."

Hearing her own voice, Carla thought she sounded like Miss Bobbins. She wondered what Miss Bobbins would do in a similar situation and had to smile at the thought.

"Well," Jonas approved, "I'm glad to see there's a trace of humor lurking somewhere within you. Want to share the joke?"

"I was thinking about the head librarian in Bedloe Falls," Carla admitted.

"The gray dragonlady who broke up our tête-à-tête in the Quiet Room?"

"Yes." A thought occurred to her. She said, "Do you know, you may very well have lost me my job, Jonas Davenport?"

"Because you took me in the Quiet Room with you?"

"No, because I took tomorrow off without asking for permission in advance. I said it was a family emergency, so Miss Bobbins pretty much had to accept that. But Friday's our busiest day. I'm afraid by the time it's over she's going to be absolutely *incensed*."

"Does she breathe fire when she's incensed?"

"Bright purple fire," Carla retorted impishly. "With yellow and orange stripes running through it."

"Awesome," Jonas said, his mouth twitching.

Carla looked at him, and she wanted to dissolve not just into laughter but into his arms. Snatching at self-control, she said hastily, "May I have your pajama bottoms?"

"Be my guest," Jonas told her as he proffered them. "I'll even play the ultimate gentleman role and turn my head away again. Okay?"

"Yes," she muttered, and tried to slip off her skirt and green, lace-and-satin panties as quickly as possible. Then she drew on his pajamas, the legs of which seemed to go on forever and ever and ever.

"I think," Carla said, "we're going to have to roll up the cuffs."

"Glad to oblige," Jonas told her promptly, and suited action to words. "Now," he went on, when he'd gotten the cuffs to a manageable length, "perhaps you'd like to use the facilities before I settle you into bed."

"Er... yes, I would," she agreed.

"Suppose I carry you over to the bathroom door...and you can try it on your own from there?" he suggested tactfully.

She started to tell him she could hobble all the way, but before she could get the first word out Jonas reached down and swept her up in his powerful arms.

He was waiting when she emerged from the bathroom. Immediately, he swooped her up again. A moment later, she was in bed, and he was drawing the top sheet and two blankets up over her.

"Now," he announced, "for the soup course."

The mere mention of soup made Carla hungrily aware that she'd skipped supper in her desire to get on the road. "Would that we had something like soup," she admitted wistfully.

"We will have," Jonas promised. "There's a vending machine in the office."

"How are you going to get through all that snow to the office?"

"By taking giant steps in my trusty seven-league boots," he said, again flashing that disconcerting grin.

He was as good as his word. In what seemed to her a remarkably short time, considering the weather conditions, he reappeared with hot chicken noodle soup and a stack of saltine crackers to go with it.

He watched approvingly as she polished off the makeshift meal, meanwhile sipping some brandy and water himself.

"No soup for you?" she asked him.

"After a while, maybe. I had a late lunch that was really a dinner."

"Jonas..."

"Yes, Carla?"

"Look, I appreciate everything you've been doing for me."

His grin was wicked this time. "Are you saying you're glad I followed you from Bedloe Falls? Glad I decided to turn in at the motel, too?"

Carla wriggled visibly, and he teased, "Well, as far as I'm concerned this is an experience I wouldn't have wanted to miss. Except, if I'd written the scenario for it, you wouldn't have twisted your knee. We merely would have been snowbound together, which might have been even more interesting."

Carla flushed and couldn't answer him. She tried to tell herself that had they merely been snowbound in the same motel, she would have managed to keep her distance from him. As it was, her trick knee had brought them together. For the first time ever, Carla was almost glad that approximately fourteen years ago she'd fallen over a tree stump.

Carla was awakened abruptly by a series of hideous sounds that seemed bent on tearing the quiet night apart.

She reached for her glasses, which Jonas had thoughtfully placed on the bedside table. Her wristwatch had a luminous dial. She saw that the hands on it stood at 1:30.

She threw back the bedclothes and gingerly tested her knee. The pain had settled down to a heavy, dull ache, and she was able to hobble across the room.

She drew back the window drapes and peered out onto a scene of incredible activity. The snow had stopped. There were three mammoth, bright yellow plows out in the parking lot doing their best to scoop up the blizzard remainders.

Carla remembered the motel keeper saying he'd contracted to have the place plowed out. Well, he was true to his word, but she almost wished that weren't the case. This meant that she and Jonas would have no problem leaving in the morning.

She became astonished at herself. Had she actually been *hoping* they'd be marooned a while longer?

The din was terrific...and getting louder. As she watched, she saw a man move into her line of vision, operating a snowblower along the top of the terrace, then moving down the steps. He was wearing so many layers of heavy clothing he had no shape at all. She watched him manipulate the noisy machine expertly, and by the time he'd finished and moved on there was a clear path straight to her car.

"Damn," she muttered under her breath, and slowly hobbled back to bed. But sleep didn't come easily. She started to think about Jonas in the very next room. He'd left the door open in case she needed something in the night. "Just call out," he'd said. She was tempted to call out now, but she doubted he'd even hear her. If he was able to sleep through the racket made by the plows and the snow machine, he'd be able to sleep through just about anything.

Still, it was tantalizing, very tantalizing, to know Jonas was so near, though her common sense was shouting that she should do everything in her power to keep him at a distance. So they'd shared an experience, she reasoned. Tomorrow was another day. She silently ran through a whole sequence of wise clichés. None of them made her want any less to go to Jonas. To watch him sleep. Perhaps to stretch out an exploring hand and touch the dark smoothness of his hair. Maybe to see how he reacted to being awakened suddenly in the middle of the night.

Carla tried to summon up thoughts, memories of Brian, which was the way she'd gotten through difficult times for years. But suddenly Brian seemed to be receding. It was as if he were standing at the very edge of her memory, and she had the feeling he actually wanted to take leave altogether, which was daunting. All these years it had been so easy to conjure up a vision of Brian's beloved features. Remembering him had kept her safe from the pressures and turmoil of life for so long.

Finally she slammed the brakes on all the treacherous corners of her mind and forced herself to concentrate on blackness, blackness, blackness. The problem was the blackness kept being superceded by an image of Jonas against a background of snow. And she knew that snow, forever, would remind her of Jonas. Snow and brandy and rare old books...

Everything became jumbled together, and Carla finally drifted off to sleep.

She was awakened by the aroma of freshly brewed coffee. Opening her eyes, she instinctively reached for her glasses. She noticed first that the door connecting her room with Jonas's had been closed. Then she focused on the man coming through the outer door that led onto the terrace.

Jonas was balancing a carton of coffee in each hand. At the same time, two of the fingers of his right hand were clutching a white paper bag.

He set the coffee containers down on the bedside table with a flourish, said, "Voilà!" triumphantly, then produced two paper napkins, opened the paper bag and withdrew a pair of glorious, plump, beautifully brown-crusted doughnuts.

Carla stared at both the doughnuts and the man in undisguised admiration. "Where did you ever get those?" she asked him.

"These are courtesy of our estimable motel keeper, whose name is Tom O'Higgins."

Carla reached for a doughnut, sank her teeth into it, then smiled blissfully. Her smile widened as she sipped the hot coffee. "I think I woke up in paradise," she murmured.

Jonas's silence alerted her. Usually he was quick with a return quip. She glanced up at him, surprised to see an odd intentness in those light blue eyes. "You're pretty easy to please," he observed.

She sensed a significance to the statement that she didn't grasp. Then filed it for future reference. Later, when she was alone, she could try to puzzle out what Jonas meant.

Later, when she was alone. It struck her that soon she would be alone again. Without Jonas in residence, that's to say. And it was surprising how desolate she felt at the thought of not having Jonas around, when yesterday all she'd wanted was to push him out of her life so she could get on with the auction.

The auction. She glanced at the bedside clock. It was almost nine. The auction was scheduled for eleven o'clock Saturday morning, approximately twenty-six hours from now.

"Why are you so anxious to have me stop things?" Carla blurted.

Jonas was sitting in a vinyl-upholstered chair near the window, munching his own doughnut, sipping his own coffee. "Stop what things?" he asked.

"The auction."

"Oh," Jonas murmured, and set aside both the remaining half of his doughnut and whatever was left in his coffee container. Then he said, a shade too indifferently, "There's no need to get into that now."

"No?" Carla queried. "If not now, when? There isn't much time left."

"I know," Jonas admitted reluctantly. "I, too, have been doing my arithmetic."

"And you still want to buy my books?"

He raised his eyebrows. "Are you suggesting you might consider selling them to me?"

"No," she said frankly. "I just want to know why you were so anxious to buy them?"

"It's not past tense, Carla," Jonas said. "I still want to buy your books. But if you're going to be as stubborn as you were yesterday," he said flatly, "why go into it?"

He sounded like someone who'd just brushed aside one business deal in favor of a better one. Carla, nettled because he could provoke her so easily, fought back a sharp retort and said, "I don't think you do many things without a good reason, Jonas."

"What's that supposed to mean?"

"I don't think you would have bothered to drive to Bedloe Falls without a good reason. I suppose what I'm saying is I have this idea you somehow know more about my books than I do."

This time Jonas lifted a single eyebrow. "Well," he said, "that would be your problem, wouldn't it? I mean to say, they are *your* books. Surely you've had ample opportunity to inventory them..."

"No," she corrected him, "that's just it. I haven't had ample opportunity to inventory them. When my grandfather died..."

"Yes?"

Carla stopped in midstream. She was *not* going to get into this, she decided. She was not going to start telling Jonas Davenport about Brian and how he'd been so ill when her grandfather died, she couldn't leave him. Later, there'd been no chance to spend enough time in Wainwright to catalog the books as they needed to be cataloged. Occasionally she'd gone up to the attic and browsed through the contents of a carton. But there were so many cartons....

"What is it?" Jonas asked sharply.

"What do you mean?"

"You look so damned sad," he accused, sounding almost angry about it. "Look, I had no idea my interest in your books would make you so unhappy."

"It isn't that," Carla said.

"Then what might it be?"

"Well..." She hesitated, then went on, "Well, sometimes one has to do something one doesn't necessarily want to do."

"Why do I get the feeling you think I wouldn't know anything about having to do something one doesn't want to do?" Jonas pondered rhetorically.

Carla sidestepped that subject. She continued, "The time has come for Jewel and me to sell the Wainwright house, and it's a fairly big house, full of a lot of things the family garnered over the years. Including the books. As it happens, I have no place for most—for almost all—of the things. Including the books. Thus, the auction. Then..."

"Go on."

"Well, yesterday you came across loud and clear, virtually insisting I should halt the auction so you can go over my grandfather's book collection before it's put up for sale. I want to know why, that's all."

She saw Jonas's wonderful mouth tighten. He said, "Obviously, you feel I had no right to make such a demand of you. Okay, I'll admit that. Also, I admit that at the time I was only interested in acquiring the books for a couple of reasons. But then . . ."

Jonas broke off, shrugged and said, "Damn it, I knew we shouldn't get into this, but now we *are* into it, so I might as well be hanged for a wolf instead of a sheep—if I'm getting that old saying right. How well do you know the Heggertys, Carla?"

Surprised, Carla said, "Why, I've known them most of my life. Skip's sister, Gwen, and I were in the same class in high school, and we were best friends. Gwen got married, years back, and moved to Alaska with her husband. Skip was a couple of years ahead of us in school. I used to spend a lot of time at the Heggertys. Mrs. Heggerty was a very dear person. She died while I was out in California . . ."

"So, the Heggertys were family friends," Jonas observed.

"No, not *family* friends," Carla corrected. "My father never knew them. And that was all before he married Jewel."

Actually, Jewel and her father had known each other by then, Carla reflected. Her father's small fabric-manufacturing business had sometimes taken him to New York, where he'd met Jewel, then a professional model. Jewel had come to Wainwright occasionally, at Thanksgiving or Christmas, mainly. Carla had liked her instantly and had suspected that maybe *she* was one of the reasons her father and Jewel hadn't married. Her father had always felt so *responsible* for her. As a result, she'd made the decision to go to college in California, in part to assert her independence, and in part to give Jewel and her father the chance she thought they needed. And she'd been right.

But she wasn't about to go into any of that with Jonas Davenport.

"How old were you when your mother died, Carla?" he asked suddenly.

"Three," she said.

"No brothers or sisters?"

"No." As she answered him, she was tempted to pose the same questions and couldn't understand why she hesitated. Maybe because Jonas's lack of comment on what she'd told him was, in its way, a shutoff.

"Are you still close to the Heggertys?" he asked abruptly. "That's to say, have you kept in touch all these years?"

The conversation was becoming a shade too one-sided. Irked, Carla asked, "What is this, Jonas? An inquisition?"

"No, I certainly didn't intend it to be," Jonas said rather stiffly. "Your knowing the Heggertys so well makes things a bit difficult, that's all."

Carla shook her head. "I'm not following you," she admitted. "For one thing, I *knew* the Heggertys a long time ago, but mostly I knew Gwen," she continued. Certainly she was not going to tell him she'd had a crush on Skip! "And, okay, I'll answer your question," she went on. "I haven't kept in touch with the Heggertys over the years. It was natural, once I decided about the auction, to call them, that's all, particularly once I found out Skip had gone in business with his father."

"I see," Jonas said.

He was staring at his "seven-league boots" as he spoke, so Carla had a chance to take a sharp look at him. His brow was furrowed, she noted, and his handsome face was uncompromisingly stern.

Jonas could be intimidating, as she'd already learned. He looked very intimidating now, but she took her courage in hand and suggested, "Don't you think you might as well come out and tell me what the problem is?"

He looked at her blankly, as if he'd never seen her before. The effect was disconcerting. And it didn't help when he said, "I definitely plan to tell you what the problem is, but not now. There'll be time enough for that in Wainwright."

Jonas got to his feet, and Carla felt as if he were dwarfing the whole room and her with it. He could not have appeared more impersonal, yet she caught a certain note of reluctance in his voice when he said, "Well, the snow has stopped. The motel lot has been pretty well plowed out. I imagine the roads are clear enough for travel by now. In any event, we're only forty miles from Wainwright."

"Only forty miles?"

"That's right."

In the blizzard last night Carla had lost all track of her bearings. She asked curiously, "Just where are we, Jonas?"

"In Tompkinsville, or right on the outskirts of it. At a motel named, The Steuben."

As he spoke, Carla noticed he'd left a good bit of his doughnut unfinished, whereas she'd wolfed hers down. Maybe that was a clue that something was really bothering him. Maybe it wasn't. She didn't know him that well. It occurred to her that, actually, she didn't know him at all.

"We'll be in Wainwright shortly," he said. "Then, believe me, Carla, I'll be glad to put *all* my cards on the table."

* * *

It wasn't that easy. Jonas left Carla so she could get dressed—no offers of help this time, not that she needed help anyway, she reminded herself as she fastened the clasp on her bra and slipped on her sweater and skirt.

Finally, Jonas knocked at the connecting door and came in, in answer to her invitation. But only to ask abruptly, "Got your car keys?"

"Yes," she said.

"Why not let me get your car warmed up for you?" he suggested. "Sure you can drive with that bad knee?"

She nodded, gave him the car keys, then went over to the mirror and surveyed her reflection. She'd brushed her hair, but she still looked...dismal. Impatiently, she smoothed on some lip gloss, even yielded to touching her cheeks with blush because she looked so pale. She thought about putting her contact lenses in, then decided that was pure vanity. At some other time, she promised herself, she'd use the contacts and some eye makeup and get dressed in her best finery, and maybe Jonas would feel that the dull moth he'd been shepherding around had suddenly been transformed into a butterfly.

To prove what? she asked herself rather dismally. This was not a fairy tale. She was not Cinderella. Jonas was not Prince Charming. Or, if he was, the glass slipper wasn't about to fit her foot.

She was closing up her suitcase and was about to hobble with it to the door when Jonas returned.

"I'm afraid we've run into a problem," he announced.

"What kind of a problem?"

"That mechanical contraption you call an automobile refused to budge," he told her.

"Jenny?"

"Yeah, Jenny. Tom, our trusty motel keeper, came over and tried to help me out, but we drew a blank. At first we thought maybe it was the battery, and we tried a jump start. It didn't work. I'm afraid your Jenny may be in the throes of a terminal illness, Carla."

"Nonsense," she retorted brusquely. "She needs a special touch, that's all. I'll get her started."

"Do you think you can walk?" Jonas asked her. "If walking's too uncomfortable, I can carry you."

"I think you've done more than your share of carrying me around," she retorted promptly.

Setting her teeth, she hobbled toward the door, aware that Jonas was watching her closely. And when she reached for her suitcase, he took charge.

"I'm going to carry you out to the car," he stated. "Then I'll come back and get your suitcase."

Before she could protest, he lifted her into his arms.

Carla was immediately torn by some very mixed emotions. Being in Jonas's arms was wonderful. All her basic instincts urged her to relax and enjoy, to snuggle against him and let her senses reel with the masculine feel and scent of him.

On the other hand, she resented being handled as if she had no mind or will of her own. She could have walked out to the car, damn it! He hadn't given her a chance.

She felt unnerved as she slid behind the steering wheel and heard Jonas say, "Let's see you wave your magic wand and get that heap of yours going."

For the next fifteen minutes Carla tried to wave her alleged magic wand. But Jenny still refused to budge.

By then Jonas had climbed into the front seat next to her and was tapping his fingers impatiently on the dashboard. Finally he asked, "Ready to give up?"

"Do I have a choice?"

"I wouldn't think so. Look, Tom can arrange to have Jenny towed to a garage, and we'll call back later and get a diagnosis. Okay? Meantime, let's transfer you over to my car and get on to Wainwright."

At that, Carla glanced at him suspiciously. "You didn't arrange this, did you, Jonas?" she asked him.

"What are you saying?"

"Did you pull something vital out of Jenny's insides so she couldn't start?"

He glared at her. "What kind of an operator do you think I am, Carla?" he demanded. "I've certainly never felt the need to do anything like that."

Chastised, Carla was ashamed, looked ashamed. She reminded herself that even if he were poor as a church mouse, anyone with Jonas Davenport's looks and charm—when he chose to be charming—certainly wouldn't need to do much more than lift a beckoning finger and most women would be more than willing to follow his lead.

Did she fall into that category?

It would be easy to, Carla admitted, and she automatically stiffened her spine. Jonas had been kind to her, even solicitous and tender at moments. At other moments he'd been autocratic as hell. Regardless, she knew she'd never forget their interlude in the snow. But she also knew that the important thing was she also not forget it had been exactly that. An interlude between then and now.

They were about to get back to "now," and she had the dire feeling that was akin to saying they were returning to square one.

Her chin held high, Carla gathered up all the dignity she could muster and hobbled over to Jonas's beautiful burgundy car.

Chapter Four

The snowplows had been working through much of the night and the early morning, but the storm just past had been such a major one the results of their work left much to be desired.

Jonas was forced to concentrate on his driving as he swung out of the motel entrance and turned north. And, he was glad to have even that much of a challenge to keep him occupied. As it was, Carla was disturbing him more than he liked to admit, mainly because he didn't know what to do about her.

She sat at his side, staring straight ahead, her lovely profile as immobile as if it had been chiseled out of milky quartz. He thought about renewing an attempt at communication, but, for once in his life, he didn't know how or where to begin.

He realized she'd suffered a loss of face with the demise of her trusty old car—Jenny, wasn't it?—and he wished he'd been more sympathetic. But it had galled him when she'd suggested maybe he'd tampered with the car just so he could get his own way.

Did he come on as that much of an egotistical bastard? *Was* he so blindly self-centered after years as a high-powered executive that he no longer had any real empathy for the feelings of others?

Jonas asked those questions of himself and answered them fairly. No, damn it, whatever else could be said of him he was not egotistical, not self-centered, and he felt a lot of sympathy for others. His problem was that he didn't always do the best job when it came to showing it. Early on, he'd had to learn the art of camouflage and concealment. But that didn't mean he didn't care.

He'd been forced into too much too soon. Circumstances had made it necessary for him to take control of the family business—and the pharmaceutical firm was big business by then, its headquarters long since removed from Wainwright to New York, with several manufacturing plants across the country. He'd gone into the business right after college—at age twenty-two—because it was expected of him and he'd thought there was no harm in yielding to the wishes of his elders for a couple of years before setting about doing what he really wanted to do.

But it hadn't worked that way. By the time he was in his late twenties, Jonas long since had scrapped his dream and by then was regarded as one of the best of the young executives heading for the top of the heap of America's business society, a pinnacle he'd never really wanted to attain.

He'd put his energies into the business because he had to. And because he had a keen, innovative mind, Wainwright Pharmaceutical had consistently done better under his leadership. It wasn't the biggest firm in its field, but it was one of the most respected and reliable ones.

In the process of being forced to exercise leadership, Jonas also had been forced to make his mark swiftly and surely, time and again. His youth, in the beginning, had been against him. The elders—in his company and elsewhere—had been waiting, a lot of them, for the favored youngster to get egg on his face. Because he was determined not to become a Humpty Dumpty, once he knew he had no choice about what his career was to be, Jonas quickly had learned to exhibit an assurance that, he knew, bordered on arrogance at moments. He was aggressive. He drove a hard bargain with himself. He also drove hard bargains with those who worked for him or sought to do business with him. But he was *fair*, damn it!

Imagine Carla Logan thinking he'd reach under the hood of that decrepit wreck of hers to commit an act of sabotage!

Jonas took his eyes off the road long enough to glance resentfully at Carla, which was a mistake. That glimpse of her softened him. She looked tired, and he imagined her knee must still be aching. Probably she also was worrying about the damned auction and still trying to figure out just what he might have up his nefarious sleeve.

He bit his lip, staring out again at the ice-patched highway. Carla's being friendly with the Heggertys, he reflected unhappily, made the whole thing a hell of a lot more difficult.

How could he come out and tell her he was virtually convinced people she'd known most of her life were crooks and were likely to take her for their own kind of sleigh ride if she persisted in doing business with them?

Musing about that and coming to no conclusions, he saw a roadside restaurant up ahead, a cluster of cars parked in front of it.

"Carla?" he queried.

"Yes," she answered tonelessly.

"Would you mind if we stop for coffee and maybe a real breakfast? I know there isn't much farther to go, but . . ."

"No," she said. "No, that's all right."

Her enthusiasm was woefully lacking, but Jonas drove into the restaurant parking lot anyway. Then, as Carla reached for the door handle, he said quickly, "Hang on. I'll help you."

"Thank you," she said coolly, "but I can manage on my own."

She was ridiculously independent. In fact, Jonas decided, she had a downright *fetish* about her independence. He wondered if maybe she'd been married to a much older man who had browbeaten her into a submission she was determined to eradicate.

He wondered a lot of things about her. What kind of music did she like? What was her favorite color? What the name was of that soft but sexy perfume she used? Did she like Greek food, which he personally doted on? The list went on and on.

He watched her march ahead of him toward the restaurant door, trying to hide her limp. It was all he could do to keep from taking her arm to steady her just a little bit, but he resisted. Nevertheless, he'd never felt so *protective* about anyone before. He discovered he wanted to take care of Carla, to watch over her, to shield her from all harm.

Who the hell did he think he was? he asked himself irritably. Sir Galahad?

They settled in a booth by the window. Their view looked out upon snow-covered meadows and distant hills shimmering like glistening spun sugar in the brilliant sunlight. The sky was an incredible blue, the color an assertion of nature's perfection regardless of the fury that same nature had been exhibiting only a few hours earlier. The day was winter perfect. Jonas suddenly wondered if Carla skied, then decided she probably didn't, with that trick knee of hers, so he didn't put the question to her.

He ordered a hearty breakfast of ham and eggs. Carla settled for an English muffin with a cup of coffee. Jonas watched her spread orange marmalade on a segment of her muffin with a slow, deliberate evenness he suspected was indicative of her inner nervousness.

He spoke impulsively. "Look," he said, "I'm sorry about Jenny."

She looked up at him, startled. "What?"

"Your car," Jonas said patiently. "She—it—evidently means a lot to you, so I'm sorry it conked out on you. Probably there's nothing wrong a good mechanic won't be able to put right."

"I don't know about that." Carla picked up another piece of muffin and started to spread marmalade on it, even though she hadn't eaten the first one. "Jenny's been through a lot."

Jonas took a hasty gulp of coffee so hot it almost scorched his throat. "Carla . . ." he began.

"Yes?"

Why was she being so damned *polite*? Jonas would have preferred to see a show of some of the feistiness she'd displayed with him at varying moments, back in the motel.

"Look," he said, suddenly determined to clear up things between them, "I think you should know I have no hidden motives where your book collection is concerned. I'm interested in old books, I wanted to buy the collection, that's all there was or is to it. If it'll make you any happier, I'll withdraw my offer."

Her glance was suspicious. "That's a rather abrupt change of heart, isn't it?" she asked. "When only last night you were determined to ride herd on me through a blizzard to get what you wanted?"

"I suppose," Jonas conceded, the words coming with difficulty, "that I . . . well, I suppose I'm somewhat accustomed to going after something when I decide I want it."

"That I can believe," Carla said dryly.

He fixed her with an accusing eye. "You are *not* helping," he stated firmly.

"Am I supposed to help?" she asked. "About *what* am I supposed to help?"

"I'm trying to make amends for my persistence," Jonas said. "They're your books, and it's your auction. I had no right to try to interfere."

He spoke simply, disarmingly, and Carla wished she could believe what he was saying. But she couldn't, and her original conclusion—that Jonas was used to getting his own way, most of the time anyway—remained unaltered. Jonas was pushy, *and* he was loaded with charisma and a charm that could turn a glacier into a flowing river. It was a dangerous combination. She didn't want to be browbeaten, neither did she want to find herself in danger of drowning.

She called what she suspected was his bluff. "Very well," she said, as sedately as Miss Bobbins might have said it, "I'll accept your offer."

She saw Jonas's eyes widen with astonishment. "You mean you're going to let me buy the books?" he asked her.

"No," Carla said. "I was referring to your second offer. You said, a few minutes ago, that if it would make me happier you'd retract your offer for the books. Well…it would make me happier."

She finished spreading marmalade on her last segment of English muffin, put it down on the plate with the rest of the muffin pieces and looked around in the hope of discovering something for her hands to do that would be better than twisting a napkin.

Jonas's astonishment faded, and he scowled. "I might have known," he muttered.

Carla saw his lips tighten, saw his chin program itself into a stubborn mode. "Okay," he said, "if that's the way you want it, that's the way it'll be."

"Thank you," Carla said, and finally reached for a piece of muffin and took a bite.

Jonas attacked his ham and eggs with a savageness that showed he was nowhere nearly as calm and indifferent as he looked. Watching him, Carla felt she was beginning to be able to tell the difference between veneer and man, and she suddenly missed, intensely, those glimpses of the man Jonas had shown her at the motel as he cared for her leg.

She remembered his warm and wonderful hands, his surprising tenderness. She remembered him trudging through thigh-deep snow to bring her hot chicken noodle soup. She felt a twisting, sweet ache, and she suddenly wanted to at least try to understand where he'd been coming from in his approach to her.

"Jonas," she asked almost gently, "why are you so interested in my grandfather's books?"

Jonas let his fork fall to his plate with a clatter. "I thought we'd finished with that topic," he muttered.

"Please," Carla said. "Look. I want to know. I mean, I really want to know. I need to know. You're not a person to do anything without a good reason."

"I believe that's an observation you've made before," Jonas said, folding his napkin and placing it beside his plate. "Shall we go?"

"No," Carla said. "That is . . . I'd like a bit more coffee, wouldn't you?"

"No," Jonas said. "And, in case you haven't noticed it, your coffee cup is almost full."

Carla didn't bother glancing down at her coffee cup because she knew he was right. "Well," she said logically, "it's gotten cold. So . . ."

Jonas said something under his breath she was as glad she couldn't make out, and beckoned to the waitress.

He remained silent as she stirred cream into her fresh cup of coffee, then sipped with exaggerated appreciation. Maybe it was the caffeine jolt, maybe it was simply that she had a fair share of innate stubbornness herself—as she was sure Jonas did—but she returned to the subject he'd vetoed with no difficulty at all. Nor did she mince words this time.

"Why do you want the books?" she asked directly.

Jonas sighed with total exasperation. "Back to that again, eh?" he asked, accompanying the question with an expression of complete boredom.

"Yes, back to that," Carla said levelly.

"Why do I have the feeling we're not about to get out of this place until I answer you?"

"Because we're not."

A ghost of a smile flitted around Jonas's expressive mouth. Carla concentrated on the smile, the mouth, and suddenly felt as if the thermostat in the little restaurant had been pushed up twenty degrees. The twisting pang she'd experienced a few moments ago returned, and this time she correctly identified it as desire. Wanting. Needing. Yearning. All for this totally unattainable man.

It crossed her mind that there could not have been two more different men placed on earth than Brian and Jonas. Brian had been slight, fair-haired, with rain-clear gray eyes and the sweetest smile she'd ever seen. He'd been gentle and loving, the most caring person she'd ever known. Able to understand, to share, to give, even though, through so much of his brief life, he'd been ill.

They'd had two wonderful years while he was in remission from the leukemia that then staked its final claim. Even the last memories—though they still had the power to bring her to tears on occasion—were worth the pain, because Brian had been so courageous, smiling right to the end.

She'd been very inexperienced when she'd married him, and he'd been a tender and considerate lover, respecting her needs first. They'd had a relationship, sexually, that she'd felt was as perfect as any such relationship could possibly be.

But now—with no sense of disloyalty to Brian—she couldn't help but think of how different, how entirely different, it would be to be made love to by someone like Jonas Davenport. He would be the aggressor, no doubt of that. The dominant, stalking conqueror.

Would there be anguish or pleasure in his conquering?

She decided that she was going to make damned certain she never found out.

She became aware that Jonas was watching her with that intentness he showed only once in a while. She would have given a great deal to know what he was thinking. She did know that he was waiting for her to get on with the subject of the books—probably so they could get out of this restaurant and he could take her home and then go about his own business.

"All right," she said, as if they'd been in the midst of a discussion. "Why do you want them?"

"Partly," Jonas said slowly, "because books have always been my escape hatch."

"Your escape hatch?"

"Yes. Books became a world to which I could retreat when I wanted to almost as soon as I learned to read," he said slowly. "They remain so. So it was something of a natural that, after a time, I got into collecting books as a hobby. I guess these days you could call me a bibliophile, a true lover of books, that is."

"A bibliophile is also a true connoisseur of books," Carla put in. "Which would imply a lover as well, I'd think."

"Very well, Miss Librarian," Jonas conceded, that hint of a smile hovering around his lips again. "Anyway, as I said, years back I got into collecting books, and a lot of the fun—which holds true for collecting anything—is in the search and the finding. In collecting, you have the challenge of a true treasure hunt. Sometimes you strike it rich, sometimes you don't. I've become pretty good at the search and finding, if I do say so myself, so..."

"So for some reason you felt you might strike it rich if you bought my grandfather's books, is that it?"

"You do come to the point, lady," Jonas observed wryly.

"The point's the thing to come to, in this case, Jonas," Carla informed him. "My next question is what makes you think my grandfather's books might be so valuable?''

Jonas looked uncomfortable. "I think I'm going to have to take the Fifth on that one," he said.

"That's ridiculous," Carla sputtered. "Why the *secrecy*? You make it sound like my books are part of some cloak-and-dagger operation."

"No, not that," he said. "I can't say any more than I already have only because it's a matter of confidence," he allowed. "I promise you that once we get to Wainwright, you'll see there's nothing at all sinister about any of this."

"But you must have *something* in mind," she persisted.

"Yes," he said. "And, believe me, if it were anyone but you involved..."

She waited, but he didn't continue. Instead, he asked, "Finished with that coffee?"

"No," she said. "And I won't be if you keep scattering incomplete sentences around. What would happen if it were anyone else but me involved?"

"I would have closed the book on the subject long before now," Jonas told her. Then winced slightly. "Bad pun," he observed.

Carla didn't care about the bad pun. She was letting what he'd just said wash over her and trying to decide how much it meant, if, indeed, it meant anything.

She decided on a change in tactics. "You said books have been your escape hatch ever since you were a kid," she reminded him. "Why did you need an escape hatch when you were a kid?"

He surveyed her soberly, and she began to fear he was most certainly going to close the book on *that* question. That fear made the answer all the more important to her.

So she held her peace and was both surprised and relieved when he said, "Yes, I needed an escape hatch when I was a kid. Like you, I was an only child. Like you, I lost my mother when I was very young. Subsequently, I didn't have much family life. Mostly penthouse apartments in a variety of cities, or houses here and there, presided over—at least as far as I was concerned—by a series of governesses."

Jonas stared down at his abandoned fork as he spoke, then admitted, "I guess I must have been a difficult brat. Most of the governesses didn't stay around very long, as I recollect. Every now and then my father would return from wherever he'd been, and I think he must have felt an urge to start all over again at those points, and one way of doing that was to sweep out the staff, move someplace else and find some new brooms.

"In between my father's appearances, my Grandmother Wainwright would come to visit now and then. Those were the good times," Jonas remembered.

"What about friends?" Carla asked. "Children your own age?" She couldn't personally remember a time in her childhood when there hadn't been children her own age around to play with.

"I didn't make friends easily when I was a kid," Jonas confessed, avoiding meeting her eyes. "My family actually wasn't *that* rich, but nevertheless in most places we lived, I guess I was considered the rich kid on the block. Other kids left me pretty much to myself, and I tended to be a loner anyway. Books were good company."

He fell silent. Then suddenly he looked up at Carla and said, "Okay, tit for tat. You said sometimes people have to do things they don't want to do, and I got the impression that holding the auction and selling your family home is something you have to do but don't want to do. Am I right?"

It was Carla's turn to hesitate. "Yes...and no," she said.

"Elaborate."

"Well...having the auction and selling the house isn't really a financial necessity, at least not in one way. But, in another, it is."

"Am I supposed to be able to make sense of that?"

"What I'm trying to say," Carla said, "is that I don't really need the money. For myself, that is. But I've felt increasingly that the house is a millstone around Jewel's neck. You see, when my father met Jewel, she was a model in New York, a well-known model. She's...well, she's essentially a city person."

"So Wainwright bores her?"

"Stop putting words in my mouth, will you, Jonas?" Carla advised. "No, Jewel isn't bored in Wainwright. She's quite content there, but she's vegetating, and she's too young and too beautiful to vegetate. However, Dad didn't leave her that much in the way of...worldly assets. Most of the contents of the house belonged to my mother—the grandfather with the books was her father—and so all those things came to me. Jewel and I inherited equal shares in the property itself. And, believe me, Jewel would never dream of selling without my pushing her."

"Then why are you pushing her?"

"Because, as I just told you, she needs to get away from Wainwright. With the money from the sale of the house, she can get herself a condo in New York and start living again, the way she should be living. Dad's been dead two years. Jewel's put the pieces of her life together very well, but they don't make the right pattern, that's all."

"You're so sure of that?"

"Very definitely I'm sure of it."

"How long have you been a widow, Carla?"

The question came so quickly she answered it automatically. "Six years," she said. And then added quickly, "But that has absolutely no bearing on any of this."

She realized she was avoiding Jonas's eyes just as he'd been avoiding hers earlier. She said, "I've had a hard time convincing Jewel that we should sell the house. She considers it my ancestral home, which isn't quite the truth, though Hendrickses *have* lived in the house for a long while."

"Do you care about the house?"

"Yes, I care about it, in a very sentimental and nostalgic sort of way. There are a lot of memories tied up with it. But you can't live with memories, Jonas. I have no plans to go back and live in Wainwright myself."

"Where *do* you intend to live, Carla?"

"Well," she said, "I'm pretty much slated for Miss Bobbins's job in Bedloe Falls, once she retires."

"And you've already said you have no place for your family possessions where you live now, nor will you be apt to have. Nor will Jewel."

"That's right. We're each choosing a few things that are special to us, including some of the books. Skip understands I intend to retain a few of the books for myself."

"So," Jonas said, "the terms of the auction are a bit more open-ended than you originally implied."

"No," Carla said quickly. "There's a big difference between a few books and objects and the—the whole thing," she said defensively.

"What's important to me," she continued, before he could interject anything else, "is to do the best thing for both Jewel and myself, and it seems obvious the best thing is to sell the house and most of the things in it. Possessions can become a burden. I thought it all over, and I decided now was a good time to have the auction because people will be looking for Christmas gifts. Also, for our benefit, it will kind of wrap everything up by the end of the year. The house may not sell immediately, but that doesn't matter. Jewel can come visit me in Bedloe Falls over the holidays, and we'll both be starting off the New Year with a clean slate."

"Mmm," Jonas said, in a way that gave no indication whether he was agreeing or disagreeing with her.

"Jewel keeps busy," she went on, "but I know she's lonely. She's gone through a lot of empty hours by herself. Sometimes there's just no way to fill hours like that. So, I want her to have the chance to get back to the city, where she can touch base with old friends. What I'm hoping is that she'll go back to modeling."

"Isn't she a bit old for that?"

"Jewel was considerably younger than my father," Carla said. "She's forty-four, and she's stunning. There's no longer an age limit on looks and fashion, Jonas. I'm sure Jewel would have no problem in getting modeling jobs if that's what she wants. But with the money we get from the house, plus what she's gotten from Dad's insurance, she won't need to work unless she wants to. Personally, I hope she'll want to. I want to see her get out and mingle and get some of her sparkle back again."

Listening, Jonas felt his curiosity brimming. There'd been a certain revealing quality to Carla's statement about loneliness and empty hours.

He posed a question. "How old are you?" he asked.

Carla blinked. "Twenty-eight. Why?"

"I just wondered." As he spoke, he was thinking that she'd been only twenty-two when her husband died. He could imagine how bereft she must have been—even if her husband was an older man who'd tried to subjugate her, as he suspected. She must have experienced a great deal of loneliness, put in many empty hours.

He wished he knew more about her husband and what kind of a marriage they'd had. She must have been very, very young when she got married. He wished he knew how she'd come to the decision to become a librarian, and whether she felt fulfilled in her job, and whether she *really* wanted to take over for Miss Bobbins one of these years.

That protective urge surged again as he looked at her finally finishing off her cup of coffee. Behind the glasses, her eyes looked huge and were as close to the color of spring violets as any eyes he'd ever seen.

Jonas suddenly had a vision of Sir Galahad on a white horse galloping into their scenario, then recognized that it was he who was wearing Sir Galahad's armor and quickly dispelled the image.

His voice was gruff as he said to Carla, "Look, I think it's time we got going."

Chapter Five

Jonas pulled up in front of Carla's house, glad the drive was over. They'd said very little to each other since leaving the restaurant. He, personally, felt he'd already said too much. He'd told her more than he'd ever told anyone else about his lonely childhood.

There were, of course, many things he *hadn't* told her. Nor had she been very revealing about herself. He sensed she had a secret heart she seldom, if ever, shared, just as he did.

He saw that the walk in front of the Hendricks house and the steps leading up to the broad front porch had been shoveled. That was a relief, otherwise—if there were icy spots—Carla was more than apt to take a flyer and wrench her bad knee again.

He chuckled inwardly as he thought about how fervently she'd protest if he suddenly swooped her up in his arms and carried her over her own threshold.

As he circled the car to open the passenger door for Carla, the front door of the house opened, and Jonas glanced up to see a tall, slender, dark-haired woman step out onto the porch.

Carla hobbled up the walk and up the steps. She and the dark-haired woman embraced with an affection that made Jonas feel envious because their mutual feelings were so obviously genuine.

He busied himself with getting Carla's suitcase out of the trunk, bent on handing it over to her and then beating a hasty exit. He was prepared to mutter something about getting in touch—which he intended to do once he'd put a couple of scenes in his act together. But, as he neared the top of the steps, suitcase in hand, Carla forestalled him by asking, "Jewel, have you met Jonas Davenport?"

Jonas conceded it was, of course, simple good manners for Carla to introduce him to her stepmother, and politeness, he'd already learned, was basic with Carla.

Jewel said, "No, I haven't met Mr. Davenport," and extended a slim, pale hand.

Jonas grasped her hand and found himself gazing into beautiful, eloquent brown eyes. Jewel was a striking woman. She carried herself with that instilled grace that becomes routine with professional models, and even in a green-and-gold warm-up suit that would have made most women look dumpy she was stunning.

She was inches taller than Carla, had none of Carla's curves but, rather, a slenderness that was almost extreme—though perfect for high fashion.

Her voice was as warm as her eyes. "I've been wanting to meet you, Mr. Davenport," she confessed. "But I didn't expect you to be bringing Carla home. Actually, I didn't expect Carla till this evening, and I was so afraid it would keep on snowing all day. What a storm that was."

"Yes," Jonas nodded.

"I worry about Carla driving around in that old jalopy of hers," Jewel confessed, while Carla frowned. "And it would be just like her to start out in a blizzard if she felt she had to get here."

Carla was beginning to feel the two of them had forgotten she was present. But before Jonas could vouchsafe any further information, she spoke up.

"Carla *was* driving through that blizzard last night in that old car of hers," Carla stated.

Jewel looked properly stunned. Then she asked, "In that case . . . what happened to Jenny?"

"I'm afraid Jenny died," Carla said unhappily.

"Carla ran into a spot of engine trouble when she tried to get the car started this morning," Jonas said quickly. "We left Jenny at a garage in Tompkinsville. I'm sure she's going to be fine."

Jonas heard what he was saying and couldn't believe himself. He actually was personifying a decrepit old jalopy that belonged in a junkyard.

"Methinks there's a tale to be told here," Jewel murmured. "How about coming in for a cup of tea, Mr. Davenport—or maybe a drink to warm you up. Then you can fill me in."

Jonas looked at Carla and saw that she was frowning. There was absolutely no invitation in *her* eyes, and even if there had been, he would have been forced to decline. There were things he had to do.

He switched on the high-voltage smile that usually devastated his competitors. "I'm afraid I'll have to take a rain check," he said regretfully, then took the plunge and added, "But I'd like to come around this evening, if that wouldn't inconvenience you."

"Take potluck with us," Jewel suggested.

"Fine," Jonas nodded, and this time he didn't look at Carla at all.

"Sevenish," Jewel said, and they left it at that.

Carla hobbled into the living room, well aware that her stepmother was watching every inch of her halting progress. She sank down in the nearest armchair.

"Whew!" she said, which was the understatement of the century. She felt she had so much pent up inside her that she would explode if she so much as dared to let any of it out.

Jewel sat down on the big, green upholstered couch, looking as if she were posing for a magazine ad. "Well?" she asked.

"I won't bother to ask, 'well what?'" Carla said. "You knew he was heading for Bedloe Falls. The least you could have done was to send out the cavalry."

Jewel chuckled. "Was he that hard to handle?"

"That depends on one's viewpoint."

"Well, then," Jewel said, "Jonas Davenport did call here yesterday morning to verify that you were working at the Bedloe Falls Library. But that was all, darling. He gave no indication he was going your way."

"He called you later," Carla pointed out.

"Yes, he called me later. But primarily to ask if I was the one insisting on holding the auction tomorrow."

"And you said it was my auction."

"Carla, my dear, it *is* your auction," Jewel said gently.

Carla sat up a shade straighter and immediately winced. But she said, with determination, "Jewel, it is *our* auction, damn it. I've told you we're going to split everything."

"That's ridiculous," Jewel replied with a weariness that was understandable since they'd been over this subject a hundred times before. "Everything that's any good in this house belonged to your mother, Carla, and it's yours. If we sell the house, I agree to a split. But the auction remains *your* auction, my dear."

"Jonas wants me to either postpone it or call it off," Carla blurted. "At least . . . he did."

She couldn't blame Jewel for looking puzzled. So she launched into the details of Jonas's appearances at the Bedloe Falls Library the previous afternoon, the later "chase" through the impending blizzard—Carla rather dramatically describing Jonas's following her—and of the motel scene in which he played doctor with her knee.

At that, Jewel's eyes twinkled. "I think most women would vote Jonas Davenport in the top ten to be marooned with in a snowstorm," she teased.

"It wasn't funny," Carla said, but then she had to smile despite herself.

"Ah," Jewel approved, "that's better."

Carla's smile faded. "He's a strange person," she said slowly. "A strange . . . personality mixture. I've known him approximately twenty-four hours, and I'd say I've seen at least six different sides to him. I already feel like asking, Which is the real Jonas Davenport?"

Which *was* the real Jonas Davenport? The autocratic scion of not one but two wealthy families and the arrogant business executive, used to using charisma or anything else he needed to use to achieve his own goals? Or was he the caring, gentle man whose touch had been so incredibly warm and sensual as he was carefully tending to her injured knee? Or was he the lonely boy who'd plunged himself into the world of books almost as soon as he learned to read, using literature as his escape hatch? Or was he . . . ?

"Carla?" Jewel said.

Carla snapped out of her reverie.

"I'm going to run a hot tub for you," her stepmother decided. "Soak for a while, snatch a bit of a nap if you can. You look as if you could use one. Then we can get down to a few things."

"What things?"

"Well, Skip Heggerty stopped by this morning to do what he called a last-minute check. I would have thought he'd finished . . ."

"Why do you say that?"

"He's spent a lot of time here this past week," Jewel said. "Especially up in the attic, going through your books. He's made a list, which he had duplicated, and he left a copy for you."

Carla, in danger of again sinking into a reverie in which Jonas was playing a disconcertingly prominent part, came to quickly. "Where is it?"

"I have it," Jewel said. "I'll give it to you later. You'll have plenty of time to look it over this evening. The auction isn't starting till ten tomorrow morning, and Skip says he'll have ample opportunity to pull out any of the books you want to keep. We've already put the china and that Dutch sink and the other things you said you wanted out in the back pantry, which had been emptied."

"Who emptied the back pantry?" Carla asked, remembering that the fairly large, square room had been full to the brim with all sorts of things.

"Well, Skip sent one of his men over, and I helped him," Jewel admitted.

Troubled, Carla said, "This auction has caused you an awful lot of work, hasn't it, Jewel? I didn't intend for that to happen. When I asked the Heggertys to conduct the auction for us, I didn't realize what I was involving you in. You're the person who's been here on the scene, and I can see, now, that a lot has been thrust on you. I wish you'd complained to me about it."

Jewel said patiently, "You can't get a house ready for an auction, can't clear out things that have to be cleared out, without a certain amount of effort, Carla. But there was nothing to complain to you about. I had nothing else to do that really needed doing."

"Regardless," Carla said, "I should have taken leave from the library, Miss Bobbins or no Miss Bobbins, and come up here and attended to those things myself. I don't know what I was thinking about. Yes, I do know what I was thinking about. I was thinking that Skip would see to it everything was handled for us. I had no intention of putting a load on *your* shoulders."

"You haven't," Jewel said brusquely. "All is in order, and tomorrow everything is going to go like clockwork. Incidentally, I made reservations for the two of us for tomorrow night at the Heritage House."

Carla looked up in surprise. The Heritage House was Wainwright's prime hostelry. It was certainly a nice place to stay, but she couldn't immediately see why she and Jewel should be spending tomorrow night there.

Then Jewel said softly, "Once the auction's over—if it's the success the Heggertys assure me it will be—there won't be much left in the house, Carla. I saw no point in holding out beds for us to sleep on for a couple of nights. I thought it made more sense to let them go with the rest of the things.

"Now," she said firmly, "no more delays. I'm going to run that hot bath for you."

Carla hobbled upstairs, let her stepmother produce a tub filled with foaming, pine-scented bubbles, but once she was reclining in a warm, luxurious atmosphere that made her feel as if she were swimming in a fragrant forest, everything crashed down.

Tomorrow night there wouldn't even be a couple of beds left in this house.

The pictures would be off the walls, pictures she'd been looking at all her life and had come to love, regardless of their monetary value or lack thereof. The bric-a-brac she'd also been looking at all her life, like the amberina vase and the rose medallion cups and the fragile milk-glass saltcellar fashioned in the shape of a swan, would be gone, too. She'd held out some of the things she really wanted to keep, but it was impossible to hoard all of the treasures that had sentimental value.

The books would be gone, too, all those books of her grandfather's—some of which she remembered from her childhood—which she'd never even had a chance to read and now never would.

There'd also been trunks in the attic, filled with the memorabilia of other generations. Had Jewel gone through all of them, weeded the contents so that the things that should be kept were being kept?

What had she been thinking of? Carla muttered the question, chagrined because she'd been so oblivious to reality where the auction was concerned. Now she could see that no one in his or her right mind would simply call in a local auctioneering firm and tell them to go to it.

Jonas, she admitted grudgingly, did have a point.

After a time, the bath water cooled and Carla reluctantly emerged from the tub, the last of the bubbles clinging to her damp skin. She toweled, slipped on the terry robe Jewel had put out for her, then headed for the room that had been hers for as long as she remembered. She stood next to the maple four-poster, looking down at the patchwork quilt that had kept her so warm and cozy on cold winter nights long ago as if she were looking at a beloved friend. Then she snuggled under the quilt, her mind twisting and turning as she tried to sort through her jumbled thoughts. In the process, she fell asleep.

It was dark when she awakened, and it was Jewel's voice that awakened her.

"Jonas is downstairs, and we're having a drink before dinner," Jewel reported. "I got out your green velvet robe. Slip it on, darling, and come along and join us."

The robe in question was a gorgeous shade of emerald that was a definite enhancement to Carla's coloring. Carla knew that, and she knew Jewel knew it, too, and suspected that thoughts of matchmaking were again swirling around in Jewel's romantic mind.

Before Jewel became too obvious, she wished she could make her see that nothing could be much more ridiculous than envisioning a match between Jonas Davenport and herself. Except where books were concerned—for she was as much of a book lover as he was—they weren't even on the same planet. Before Jewel got carried away, that fact was going to have to be conveyed to her.

Nevertheless, Carla shrugged into the robe, paused to brush her hair, add a touch of makeup and a daub of perfume and then, looking in the mirror, very nearly changed her glasses for her contact lenses. Only at the last instant did her honest dislike of vanity cause her to opt for the glasses.

Someone had built a fire in the living room. Golden warmth radiated from the hearth, and on either side of that hearth Jewel and Jonas were occupying armchairs while engaging in an earnest conversation.

Carla, pausing on the threshold, heard only a snatch of their words before Jonas spotted her and shot to his feet.

"Come, take this chair," he invited, indicating the chair he'd been sitting in, which, undoubtedly, would be warm and cozy, not only from the heat of the fire but from the presence of his well-toned body.

"No, that's all right," Carla said, heading for the chair beside Jewel's.

"This one's more comfortable," Jonas insisted, taking her arm and nudging her toward the chair.

She fought back the instinct to throw off his arm and make a snappy retort. She *could* choose her own chair, damn it! He didn't have to assume instant command of absolutely everything.

Just looking at him made her feel perverse, for no good reason.

Jonas was wearing a creamy, thick wool Irish sweater and snug-fitting black slacks. His dark hair made her think of midnight velvet, or maybe of a material yet to be invented that combined all the best attributes of velvet and satin. The firelight emphasized his tan and made his eyes look all the lighter. The effect was . . . dazzling.

Carla quickly forced her eyes away from him, headed for the chair of her choice and sat down.

Jonas accepted his defeat with grace. "Jewel and I are having bourbon and branch," he said agreeably. "Is that okay with you?"

"No," she said. "I'd rather have white wine."

"I'll get it," Jewel said hastily, and beat a retreat before Carla could protest that she was perfectly capable of getting her wine herself.

For a strangely tense moment, Carla sat very still, staring down at her hands as she tried to assemble a poise she hoped would stand up against Jonas. She stole a glance at him. He, in turn, was staring at the fire. Sometimes he looked larger than life to her, and that was the case now. It wasn't his physical size; it was a kind of aura. That air of total assurance could be so irksome. Right now she found him daunting.

He spoke without looking at her. "Jewel and I were talking," he said.

"So I gathered," Carla commented dryly.

"Carla, look, I'm not trying to press my case about the books," he said, the words spilling out of him as if this was something he had to get off his chest. "You wanted me to withdraw my offer, I've withdrawn it. Nevertheless . . . Jewel said Skip Heggerty left a listing of the titles for you this morning."

"Yes."

"Have you gone over it?"

"No. Jewel was going to give it to me, but she hasn't yet. I fell asleep and . . ."

She let the words trail off. Why did she feel so impelled to explain herself to him?

"Do you remember anything at all about your grandfather's books, Carla? What I mean is, did you ever really *look* at them when you were younger."

"Of course," she said. "Grandpa gave me such a love of books that I later decided I wanted to be a librarian. He taught me how to recognize first editions and that sort of thing."

"Do you remember any particular titles in his collection?"

"Why do you ask?"

"Don't sound so suspicious. I just wondered, that's all."

"Jonas," she said patiently, "I went out to California to college when I was just a bit over eighteen years old. I lived out there for several years. Grandpa died while I was in California. When I came back East, it was to go to Bedloe Falls and assume my job at the library there. I've spent very little time in Wainwright since coming back six months ago."

"That's not what I asked you."

"Well, you asked me about the books. Occasionally, when I've been back here, I've rummaged through some of the books, but I just haven't been able to get down to doing a thorough job with them . . ."

"You still haven't answered my question, Carla."

"*What* question?"

"Do you specifically remember any titles you saw when you were younger? First editions, maybe? Something rare, maybe?"

He was exasperating her. Despite his saying that he had withdrawn his offer to buy her books, he still seemed awfully interested. And she wondered why. Jonas, she was certain, wouldn't waste his time in being interested in anything that wasn't worth his interest.

"Well, since you're so insistent about this," she said, "yes, I do remember some of the books. For example, Grandpa owned a rather rare three-volume set of old leather-bound books called, *The Adventurer*. It was published in 1793. There were also some Washington Irving first editions and a couple of Mark Twain ones."

"Would you look at Skip Heggerty's list and see if the books you've just mentioned are on it?"

Carla's eyes widened. "Just what are you suggesting, Jonas?" she asked.

"I'm not *suggesting* anything, Carla. I'm just asking you to do something that's really very simple."

To Carla's relief, Jewel came back with her glass of wine at that moment. Then Jewel noticed that Jonas's glass was empty, but when she suggested she make him a refill, he promptly offered to make it himself and to give her half-empty glass what he called "a bit more character," as well.

When he'd left the room, Jewel eyed her stepdaughter and said, "You look like a thundercloud, Carla. What went on between you and Jonas while I was out of the room?"

"He is so *persistent*," Carla complained.

"In what way?"

"In any way that suits him," Carla said sourly. "Or about anything that suits him. Now he's harking back to the books, and he told me this morning he'd withdrawn his offer to buy the whole collection."

"Because you wanted him to, I presume."

Carla looked up quickly. "Did he tell you that?"

"No. But sometimes it's easier to read between the lines than it is to read the text, honey. Carla . . ."

Carla had been watching the fire. Now Jewel's tone of voice wrested her attention away from the hearth. "What is it?" she asked her stepmother, not liking the gravity she was seeing on Jewel's lovely face.

"I think you should give Skip Heggerty a call and tell him you're going to have to postpone the auction for a week. If you like, I'll make the call for you. Obviously, that knee of yours is acting up on you. We can use it as an excuse.''

''Why should we need an excuse, Jewel?''

''Because this is last minute, because the auction has been advertised, because Skip will have to get some quick notices up, maybe take some radio time and post signs out in front of the property between now and ten o'clock tomorrow morning,'' Jewel said.

''Maybe what I should have asked was why we should even consider postponing the auction,'' Carla countered. She was remembering her feelings as she'd looked at her maple bed with its heirloom quilt. She'd been psyched for this auction—had gotten herself psyched—but if she got the chance to react to the sight of many things as she had to the bed, she was going to start wavering. She wondered if she postponed the auction if she could possibly bring herself to reactivate it. The temptation to call it off altogether, to try to come up with another alternative by means of which Jewel could get out of Wainwright and go back to New York, was so tempting . . .

''Carla,'' Jewel said in an unusually peremptory tone for Jewel.

''Yes?''

''There's no point in my telling you why I think you should postpone the auction unless you stop woolgathering and listen to me.''

''All right, I'm listening.'' As she spoke, it occurred to Carla that Jonas was taking his time about making a fresh drink for himself and fixing up Jewel's drink. Was he deliberately remaining offstage so Jewel could work on her about the auction? Had he managed to mesmerize Jewel to carry his banner for him in just a short fireside chat with her?

"I know you've known the Heggertys a long time. I know you were in love with Skip when you were both in high school . . . or thought you were," Jewel stated.

Carla hoped fervently that Jonas didn't also have a habit of eavesdropping.

"Jewel," she protested, "that was forever ago. And Skip was a senior when I was a sophomore. He didn't even know I was alive."

"Nevertheless, you have known the family a long time, and it's not easy to hear things about old friends."

"What kind of things?"

Jonas had started in along this vein back at the motel. Then he had suddenly shut up tighter than a clam.

"Unfortunately," Jewel continued, "the Heggertys do not have the best of reputations in their business. There was no way you could have known that. You haven't been around Wainwright that much. I'm afraid I haven't circulated that much, either, these past couple of years—so I'm not very conversant with town rumors."

"Certainly you don't believe the kind of gossip that flies around a town like Wainwright," Carla said, disbelievingly.

"Sometimes where there's smoke there's fire," Jewel rejoined quietly. "Anyway . . . Jonas has had occasion to learn a number of things about the Heggertys, and, frankly, I'm sorry you chose them to conduct the auction, Carla. I know you have a contract with them. I don't know how legally binding it is. But I think you should postpone the auction until we can find out. Then . . . we'll take it from there."

"I have the feeling that Jonas has put words in your mouth," Carla said, not bothering to either keep her voice lowered or to hide her indignation. "Damn Jonas! I should think he'd have enough to do keeping his fingers in all those big business pies of his without butting in where he isn't wanted."

She caught Jewel's warning glance, but it was too late. Jonas was standing in the doorway with a glass in either hand, and if someone who had his kind of tan could be said to have suddenly gone pale, then he'd suddenly gone pale.

He crossed the room, his shoulders rigid, handed Jewel her drink and then sat down in the chair by the fireplace. He was expressionless, but his mouth was set in a tight, telltale line.

Carla stared at him helplessly, saw him take a hefty swig of his drink then heard him admit, "She's right, Jewel. I have butted in. So my course of action, at this point, is pretty clear. I'm butting out."

He set the drink aside and stood up again. Ignoring Carla, he said to Jewel, "I hope you'll understand if I renege on your potluck supper invitation. Thanks for the drink, anyway, and I'll be getting on my way."

He turned toward Carla in parting, evidently unable to resist one last thrust. "Go right ahead and have your own stubborn way about your auction," he told her. "After all, why the hell should I care if your old high-school sweetheart sweeps the magic carpet right out from under you?"

Chapter Six

Jonas beat a hasty retreat. Jewel followed him. Carla heard their voices out in the hall, but she couldn't make out what they were talking about.

Jewel came back to say, "I tried to persuade him not to leave, but he was adamant. He looks like the Rock of Gibraltar, but I'm afraid you've hurt his feelings, Carla."

"I doubt he wounds that easily," Carla retorted.

Jewel cast a speculative eye on her stepdaughter. "What is it with you two?" she demanded. "As far as I can make out, you only met each other yesterday afternoon. It's difficult to think two people could become so programmed to disagree in such a short time."

"Jonas is used to running things," Carla said, "and I don't like to be run."

She spoke as if the explanation were a very simple one, but she knew the difficulties between Jonas and herself were far more complex than she was admitting. Her problem was that Jonas either exasperated or intrigued her, from moment to moment and in varying degrees— and she didn't know how to handle such emotional switches.

No, she conceded honestly, taking the matter of her feelings toward Jonas a step further along the way, her *real* problem was that she was almost afraid of Jonas. Not, certainly, because he'd ever do her any harm—if she'd ever been convinced of anything she was convinced of *that*. She was even willing to believe that *he* believed he had her best interests at heart.

Her uneasiness about him lay in a different direction. He intimidated her, even when he was being charming. Perhaps most of all when he was being charming. He seemed to her the epitome of everything she wasn't, and deep down she was convinced her first feelings about him had been the correct ones. The two of them lived on different planets. She'd be squashed flat in Jonas's world, he'd be bored stiff in hers. A mutual love of books just wasn't enough of a binder.

Carla thought further, then reflected morosely that her *biggest* problem where Jonas was concerned was that when she wasn't trying to stand up to him, he made her melt. He was a very sexy man, even when he wasn't trying to be sexy. Certainly he hadn't been trying to be sexy when he was caring for her bunged-up knee, but if he'd paused to take her vital signs, she was sure her blood pressure would have been up, her pulse racing and her respiration rate equally out of whack.

She could only hope he hadn't been aware of her involuntary response to him. Otherwise, she would be enormously embarrassed. She hated to think of his amusement, should he review their few hours together and suddenly come to realize that snowbound, back at the motel, she'd been anything but the prim, aloof librarian she'd tried to appear to be.

As Carla was thinking, Jewel had kept herself busy poking what was left of the logs in the fireplace. Now Carla became aware that Jewel had turned away from the hearth and was watching her, that speculative expression in her lovely dark eyes again.

She was surprised when Jewel said suddenly, "I think you're doing Jonas a disservice. I think you should have listened to him. I *did* listen to him."

Jewel drew a long breath and continued, "I've seldom stuck my neck out when it's come to giving you advice, Carla. I've never felt I had that right, and your father warned me, a long time ago, that you were born with a will of your own. But..."

Carla waited. Finally she prodded. "But what?"

Jewel plunged. She said, "I say again, I think you should call either Skip Heggerty or his father and simply say you've had a minor accident and you're not up to holding the auction tomorrow."

Carla heard this and shook her head. "I can't believe you, Jewel. Ten minutes with Jonas Davenport and you've let him convince you we're about to do the wrong thing."

"Only because he can back up what he's saying, Carla," Jewel shot back, "and I think it would have been downright foolish of me not to listen to him."

"All right," Carla agreed, "you heard what he said, and evidently you think he has grounds to prove the Heggertys are dishonest."

"*Dishonest* is a strong word."

"Is there a weaker one for the same thing?"

Jewel sighed. "Your father also warned me that you could be the stubbornest child alive. Don't look like that.

Believe me, I know you're not a child but, rather, an exceptionally strong-minded, capable and resilient woman—despite that helpless-kitten appearance of yours.''

Helpless kitten appearance, indeed!

"I am not trying to get you to call *off* the auction," Jewel went on, "even though you know I've never been much for it. I know your motive, even though you've never spelled it out in so many words, and surely no motive could be more generous. You want to auction off your things so we can sell this house and I'll have the money to move back to New York. You think I'm withering away here in Wainwright—"

"Well," Carla interrupted bluntly, "aren't you?"

"Not really," Jewel answered, to her surprise. "At least, not in the way you think I am. I loved your father very much, Carla. It's taken me a while to adjust..."

"Becoming a widow is something it takes anyone a while to adjust to."

"I know. And I'm not saying there's any reason why I should think my lot any more difficult than that of any woman who's been through the same thing. But... your father's death was so sudden. He got up one morning looking like the healthiest man in the world, and by noon he was... dead. He'd just had a physical. We'd no idea there was a serious problem with his heart...."

Jewel paused, then said softly, "Forgive me. I didn't mean to bring that up. And, believe me, I'm well aware of what you went through with Brian."

"No," Carla said, "no, you're right. I knew for a long time that Brian wasn't going to live. I knew when I married him that he had leukemia and was in remission. He never tried to keep his illness from me. Then... he was sick for so long I... well, I guess I began adjusting to the fact Brian was going to leave me long before that actually happened...."

"Which didn't make anything less difficult for you," Jewel put in. "I've never told you this, Carla, but I admire you tremendously. You had your mourning period, then you went out and did something about yourself. Got yourself into a career you'd always been interested in. I'm very, very proud of you, and your father would be, too. But..."

Carla smiled faintly. "Must there always be buts, Jewel?"

Jewel returned the smile. "There usually are," she conceded. "Carla, dear, I'm not about to try to tell you what to do, but I am going to ask you to think this over, and I really hope you'll call Skip, even if it's only to delay things for a couple of weeks. I'm in no hurry...about anything. Eventually, yes, I would like to go back to New York. I have a lot of friends there. I admit it's my world. But I've had some very happy times here in Wainwright. The best times of my life, actually. I'm sure I'm going to miss this house, the people I've met here, the town itself, the beautiful countryside...."

When Carla didn't immediately answer, Jewel said, "I have the feeling I'm not doing a very good job of persuading you. So I'm going to make it an outright request. *Please* call the Heggertys."

Carla frowned. "Jewel, even if I agreed it would do no harm to postpone the auction for a couple of weeks, this is *very* late in the day," she pointed out. "The auction has been advertised, everything's set to go..."

"The Heggertys can get the radio station to broadcast the postponement," Jewel said. "Signs can be put out in front of the house. Next week, the new date can be advertised in the papers."

"I don't think the Heggertys are going to agree to that without a *very* good reason," Carla said doubtfully.

"You have the reason."

"Jewel," Carla said patiently, "do you really believe that if I tell Skip I twisted my knee, that's going to convince him the auction should be stopped? He may even remember I have a trick knee. I used to be limping some of the time when I went to his house with Gwen.

"Anyway," she continued, "my knee feels a lot better. By tomorrow, it'll be fine."

"It won't *look* fine if we dig out your grandfather's cane and you go hobbling around on it," Jewel said. "And stop looking as if that would be the ultimate chicanery. You can take the tack with Skip that two weeks from now it'll be that much closer to Christmas. People who haven't done their shopping will be that much more eager to snatch up a bargain or two. And the genuine dealers and collectors don't care what the calendar date is anyway."

Carla laughed. "I don't think I'm hearing right," she said. "This is a new Jewel I'm seeing. I'd never have believed you could be such a conniver."

"*Expedient* is the word for what I'm suggesting," Jewel corrected, then paused for a moment of thought. "Okay," she decided. "Let's strike a bargain. While I heat up our supper, you go over the book list Skip left here and see how it strikes you."

That seemed fair enough. Jewel brought the list, which took up several pages of computer type. Carla sank back with a second glass of wine and started reading through the list, convinced that she'd immediately stumble upon the inclusion of the three-volume *Adventurer* set as well as the Irving and Twain first editions.

She didn't.

She went through the list a second time, then a third time. There was no doubt about it, the titles were missing. Which, she quickly told herself, didn't necessarily mean a thing. It was years since she'd seen those books. Before his death her grandfather could either have loaned or given them to someone. Or maybe the missing volumes were somewhere else in the house, though she couldn't see why they would have been separated from the rest of the library.

She was still muddling that over when Jewel called her to supper.

They ate at the kitchen table. It was warm and cozy in the big, old-fashioned kitchen, and once again Carla was threatened by a nostalgia trip.

She brushed it aside and made herself think about the books and the auction in a more practical manner.

Knowing that there had been books—quite a few books—that weren't on Skip's list *did* put a different complexion on things. In view of that, Jonas and Jewel were right, she had to concede. It made sense to postpone the auction until she'd had the chance to go through the books in the attic herself, and also to scan other areas of the house where the missing volumes just might have been placed.

Further, though she hadn't told Jonas this, she didn't have a contract with the Heggertys, at least not a written contract. Skip—evidently with thoughts of her long-time friendship with his family in mind—had felt that a verbal agreement was good enough, and so had she.

Jewel was clearing away the dishes when Carla made her announcement after first glancing at the kitchen clock and noting it was slightly after eight.

"I'm going to call Skip," she said.

She was grateful when Jewel didn't make a big thing of her sudden acquiescence. Jewel merely said, "Good," and let it go at that.

Skip Heggerty's wife informed Carla that Skip was watching a basketball game, inferring that under such circumstances he didn't like to be disturbed.

Carla couldn't remember ever having met Skip's wife—he must have married while she was in California—and so didn't know whether this was a local girl who might have been in school in Wainwright when she was or an out-of-towner. Thus she said politely, "I'm sorry, Mrs. Heggerty, but I really have to talk to him."

Skip, answering the phone, sounded gruff. "What can I do for you, Carla?" he asked abruptly.

"Skip, something's come up," Carla said. "I've had . . . well, er, I've had a minor accident."

"I'm sorry to hear that. Where are you?"

"Here at the house. A friend drove me up this afternoon. But I've done quite a job on my knee, and I can barely walk," Carla told him, uncomfortable with the fibbing.

"That's too bad," Skip said, managing in the saying to convey that he couldn't see what her injured knee had to do with him.

Carla came out with it. "We'll have to postpone the auction, Skip," she announced.

She could picture Skip holding the phone receiver away from his ear, looking at it quizzically, then clamping it in place again.

"What was that you said?" he asked.

"We'll have to postpone the auction, Skip."

"Carla, what does your *knee* have to do with the auction?"

"I can't get around," she said. "That is . . . it's quite painful, and I can only get around with difficulty."

"So you can sit in a chair," Skip said bluntly. "You don't have to go anywhere."

Skip's tone of voice reminded Carla of his father, whom she'd never especially liked. She could remember long-ago times when she'd been at the Heggertys with Gwen and had overheard Mr. Heggerty talking to someone on the phone about business. Depending upon his position in the situation, he'd tended to be either overly conciliatory or almost rude.

Skip, by his tone of voice, was being almost rude.

A coldness crept into Carla's own tone. "There's more to it than that," she informed Skip. "As you know, not everything in the house is scheduled for auction."

"What do you mean?"

"We agreed, Skip, that I'm to keep certain things I want."

"Your stepmother already stored the stuff you want to keep in the back pantry," Skip informed her. "One of my men went over the other day to help her move the heavy stuff."

"There are other things," Carla said vaguely, "as well as some of the books."

"Hell, Carla," Skip erupted, "I left a list of the books for you. All you have to do is circle the ones you want to keep and I'll see they're put aside as we get to them."

"No," Carla said.

"No *what*?" Skip demanded irritably.

"I need to inventory the house one more time, Skip," Carla said. "It was my plan to do that tonight. Now I can't. And I'm not about to wish, years from now, that I'd kept something I didn't."

"Carla," Skip said, "most people feel like you do on the eve of an auction." The entire tenor of his tone had changed. Now he sounded to Carla the way Mr. Heggerty used to sound when he was being conciliatory, and she decided she almost liked Skip better when he was rude.

"The thing is," Skip went on, "people get to thinking about stuff that's been in their family, stuff they've been living with all their life, and suddenly they get sentimental about it. They don't want to part with it, they also don't want to keep it. Believe me, the feeling passes. You can talk to any of our clients once the auction is over and they've had time to readjust, and they'll tell you it was the best thing they ever did."

Carla was tempted to ask him to give her a satisfied client list.

Instead she said, "I don't think it'll work that way with me, Skip. Every time I've had to do something in haste I've repented at leisure—to quote a very old saw. This time around, I don't want to make any mistakes. So, again, the auction will have to be postponed."

The oil went out of Skip's voice. "We can't do that, Carla," he said flatly.

"What do you mean, you can't do it?"

"My father won't go for it."

"I'm afraid your father is going to have to go for it, Skip."

"You don't back out on an auction at the last minute, Carla," Skip informed her. "It's illegal to do so, for one thing. For another thing, we've spent money advertising this auction in the newspapers, on the radio and on a couple of TV stations that cover this area. We've hired extra personnel to handle things tomorrow. There are dealers in town who've come from Utica and Albany and

New York, among other places, because of our advertising. So you don't just call it off, Carla."

Carla found herself wishing that Jonas was around so she could consult him at this point.

Then she reminded herself that it was her business. She'd already complained enough about Jonas butting in on it, and she was going to have to handle it herself.

"Skip," she said, "I'm sorry you're taking this approach. But, since you are, I'm going to have to remind you I don't have a legally binding contract with you."

"The hell you don't," Skip shot back.

"We have a verbal agreement, that's all. You said it was enough, I also thought it was enough."

"It was enough," Skip said. "Our advertising is, in itself, proof that we have a contractual agreement. Carla, once you agree to an auction, you can't back out. If you do, the auctioneer has a perfect right to get a court order and sell your things right out from under you."

Was he bluffing or was what he was saying the truth?

Carla didn't know, but not knowing did nothing to lessen her surging anger. If he was bluffing, damn it, she was going to call his bluff!

"So, get your court order," she told him, and hung up the phone.

The receiver was no sooner resting in its cradle than Carla regretted having let her temper get the best of her. It was a temper she usually managed to control—but she had been through a lot the past couple of days, and Skip's unexpected attitude had brought her to the boiling point.

Jewel had left her alone in the kitchen to make her call. Now, she got to her feet—the knee did hurt, damn it—and hobbled to the door, calling Jewel's name.

Jewel appeared like a genie sprung from Aladdin's lamp. "Well, how did it go?" she asked, and then took a good look at Carla's face and said, "Whew!"

Carla hobbled back to the table and sat down. "I think I could use a drink," she informed her stepmother.

Jewel showed her surprise. Carla wasn't much of a drinker. But she only asked, "How about some brandy?"

"Sounds just right," Carla muttered. "A lot of brandy, Jewel."

Jewel brought her a moderate measure in a snifter and, at once, the aroma of the brandy brought back memories of last night in the motel with Jonas. He had been so terrific to her. And she'd really been such an unappreciative little snot.

She asked suddenly, "Got a phone book, Jewel?"

"Yes," Jewel said. "In the top drawer, right behind you."

Carla reached for the phone book and thumbed through the *D*'s. Then, putting the phone book back in the drawer, she said, "I might have known."

"Couldn't find the number you wanted?" Jewel asked.

"No. But then I might have known Jonas wouldn't be listed."

"He isn't," Jewel said, "but I can solve your problem. Jonas gave me his unlisted number...just in case we needed anything."

Jewel reached in the same drawer, withdrew a slip of paper and handed it to Carla. "I'd like to catch the TV news," she said tactfully. "If you want me, just holler."

It took Carla a long and thoughtful moment before she punched out Jonas's phone number.

In all fairness, she conceded, she owed him this call, even if she didn't need to talk to him about the auction.

The phone rang four times, and she was about to hang up when he answered. His "Hello," sent a warm shiver straight down her spine, and she marveled at that. She'd never known, before, that shivers could be warm.

"Jonas?" she asked tentatively.

"Yes."

"It's . . . Carla."

"I recognized your voice," Jonas said abruptly.

"Jonas . . . I . . ."

"Yes, Carla?" he asked patiently.

She came out with what she had to say in one swift sentence. "Jonas, I was bitchy to you tonight, and I apologize."

The silence was intense.

"I wish you'd stayed for supper," she added.

Jonas's chuckle was low and surprisingly musical. "So do I."

"Look, I felt at a . . . disadvantage. And that's the way I retaliated. I shouldn't have." Funny, how much easier it was sometimes to say something to someone over the phone rather than straight to his face.

"Why did you feel at a disadvantage, Carla?"

Jonas's voice was low and soft and . . . caressing.

"Well," Carla said, working her way through a whole series of warm shivers, "I guess you could say I've psyched myself up for this auction, and I'm afraid if I postpone it I won't be able to psyche myself up again."

"That's understandable."

"Nevertheless," Carla went on, "I did call Skip Heggerty a while ago. I told him I'd had a minor accident— my knee—and there was no way we can hold the auction tomorrow."

"Did Heggerty go along with that?"

"No."

"Carla, you do have a copy of your contract with him, don't you? I mean, there? It isn't in Bedloe Falls?"

"We don't have a contract, Jonas."

"I don't understand."

"When I approached Skip about holding the auction, he didn't press the point of a written contract," Carla explained. "We'd known each other for years, after all. He said a verbal agreement was good enough for him."

"Then there must have been some benefit involved for him," Jonas said, a hard edge creeping into his voice.

"I don't know about that. Now Skip says since he and his father widely advertised the auction that proves there was an intended sale, which makes the whole thing as legally binding as if we had a written contract. He said he could get a court order and sell my things right out from under me."

"And what did you say?"

"I told him to get his court order, and then I hung up on him," Carla snapped, the angry fire she'd felt over Skip's statement flaring up.

To her surprise, Jonas chuckled again. "I'd like to have heard that," he admitted. "Also, I daresay Skip's consulted with his father by now and is probably trying to get back to you at this very minute. Carla, don't give ground. Do you know Brad Shapiro?"

"No."

"He's a lawyer, a good lawyer, and also a close friend of mine. He moved to Wainwright a few years back— probably when you were out on the West Coast. I'm going to call him and . . ."

Jonas was taking over again. Carla sighed and said, "There's no need for that, Jonas."

Silence descended, but just for a few seconds. Then Jonas said carefully, "With your permission, Carla, I'll call him. I can sketch out what's going on, and then he can get in touch with you. I know you don't much like taking advice from me, but I'd suggest you don't talk to the Heggertys until you first talk to Brad.''

The way he spoke made Carla feel as if she'd been rightfully chastised. ''Thank you, Jonas,'' she said. ''I'll have Jewel answer the phone until Mr. Shapiro calls.''

''Good.'' Again, there was a pause. Then Jonas said, ''Do you mind if I ask what caused you to consider postponing the auction?''

It was Carla's turn to hesitate. But then she admitted, ''I went over the book list Skip left for me.''

''And?''

''Well, some volumes that I do remember distinctly— volumes I'm fairly certain are quite valuable—were not on the list.''

''I see.''

''Jonas,'' Carla said hastily, ''that doesn't mean the Heggertys are guilty of anything. My grandfather could have given those books away. Or loaned them to someone who never returned them. Or they may be stashed somewhere else in the house....''

''Did you tell Heggerty you'd found some volumes missing?''

''No.''

''Well,'' Jonas admitted, ''that's a relief. You may be right, of course. There may be a perfectly acceptable explanation for the absence of those books you remember. Until you make sure, tell Brad about the missing volumes and no one else, okay?''

Jonas spoke so gently she couldn't accuse him of trying to take command again. She melted, listening to him, and suddenly wished that he were sitting here at the kitchen table with her.

She wished, even more, that she could snuggle into his arms right now. She wanted to rest her head on his shoulder and just relax for a little while with his warmth and strength to sustain her.

Jonas said, "I'd better call Brad. Fortunately, I know he's home. I spoke with him about something else a short while ago. So he should get back to you before long, Carla."

"Thank you, Jonas," she managed.

Jonas chuckled again. "You owe me one potluck supper," he reminded her. "But we'll take that up tomorrow."

Chapter Seven

It's true that auction contracts are binding, Mrs. Logan," Brad Shapiro said carefully. "Or can be. Let's assume you have a legally binding contract with the Heggertys and you decide tomorrow you're going to lock them out of your house so they can't conduct the auction. They *could* get a court order and sell anyway. Provided that..."

Carla waited for him to continue and, when the pause lengthened, put in, "Provided that *what*? Mr. Shapiro?"

"Well, there are circumstances under which I feel reasonably certain a court order would be granted," Brad Shapiro said cautiously. "However, Jonas has spoken to me, and he thinks there's a fair chance an order would *not* be granted in this case. Of course, that's something that will have to be checked out, and I doubt I can do much until Monday morning, by nature of the fact that the sources I'll need to contact won't be open for business again until then."

"So," Carla said unhappily, "what do I do in the meantime?"

"Since you're a friend of Jonas's," the lawyer said, "I'll give you some off-the-record advice that may sound pretty unprofessional. You're going to have to stall for time if you're determined to delay the auction. Your best course, in my opinion, is to bluff this out. The Heggertys *could* get a court order, even on a Saturday morning. Although the courthouse wouldn't be open for routine business, there are always emergency channels.

"As I've said," he continued—while Carla, listening, could feel her spirits plummeting—"I don't think they'll go that far. I think, from what I know of the Heggertys, they'll try to bully you. That's where you're going to have to retaliate, by either bluffing them out yourself, as I suggested, or by taking the chance of calling *their* bluff."

Brad Shapiro concluded their conversation by giving her his phone number and telling her to contact him as soon as there was anything definite settled—one way or the other—with the Heggertys.

She hung up the phone and groaned. By now, Jewel had joined her and was sitting opposite her at the kitchen table. Carla grimaced and told her stepmother, "This is really unhinging me."

The phone rang.

"Shall I?" Jewel suggested, and, at Carla's nod, she picked up the receiver.

Jewel immediately cued in Carla to the identity of the caller by saying, "Mr. Heggerty? Yes, I know Carla spoke to Skip earlier. No, I'm afraid she can't come to the phone. The doctor said it was imperative she stay off her leg, and she's overdone it as it is. She's in bed."

Jewel's lips tightened as she listened to whatever it was Mr. Heggerty was saying, and Carla began to make motions, indicating that she should be handed the receiver. But Jewel shook her head.

"I'll go upstairs and take the portable phone in to Carla," Jewel said finally. "But I can assure you, if she's fallen asleep, I'm not going to wake her up. The doctor was adamant about her getting some rest. She'll call you as soon as she wakes up."

With that, Jewel hung up.

The two women faced each other across the table. Carla was scowling. She said, "I appreciate what you were trying to do, Jewel, but you should have let me speak to him."

"We'll wait ten minutes, and then you can call him back," Jewel said logically. "If you want to, that is. What a thoroughly unpleasant man he is!"

"Yes, and I'm afraid Skip's taking after him," Carla admitted unhappily.

She was tired, frustrated and worried, and her knee really *did* ache. But, above all, she was disillusioned. It was naive, of course, to feel such a sense of betrayal over Skip's attitude, but she did. She reminded herself she hadn't exactly sailed through life thus far on a rosy cloud. But friendship always had been tremendously important to her, and wasn't loyalty a basic part of friendship?

Of course, if one were going to be literal about it, it was Gwen Heggerty who had been her friend, and she wondered what Gwen would think of her brother's actions. She wished Gwen were closer than Alaska.

She'd never liked Mr. Heggerty anyway. But Skip... well that was different. She'd been so smitten by him....

"Carla, what *is* it?" Jewel demanded.

"I guess I'm seeing the dark side of someone *I* trusted, and I don't much like it," Carla said solemnly.

She reached for the phone. "Okay," she said. "Here goes."

"Want me to leave the room?" Jewel asked diplomatically. "I know you've never much liked talking on the phone with people around."

"You're not 'people,' Jewel. Please stay. This involves both of us."

William Heggerty answered on the first ring. He'd evidently simmered down in the few minutes since he'd talked to Jewel, but Carla disliked his phony cordiality even more than she would have his undisguised hostility.

"Sorry to hear you've had an accident, Carla," he said. "I think I've come up with the solution to your getting around the place tomorrow, though. The pharmacy closes early this time of year, but I'll give Don Williams a call as soon as I finish talking to you, and I'm sure he'll open up for me."

"There's nothing at the pharmacy that would help me, Mr. Heggerty," Carla pointed out.

"Oh, yes, there is," the auctioneer informed her. "All we need is to rent you a wheelchair. Then you can get around just fine. You're just a little bit of a thing. Skip and I can carry you up and down stairs, and your stepmother can push the chair for you if you can't manage it yourself."

Carla flared again. It suddenly seemed to her that all her life people had been telling her what to do and how and when to do it, Jonas being one of the latest examples. Jewel and Jonas, she thought to be fair, had been motivated by entirely different considerations than William Heggerty's, of course. William Heggerty was thinking of himself. The others, she thought grimly, had mainly been trying to protect her, because evidently there was something about her that seemed to cry out for protection when all she really wanted was to pursue her own independent way.

No doubt about it. She was overdue for an image change.

"There is no possible way I could do the things I need to do before the auction from a wheelchair, Mr. Heggerty," she informed the auctioneer. "I want the auction postponed for two weeks. That will still give us plenty of time to capture the Christmas-buying crowd. And if the dealers are that interested in what we have to offer, I'm sure they'll come back from New York or Albany or Utica or wherever."

The syrup went out of William Heggerty's voice and was replaced by flint. "You just don't back out like that," he informed Carla. "We've put a lot of time and money into tomorrow's auction, and I can assure you, young lady, we have the legal right to conduct it, whether you want us to or not. If you wanted to renege, you should have thought about it a whole lot sooner. Before we advertised, hired extra help—"

"If you'll send me a bill for your advertising and the cost of the extra help, Mr. Heggerty, I'll see to it you have a check by return mail," Carla shot back.

"It's not that easy, young lady," Heggerty retaliated. "How would you expect me to bill you for the time Skip and I have put in on this? Set some sort of hourly rate? It would in no way compensate, I'll tell you that."

He finished decisively, "We'll be at your place by 8:00 a.m. prepared to get everything ready for the 10:00 a.m. sale."

"You won't get in," Carla said.

"What's that?"

"Every door, every window, will be locked and bolted," she said. "If you try to *break* in, I can assure you I'll call the police in a hurry."

"Well, I can assure *you*," Heggerty said, "the police will be on our side. We'll be within our legal rights."

"I doubt that," Carla retorted, with far more assurance than she felt. "The police would hardly allow you to break and enter without some sort of a court order. Even then, I think breaking and entering—and that's just what it would be, Mr. Heggerty—would be considered illegal. Certainly, the police would have to consult a judge. Don't you think that might be difficult early on a Saturday morning?"

She tried to speak politely, professionally, as if this were a library matter she was dealing with. She tried to keep the increasing rancor she was feeling toward this man out of her voice.

Evidently she succeeded, at least to an extent, because William Heggerty said, though without any trace of admiration in the saying, "You are a cool one, Carla. Regardless, I'll have my court order, first thing in the morning. Then we'll see whether the cops can ferret out a judge to deal with legalities."

As Carla replaced the phone receiver, Jewel said, "Was that a win, a loss or a draw?"

"I'm not sure," Carla said dubiously. "I tried to bluff, as Brad Shapiro suggested I do. I guess you could say Skip's father called my bluff. But whether *he's* bluffing or not, I really don't know."

"Sleep on it," Jewel advised.

"Sleeping on it" was a lot easier said than done. Carla woke up in the wee hours, couldn't get back to sleep and tried to escape via a mystery novel about chicanery in high places in Washington.

The story was good, exciting, but she couldn't concentrate on it. When she finally did drift off, she had some mixed-up dreams she was glad she couldn't remember when she awakened again.

Jonas Davenport arrived shortly after seven o'clock, bearing some freshly baked muffins he'd bought at an early opening bakery in town.

Jewel produced coffee, boysenberry jam and sweet butter. Jonas huddled at the kitchen table, looking terrific in an oatmeal-colored Irish sweater and stone-washed jeans.

Carla felt wretched. The lack of sleep showed. Wearing a faded old blue wool dressing gown, her face scrubbed, her hair put back in a ponytail and her glasses perched firmly on her nose, she felt she must surely be one of the most unattractive women on Earth.

Jonas, however, thought she looked terrific. It was difficult for him to take his eyes off her, something he was afraid Jewel would notice—Jewel, he'd already discovered, was *very* perceptive.

He'd already apologized for looming up so early, without prior announcement and had explained he wanted to be around just in case the Heggertys decided to enforce their allegedly legal claim.

Carla, hearing that, had immediately run the gamut from gratitude to annoyance. She appreciated Jonas giving up his Saturday morning. On the other hand, she wished he were motivated by something other than her apparent need for protection. She was a *woman*, not a helpless, floundering girl, damn it.

"This is sort of like living with a time bomb," Jewel said suddenly. "I expect the Heggertys to start breaking down the door at any instant."

"It won't come to that," Jonas said.

The statement was enough to cause Carla to glance at him. How could he be so *sure*, unless he knew something she didn't know?

The glance caused their gazes to lock. And Jonas's light blue eyes seared all the way through her. If there was any ice left in her to melt, it melted. She gulped and reached for her coffee cup.

"Why do you say that, Jonas?" Jewel asked.

"Because I don't think the Heggertys would want to risk getting the law involved in this," he stated, his eyes still on Carla. "I don't think they want to call attention to themselves or their business operation."

Finally, he broke eye contact, and Carla sagged a little. "I could be wrong," he admitted. "All we can do is wait and see."

Jonas was right. Skip Heggerty phoned shortly before eight and, when Jewel answered the phone, asked to speak to Carla.

"If it were anyone but you," Skip said, "we wouldn't be doing this, Carla. I want you to know that. I hope you'll appreciate it. This is going to be a helluva lot of trouble for us, but we'll agree to a two-week postponement. One of my men is on the way over to your place. He's going to put up a few signs around your property announcing the postponement and the new date, and he'll tack one to your front door. A lot of people are going to be madder than hell. Some of the dealers may try to get in anyway. I'm going to have to ask your word that, if they get by you, you don't make any sales."

"I wouldn't do that, Skip," Carla protested.

"Good. We'll trust you won't. Like I said, if it were anyone but you, Carla..."

Carla forced the words out. "Thank you, Skip."

The temporary victory announced, Jonas took his leave. He said that he had things to do during the day, but he asked if he could come by in the late afternoon and bring someone with him.

Jewel gave a quick affirmative before Carla had a chance to say anything.

All day long, though, Carla wondered who it was Jonas was going to bring with him.

A fiancée, maybe? Was Jonas involved with someone, even though—as she recalled—Jewel had said he tended to turn his back on women, at least the ones who pursued him. And evidently a fair number fell into that category.

She spent the day going through the downstairs rooms in the house and listing a few things she wanted to remove to her "hoard" in the pantry over the course of the next two weeks.

She also faced up to the fact that she was going to have to ask for a two-week leave of absence from the Bedloe Falls Library. There was no way she could leave Wainwright until the auction had been held and this whole affair was concluded. She would need the time in between to catalog the books.

She managed to reach Miss Bobbins at home, shortly after noon. Miss Bobbins heard her request and issued a sharp, emphatic, "No. I can appreciate you may have some home affairs to handle, Mrs. Logan," Miss Bobbins added, "but I cannot allow the library to be understaffed for that long. You may remember that Marie Doane will be on vacation starting Monday."

Marie Doane was an assistant librarian, and Carla knew that she and her husband had been planning a Caribbean cruise for a long time. She had no wish to jeopardize Marie's plans. On the other hand, she felt Miss Bobbins was being unreasonable.

"A couple of members of the Friends have had library experience," she pointed out to Miss Bobbins. "I'll call them if you like. I'm sure they'd be glad to volunteer some hours to help you out."

"Mrs. Logan, you are being *paid* for your services," Miss Bobbins reminded her. "We can't expect members of the Friends to take over professional responsibilities without recompense."

One more thorn, Carla thought wearily.

She said frankly, "I can't make it in there on Monday morning, Miss Bobbins. For one thing, I have no car. My car is in a garage in a town about forty miles from here, and I don't think they're going to be able to fix it."

It was only beginning to occur to her that if such were the case, she was going to have to get another car to replace Jenny.

Yet another thorn.

She and the head librarian ended their conversation on a mutually unsatisfactory note.

"She is a mean old lady," Carla said resentfully to Jewel, once she'd mulled over the conversation. "She doesn't take anything except the library into consideration. The library's her whole life. She's not even human about anything else."

She heard her own words and remembered when— back in the motel as Jonas was ministering to her leg— she'd chuckled over what Miss Bobbins's reaction might be to being placed in a similar position and then had suddenly decided the speculation wasn't all that funny.

She'd wondered if, one day, she might become like Miss Bobbins herself. She thought about that now and didn't like any part of the thought.

Jewel had taken on the task of transporting some of the small things Carla wanted to keep out of the auction to the back pantry. She paused to ask, "What are you going to do?"

"I'll have to go over Miss Bobbins's head. What else can I do? I don't like the idea of going over anyone's head, but she hasn't left me a choice. I'm not going to put my job on the line just because she's so hard-hearted and pigheaded."

"So?"

"I'm going to call the chairman of the board of trustees," Carla announced.

Wilfred Emerson, the trustees' chairman, had been delighted with Carla when he'd interviewed her and had urged Miss Bobbins to hire her. He, at least, Carla felt, was on her side.

She was right. Emerson said, "Take your two weeks and think no more about it. I'll straighten it out with Angie, without ruffling any feathers."

It seemed incredible to think that anyone might call Miss Bobbins, "Angie."

"Angie and I went to high school together," the trustees' chairman added. "Would you believe we even dated a little, way back then?"

Carla wouldn't believe.

"She's a damned good librarian," he went on, "but she does have tunnel vision about some things. Regardless, I think, before long, she's going to realize herself that she's ready for retirement. And you know what the whole board favors then."

Carla knew she was favored to become the next head librarian.

"Don't worry about this," Mr. Emerson said in parting. And Carla decided to take him at his word.

The day wore on. Her leg was a lot better, but it began to get achy again after lunch, and, at Jewel's suggestion, she gave in to the message her body was sending her and took a nap.

It was nearly dark when she woke up, and for a moment she was afraid Jonas might already have arrived. But darkness came early these December days, and when she went to listen at the head of the stairs, there was only silence below her.

Compelled by an instinct she wasn't about to analyze, she got out a deep blue velour leisure suit Jewel had given her last Christmas and slipped it on. She put on a little makeup, brushed her hair and fluffed it around her shoulders and again thought of dispensing with the glasses in favor of her contacts. But that, she decided, would be a shade too obvious.

The doorbell rang just as she reached the foot of the stairs. She opened it to find Jonas on the threshold, a small, elderly woman at his side.

Martha Daniels, the Wainwright librarian. It was years since Carla had last seen her—she'd yet to visit the local library on her recent excursions to Wainwright—but she recognized her immediately.

Miss Daniels was probably about Miss Bobbins's age, but there all similarities ceased. She was short and plump, with a pretty face, curly iron-gray hair and an entirely different attitude, which was the most important thing of all.

When she'd been a teenager at Wainwright High School, Carla couldn't ever remember Miss Daniels saying hush to any of the students in the library researching projects, even though, more often than not, they got to giggling.

Miss Daniels, at Jewel's suggestion, accepted a glass of sherry. Carla, to her own surprise, asked for some brandy. Jonas went out to the kitchen with Jewel to help get the drinks. Jewel had already made a fire in the living room. The room looked cozy and inviting, with its well-used, old, upholstered chairs and the big couch, the few really nice antique tables, a secretary desk and paintings, touched with the patina of age, hanging against walls papered in a very soft shade of apricot.

It was a nice room, Carla thought. A very nice room. She'd always taken it for granted, the way people tended to take so many familiar things for granted. She was only beginning to appreciate this house and everything in it, she thought ruefully—when it was too late.

She and Miss Daniels discussed libraries while they waited for Jewel and Jonas to come back with the drinks. Miss Daniels, Carla discovered, was a lot more innovative than Miss Bobbins. She was fully up to date on all the latest library aids. She knew as much as Carla did about computers, audio-visual equipment and the other types of electronic equipment that tremendously expanded the scope of even a small-town library.

Miss Bobbins, on the other hand, resisted change.

Upon Jewel and Jonas's return, the quartet settled around the fireplace. Jonas, after sampling his bourbon and branch water, got straight to the point.

"I know you've had the feeling I was holding out on you, Carla, and that I knew something about your grandfather's books you didn't know," he said. "You were right. But I didn't feel I had the right to go into specifics until I had the chance to talk to Miss Daniels.

You see, it was she who steered me in the direction of your grandfather's books.''

"You, Miss Daniels?" Carla, genuinely surprised, posed the question directly to the librarian, bypassing Jonas.

Jonas noted the route she was taking and frowned. He was beginning to get the impression that she avoided directness with him whenever she possibly could, be it eye contact, voice contact—whatever kind of contact.

Did she find him that formidable? Or did she simply dislike him? It could be a matter of chemistry.

No, damn it, Jonas decided. Whatever else, she did not dislike him. He'd had occasion to note her reaction and feel her responses on a couple of occasions. And once they got her books, the auction and the Heggertys out of the way, he planned to do a little private investigation into the mystery of Carla Logan.

Miss Daniels said, "Well, knowing of Mr. Davenport's interest in old and rare books, Carla, I felt he ought to be informed about your grandfather's books once I learned you were putting them up for sale at auction."

"What about my grandfather's books?" Carla asked warily.

"Your grandfather had an amazing collection," Miss Daniels said. "Of course, he'd been collecting books most of his life and had inherited some pretty fine old volumes, as well.

"Once, years back, your grandfather asked me if I'd catalog the books for him," Miss Daniels went on.

"And did you?"

"Yes, though in an informal manner," the librarian reported. "I didn't catalog the books in the way you, as a professional librarian, would think of as cataloging.

What I did was to list the volume titles, authors, publication dates and publishers. I would never have had time to do the thorough job for your grandfather I would like to have done. But I did make a comprehensive list, and, at the time I gave it to him, I told him he really should have the collection cataloged properly and then he should get hold of someone—in New York, perhaps—and have an appraisal made. I think it's something he intended to do but just never got around to doing.''

"I never found a list of the books," Carla said slowly. She sat up straighter. "Miss Daniels, do you still have a copy of that list?"

Miss Daniels smiled. "Yes," she said. "Your grandfather was a dear, I adored him—everyone in town did— but he did tend to be absentminded. I felt certain he'd probably lose or misplace the list I gave him, so I kept a copy at the time. Now Mr. Davenport has had that copy duplicated, so..."

Carla stared resentfully at Jonas. All this time he'd known exactly what books were in her grandfather's collection—her collection—and she didn't. It was another example of his high-handedness, his assumption that it was his right to take charge.

Jonas said, "Before you lacerate me visually, Carla, let me say that I didn't feel privileged to pass the list along to you until I'd spoken to Miss Daniels. What she's told me—about the book collection and a few other things as well—was told in confidence. I don't violate confidences," Jonas concluded, a stubborn set to his chin.

He reached for a slender leather briefcase he'd propped against the chair he was sitting in. "Now," he said, "here is the list. I had six copies made. You'll find all six and Miss Daniels's copy are present and accounted for."

"You didn't keep one for yourself?"

"No," Jonas said coldly, "I didn't."

Why was it that under circumstances like these he always made her feel ashamed of herself? Carla wondered.

Again she avoided Jonas and addressed Miss Daniels. "Your list is going to be enormously helpful," she said. "I've already discovered that some volumes I personally remember aren't on the title list Skip Heggerty gave me yesterday. As I've already pointed out, Grandpa may have sold those books or given them away or loaned them. But the main reason I postponed the auction was to have the chance to find out."

She couldn't resist glancing at Jonas as she said that. She'd expected he'd look triumphant, but he didn't. Instead, there was something else in those light blue eyes. Approval? Was that what Jonas was showing her?

Maybe, in part, but she was seeing more than that. There was an expression in Jonas's eyes that made her wish she were alone with him right now. They needed a confrontation to get things straight between them. But, from the way he was looking at her and the way she was feeling, Carla suspected that more than a meeting of the minds between Jonas and herself was going to be inevitable.

Chapter Eight

Carla went up to the attic Sunday morning. It was an overcast day, more snow threatened. It was gloomy in the big old attic, with its high rafters and a planked wooden floor that creaked under her footsteps. She switched on both of the yellowish lights that hung suspended from beams and looked around her.

She was surrounded by trunks, cartons, an old dress frame, an ancient sewing machine, discarded floor lamps, chairs and tables, a tennis racquet with half the strings missing...the list went on and on.

How could she have thought of letting all of this go at auction without so much as looking it over first? There was such a thing as dwelling on the past and the possessions accumulated from it. But it was equally bad to try to negate that past and to be foolish enough to disregard completely things that might not only have intrinsic value but considerable sentimental value as well.

She started opening a few of the boxes of books, and soon was staggered. There were cartons and cartons and *cartons* filled to the brim with old books. Miss Daniels had said the collection was a large one, and Carla had already known that herself. But she hadn't realized *how* large. She hadn't counted the titles on Miss Daniels's list but she felt as if she were looking at thousands of books. A whole sea of books.

Many—maybe most of them—probably would be worth little, if anything. There was a vast distinction between plain old books and rare old books, and probably most of these fell into the plain category. Even so, the only way to evaluate them was to go through everything.

Daunted by the magnitude of the task, Carla let herself be diverted by an old photo album she found on a table, and she sat down and thumbed through the pages, recognizing few, if any, of the people depicted.

She was still trying to identify photos of her grandfather at an early age when she heard footsteps on the attic stairs. Jonas emerged and smiled at her cheerfully.

"Jewel told me what you were doing," he said. "I thought maybe you could use a hand."

"Thanks," she said, at once on edge merely at the sight of him. "I don't think so."

"Well," Jonas said, "that's at least one of the more polite rebuffs I've ever received."

Rebuff or no rebuff, she could see that he was not about to leave. He pulled another straight-backed chair out of the shadows and placed it next to the one she was sitting on. "We need to get a couple of things straight, Carla," he said as he sat down.

"About what?"

"About the Heggertys, for one thing," Jonas said. "About the books, for another thing. Maybe even about us."

Carla could find no ready answer.

"About the Heggertys, to begin with," Jonas began, leaning forward as he spoke so the old chair squeaked in protest under his solid weight. "I couldn't be more specific until I'd spoken to Martha Daniels."

"Miss Daniels does seem to figure prominently in your scheme."

"I'm not sure I like the word 'scheme.' No matter. It was Miss Daniels who first alerted me to the fact the Heggertys may not be entirely aboveboard. I'd heard rumors about them from various people who'd worked for me—principally in connection with my house, which I've been renovating. I didn't pay too much attention to the rumors because I know enough about small towns to realize rumors can fly without wings and often don't have much validity. But when Miss Daniels mentioned she wished you hadn't put your auction in the hands of the Heggertys, my curiosity was aroused."

When Carla didn't answer, Jonas plunged on. "From what Miss Daniels told me about the collection, I decided I wanted to acquire it for myself," he admitted. "A couple of years ago I went into partnership, silent partnership, with a friend of mine who has a book shop in Utica that specializes in rare books."

"Aha," Carla murmured.

Jonas bypassed the suggestive word. "I checked with Fred, my friend, and he told me he'd had some dealings with William Heggerty and Son. They'd come into the store now and then with some pretty choice old volumes. Fred, initially, accepted the offerings at face value and bought them for what he considered a fair price.

Then he began to wonder where the Heggertys were getting all the books.

"Utica, of course, represents a relatively small market where rare books are concerned. It stands to reason the Heggertys might have been able to get more for what they had to offer in New York or elsewhere. On the other hand, it's only a couple of hours' drive to Utica, which makes it a much easier disposal point. And, considering they got the books for nothing, the transactions were always pure profit."

"What are you saying?" Carla asked sharply.

"I suppose I'm saying I think the Heggertys stole the books they offered for sale to Fred," Jonas admitted unhappily. "I can't really think of a kinder word for it. Maybe they paid for the books—a pittance, I'd bet. Maybe they just *took* them from the contents of a house they were auctioning, with their clients being none the wiser."

He held up a warning hand as Carla was about to interrupt him. "Hear me out, Carla, please," he urged. "It isn't easy for me to be unloading all of this on you. If the Heggertys peddled off rare books they'd come by, what else have they been peddling? Paintings? Collectibles? Antiques? A lot of their operations are in relatively rural areas around here. There are many older people planning to sell out, to get away from the cold winters and move to Florida. I'd say nine-tenths of the time most of their salable stuff has been passed down, generation to generation, thus acquiring value. You know the way people go for the old these days. They even buy junk if it's old. If it's good old, they're willing to dip into the cash reserves to acquire it.

"Anyway, after talking to Miss Daniels and then to Fred, I began to see the Heggertys might have quite a little vein of gold they were mining. So I went back and listened to what some of the people who'd been working for me were saying. The reports were all negative, and, believe it or not, I hate to be telling you this. I have an idea of how you felt about Skip Heggerty when you were a girl. I've seen him...and I admit he is a handsome devil, even with that slight beer paunch he's developed."

The expression on Jonas's face was pretty comical as he brought up the subject of Skip's slight beer paunch. Carla nearly laughed. Jonas was so much better looking than Skip, there was no comparison. She sobered. The surprising thing about it was that Jonas honestly didn't seem to realize that.

The impulse to laugh faded away. She put together what Jonas had just told her and said, "So...you're calling Skip and his father a couple of crooks, is that it?"

"Them are strong words, lady," Jonas said, making a sorry attempt to lighten things up a little.

"You're the one who's been speaking them," Carla pointed out. "Your friend Brad Shapiro made a few inferences on the phone last night about Skip and his father, too. He also doubted they'd go for a court order to hold the auction, even though it might be within their legal right. Have you any ideas about why they agreed to the postponement?"

"Yes," Jonas admitted reluctantly. "Most auctioneers are licensed professionals. Very reputable. They do business strictly according to the line of the law, and so they have the law on their side. And, if they have a contract, they can, indeed, get a court order and hold the auction as scheduled, if only to recover their own costs. Obviously this isn't the case with the Heggertys."

Jonas stretched out his legs and regarded the top of his black leather boots contemplatively. "I've been doing all the talking," he said uneasily. "How about a little input?"

Carla posed a logical question. "What am I supposed to say?"

"I have this feeling I'm tearing down the fabric of your dreams," Jonas said unhappily.

"Because of Skip Heggerty?"

He nodded.

"I can't imagine what you've heard around town about my long-ago crush on Skip—of which, I'm pretty certain, he was completely unaware," she said with amusement.

"Don't bet on it," Jonas muttered.

"Jonas, I was about fifteen years old and homely as sin. You should have seen me in those days. Braces, big glasses—"

"I think you've always underestimated yourself, Carla."

The quiet statement threw her a curve.

Before she could come up with a good answer, Jonas said, "Beauty shows through," and then he quickly changed the subject. "Brad's already done some homework, and the fact has emerged that the Heggertys are not licensed auctioneers. They seem to conduct their sales on the buddy system. They've been around Wainwright forever, so people trust them. Unfortunately, most of the people we're talking about really don't know when they've been fleeced simply because they're not up on market values, for which they can't be blamed. I imagine they're delighted when the Heggertys hand them a substantial check for stuff they may have been thinking of carting off to the town dump.

"Brad points out that if the Heggertys *were* licensed, the chances are they would have gone after their court order and as of yesterday your household contents, books and all, would have gone under the gavel. As it is, Brad's conclusion is that they agreed to a postponement, supposedly for old times' sake. Right?''

"Yes."

"You told them you still want to hold the auction?"

She nodded. "Two weeks from yesterday, as you must know," she said. "There are signs stuck in the snow out in front and a big notice tacked to the front door."

"Good thing the forecast was for another blizzard yesterday, though it didn't materialize," Jonas said. "Otherwise, you probably would have been swamped with dealers, anyway. Dealers can be aggressive."

"Do you speak from experience?" Carla asked him.

"What am I supposed to assume from that question, Carla?"

"Well, you're a dealer in books yourself, aren't you?"

"No," he said shortly. Visibly exasperated, he continued, "I *collect* books. I love books. I think I already went through that with you. One of the biggest rooms in my house, now that I'm renovating it, is to be the library.

"I already told you I'm a *silent* partner in my friend's business," he went on, "and I do mean silent. I admit that what I wanted to do was buy your book collection, take from it what I'd like to see in my own library, pass on the other good stuff to Fred and donate the lesser volumes to charitable organizations, where maybe they could bring in a few dollars at bazaars and book fairs. Believe it or not, those were my sole motives."

That hurt note had crept into Jonas's voice again, but it was short-lived. He said brusquely, "Well, I guess I'd better be getting along."

He and Carla stood up at the same instant. They were close enough so that body contact was unavoidable.

Jonas, she discovered once again, really towered over her. Nevertheless, she looked up and met his eyes, and for a relatively long moment the two of them stared at each other.

Carla couldn't believe herself, but it was she who made the first gesture. She reached out a tentative hand and said slowly, "Jonas?"

She saw his throat work. "Yes," he managed huskily.

"I always seem to be doing you . . . an injustice. I must come on as if I'm the most suspicious person in the world, and I'm not, really. It's just that I . . ."

"Yes?" Jonas queried, his voice a shade huskier.

"Well, I guess I feel the need to handle things myself, sometimes. Can you understand that?"

"Yes," Jonas said, downright hoarse at that point.

"Sometimes I need some breathing space, that's all," she went on. "It's difficult to explain, but sometimes I just need to do things my way. But with the Heggertys, I admit I've made a mess of things. And I appreciate the effort you've gone to to get all this information together and to tell me the way it is. Believe me, I don't . . . disbelieve you. As I said, I'm appreciative. I'm really appreciative, Jonas."

He waited. Carla waited. Then she stood up on tiptoe, flung her arms around his neck and gently kissed him square on the lips.

"Thank you," she said.

She stepped back and saw that Jonas looked as if he were in shock. The shock didn't last long. He reached for her, drew her to him and this time he bent his head so the kiss was a lot easier. Their mouths fused, and a drafty old attic in December became a tropical paradise where palm fronds swayed gently in the breeze, lilting music filled the air and the sun spilled a golden radiance over everything....

There was no telling what might have happened, Carla told herself later, if Jewel hadn't chosen that moment to call up the stairs, "Hey, you two? How about some lunch?"

Jonas stayed for lunch. He also stayed for the potluck supper he'd missed a couple of nights earlier.

In the intervening hours, he and Carla started going through the cartons of books. They each, as if by unspoken agreement, took pains to stick strictly to business.

Jonas inaugurated a book search method whereby they took a couple of new, empty cartons up to the attic to start working with. One carton was marked, Keep, and the other carton was marked, Sell. Then, while Jonas conferred with Carla about each book and placed the volume in the proper carton, Carla scanned Miss Daniels's list—which, fortunately, the librarian had alphabetized—and checked off the titles.

By the time Jewel called up to suggest they stop work for the day and come down and indulge in a cocktail hour, they'd gone through a number of cartons. But there were still so many left to go through that Carla began to see this was going to be a lengthy process, and she was honestly thankful for Jonas's help.

Jonas, comfortably ensconced in front of the living-room fireplace again, with a glass of bourbon and branch in hand, said, "It's going to take weeks to get through all the books at the rate we're going. I wish I could think of a way to expedite the process, but I can't."

"I could help," Jewel volunteered.

"That'd be kind of an imposition," Jonas said before Jewel could say anything.

"Not at all," Jewel protested.

"Okay, at moments when you feel you have spare time on your hands," Jonas agreed.

Once again he was on the verge of taking over, in Carla's opinion, and she forestalled him. "There's no reason why either of you has to go any further with this," she said firmly. "I can perfectly well handle it myself." She added, unless she seem *too* ungracious, "Though I certainly appreciated your help in getting me started today, Jonas."

Jewel said, "Carla, it would take you forever, going through all those books on your own."

"Nonsense," Carla retorted brusquely. "I'm used to dealing with books, remember?"

"Regardless..." Jewel let whatever it was she had been going to say evaporate. She knew her stepdaughter.

Jonas favored Carla with a long, level glance. There was no smile on his face, no humor in his voice as he asked, "Do you really want to handle the books by yourself, Carla?"

"You mentioned that it would be an imposition to ask Jewel to get involved," Carla told him, quickly adopting some evasive tactics. "It would certainly be an imposition for me to suggest you spend any more time on the books. I'm sure you have other things to do, Jonas."

"Sure I have other things to do," he agreed easily. "But the mystery element involved in your grandfather's collection is pretty fascinating to me as a collector. Let's say I want to be in on the denouement. I want to be around when you discover whether or not some of the choicest books really have disappeared. And the only way to do that is to work side by side with you. Anyway, it makes sense. Two people can do a job twice as fast as one person can, unless one of the individuals is a hopeless clod.''

Jonas waited. Carla didn't say anything.

''I, too, am used to dealing with books,'' he added. ''Once I get my library set up, I'll show you *my* collection. In fact, when the library's ready, maybe we can arrange a tit for tat deal. You can help me shelve my books and get them in some sort of order so when I want something, I can find it.''

As she heard that, Carla's heart sank. It hit her that once the auction was over and the house sold, she would be leaving Wainwright for good. Thereafter, her life would be centered in Bedloe Falls.

Bedloe Falls was a nice town, but suddenly it held very little appeal to her.

Jonas still looked serious and somehow distanced as they ate the excellent supper Jewel had prepared for them. He left early, pausing at the door only to say, ''By the way, Carla, I forgot to mention it, but Brad wants to see both of us at his office at nine-thirty tomorrow morning.''

Carla nodded, not bothering to point out that he might have consulted her first before making an appointment for her. It didn't seem to matter that much.

What did matter was that her world was turning over, thanks to Jonas. She told herself hastily that that wasn't his fault nearly as much as it was hers. He hadn't really done anything. She'd been as responsible for that kiss up in the attic as he'd been. Her determination to stand up for herself and resist him was in danger of going straight down the drain.

It would be so easy, so very easy, to fall in love with him.

Chapter Nine

Carla instantly liked Brad Shapiro. He was slim, dark, not at all good-looking, but he had a personality that made looks unimportant.

They settled down in his office, which was on the second floor of an old red brick building on Wainwright's main street. They exchanged pleasantries, mentioned that it *still* looked like there was another blizzard on the way, though no further snow had materialized yet, and then got down to the subject at hand.

"I was reasonably sure from various things I'd heard around town that the Heggertys weren't licensed auctioneers," Brad said frankly. "Yesterday being Sunday, it was hard to check as much as I wanted to, but I learned enough. They aren't licensed, nor do they pretend to be if anyone asks. Thing is, most of the people they deal with don't ask."

He leaned back in his chair, tapping the tips of his fingers together. "I don't want to sound like I'm insulting anyone's intelligence," he said, "but the Heggertys do prey on people. Their ace in the hole is that they've been around this area for a long time. They know a lot of people. William knows folks in his parents' generation as well as his own. Skip fills in with the younger set. So it's a natural that when someone around here wants to auction something, they think of the Heggertys.

"The Heggertys are also good at handling their own PR in that respect. Skip makes a good front man. William's astute. Depending on the prospective client, he knows exactly when to send Skip out to make a pitch for a job and when to do it himself.

"As I hear it, the licensed auctioneers in this part of the state have been trying to put the Heggertys out of business for a long time. Trouble is, thus far they haven't actually been able to catch father and son in any wrongdoing."

Carla listened and felt sick at what she was hearing. Gwen's brother. Gwen's father. This was very hard to take in.

"Isn't there a chance they actually haven't been guilty of any wrongdoing?" she asked.

"Well," Brad said, "in our legal system, as you well know, you're innocent until proven guilty. But I think it would be naive to pretend the Heggertys haven't been indulging in some dirty pool, Carla. If you think just of the books the Heggertys have taken in to Fred's bookstore—Jonas's partner—you'll start to wonder. Maybe they came by those rare books in a perfectly legal fashion. Maybe, again, they didn't.

"I hear by my rather tenuous grapevine that some interesting paintings have turned up in other places, offered for sale by the Heggertys, as have a few antiques. Small pieces, thus far, easily transportable. The Heggertys evidently head for the Utica-Rome-Syracuse market. They usually don't repeat with the dealers they approach often enough to arouse suspicion, though they did in Fred's case. But we might say that Fred may be a shade sharper than a lot of people.''

"So you're telling me that Skip and his father *steal* things that were meant to be auctioned off, without the owners becoming aware of what they're doing."

"'Steal' is a strong word," Brad conceded. "But from what I've discovered, I do suspect that some of the things they peddle later have been acquired from stock given to them to auction. Maybe sometimes they buy what they want for a minimum sum, convincing the owner whatever it is wouldn't bring much anyhow. A lot of people are woefully ignorant about the value of the things they possess, especially when they've inherited those possessions.

"Again, as I hear it, what the Heggertys usually do is to go through a house, make an inventory and then talk over the sales prospects with the client. They quickly sense whether or not the person they're talking to knows anything about market values. Sometimes they'll offer to buy some of the stuff themselves, then and there. Sometimes they make a deal where an auction is avoided altogether, and they just cart off a lot of things they've convinced their client aren't worth much but—maybe for old times' sake—they're paying more than a fair price for. They use varying methods, I'm sure.''

"I don't imagine it's all that unusual to offer to purchase certain items in advance of an auction, is it?'' Carla suggested.

She wasn't thinking of Jonas as she said that, but once the words were out, she saw that he was flushing and an angry glint had crept into his light eyes.

He said flatly, "I offered to buy Carla's books in advance of the sale, Brad. That's what she's referring to."

Brad looked honestly appalled. "Certainly you're not comparing any offer Jonas might have made with the route the Heggertys take, are you?" he asked bluntly.

Carla didn't dare look at Jonas. "No," she said. "I was merely trying to make a point."

"For the sake of the record," Jonas said tightly, "she turned me down."

What could she say? Carla thought, feeling pretty dismal at this point. She *had* turned him down.

Were it today, would she turn him down? She wasn't sure. She did know that she would listen more than she'd listened to him either at the library in Bedloe Falls or in the motel.

She knew a lot more about Jonas now than she had then. He wasn't greedy. He didn't amass things just for the sake of amassing them or because he had enough money to buy anything he wanted. He genuinely loved books. She'd seen that as they went through the cartons up in her attic. He'd handled the old volumes with a gentle touch, a reverence she liked.

He'd handled *her* with a gentle touch and a reverence she'd liked, but at the same time his kiss had been fired with passion....

Oh, Jonas, she mused silently, *where have the two of us come from and where are we heading for? What am I going to do about you? If I let you into my life much further, it's going to be terrible to have to let you out again. And, we're too different. We don't belong together.*

She sighed involuntarily, looked up and met Jonas's eyes again and, this time, saw not anger but an odd expression she couldn't read.

Jonas said, "Well, Brad, I think we've taken up enough of your time on this, for the moment. Carla and I are going through her books. In a few more days we should know what titles are missing, which, I realize before you tell me so, doesn't necessarily prove a thing. Unless..."

"Unless?" Brad prompted.

"Well, unless the missing volumes are rare ones and at some point they show up for sale. The Heggertys might approach Fred again. It's been a long while. Were they to do that, it'd make things relatively easy for us. But, there are also other ways...."

"We'll have to wait and see," Jonas concluded.

Downtown Wainwright looked as if it were modeling for a Christmas card illustration. Snow covered rooftops and bordered windowsills. Shops were lavishly decorated for Christmas. Fragrant green wreaths with big red ribbon bows ornamented house doors.

Christmas in California had never seemed like Christmas to Carla, regardless of the fact the Westerners went the full route where Yuletide decorating was concerned. Brought up in the North Country of New York State as she'd been, the climate had been wrong for her.

Since coming back East, Christmas hadn't seemed like Christmas, either. Last Christmas had been the first one since her father's death, and neither she nor Jewel had felt much like celebrating. They'd exchanged presents, but they'd kept decorating to a minimum.

Now she said suddenly, "This year, I want a tree."

"What's that?" Jonas asked.

"I—" She stopped what she was about to say before she went any further. She was remembering that by Christmas the auction would have been held, the house stripped bare. She and Jewel had already decided they'd have Christmas together in Bedloe Falls this year, or else maybe go down to New York over the holiday.

Jonas said, "If you were talking about a Christmas tree, I can't see there'd be any problem in your having a Christmas tree."

"There won't be any place to put it," Carla murmured.

He shot a sideways glance at her. "That's not necessarily so," he said, and then quickly changed the subject.

"Brad will keep looking into this whole thing with the Heggertys," he told her.

Carla knew how lawyers' fees could run up. "Brad was very kind to use up a part of his weekend on my behalf," she said. "But . . . I can't afford to give him carte blanche from here on in, Jonas."

"If you're worried about money," Jonas said, "Brad is doing this out of friendship."

"How can that be? He doesn't even know me."

"He knows *me* very well," Jonas pointed out. "We exchange favors, now and then."

"It's me he'd be doing a favor for, not you."

"Look, lay off it, will you?" Jonas suggested. "Brad's glad to be doing this. He doesn't like the kind of chicanery the Heggertys seem to be practicing any more than I do."

"But . . ."

They were at his car. Jonas said firmly, "No buts. Now, get in, will you?"

He held the door. Carla got in the car. But no sooner was he behind the wheel than she turned to him to say, "Look, Jonas, there's something you and I have to straighten out."

"And what would that be?" Jonas asked with exaggerated patience.

"You've got to stop... taking over all the time."

"Is that what you think I do? You think I take over?"

"You take over," Carla stated firmly.

She glanced at Jonas. He was staring down at the ring of keys he was holding. He looked uncomfortable, which surprised her. He sounded uncomfortable as he said, "I'm sorry. I'm honestly sorry. I know what you're saying, and you're perfectly right. This *is* your business. If you want Brad to stop looking into things any further, just give him a call when you get home and tell him so."

"Jonas..."

"No, Carla, I hear you," Jonas said. "And what goes down from here on is entirely up to you. As it happened, I had some knowledge you didn't have, so I hated to see you go ahead with the auction. I think you might agree, now that at last some of the facts are in, that it was a valid concern."

"Yes," she admitted. "It was a valid concern. And...I appreciate your having been concerned."

"Thank you. However, you now know what the score is—or is likely to be—so you have the reins in your own hands. If you want me to butt out, Carla, just say so."

He waited. Carla waited. She knew there was no possible way she could tell him to butt out.

After a moment, Jonas extricated the car key from his key ring and slipped it in the ignition switch.

"Back to the books," he said.

* * *

Jonas's hands were clammy on the steering wheel for the first couple of miles of their drive back to Carla's house. Also, he felt like he was suffering from a lack of oxygen. He'd been holding his breath while he waited for her answer.

Working with her on her books—and staying in her life—was tremendously important to him right now.

The relief had been profound when she hadn't answered him. True, she hadn't told him *not* to butt out, but he knew Carla well enough to be sure that if that's what she'd wanted, she would have taken advantage of the opportunity he'd just given her.

She was so entirely different from anyone he'd ever known. Especially, any woman he'd ever known. He had dated his share of users, women out for his money and influence. He admired Carla's independence—even though at times it irked the hell out of him. He very much admired her gutsiness. His problem was that he wanted to take her home with him and take tender loving care of her forever and ever. She did inspire the damnedest feelings in him.

He knew she didn't like his tendency to take over, and he'd honestly been trying to curb it, though certainly not with one hundred percent success. She also didn't like his tendency to protect her, but he didn't seem to be able to restrain himself when they got into a situation where he thought she needed help.

Well, at least she was going along with his continuing to work on her books with her, and that was a minor victory.

When they were through with the book cartons and had explored other parts of the house for books that might have been stashed away elsewhere, would the

Heggertys be revealed as the crooks he thought they were?

Tune in tomorrow, Jonas thought ruefully, and brought his car to a stop in the driveway at the side of Carla's house.

They put in a couple of hours before joining Jewel for a light lunch, then went back to work again. Carla was *all* work today, and watching her, Jonas felt he might very well be going quietly insane. He'd been fighting down a lot of heavy feelings toward her, but he knew he couldn't keep on with the battle forever. He wanted her too much. Each time he looked at her, he wanted her more than he had the time before.

The wanting was not simple, though. Nothing about his relationship with Carla was simple, he decided grimly. This was not just a matter of sex, pure and simple, and he had the experience and the self-knowledge to recognize that. Desire for Carla was mixed with a kind of caring he'd never felt before. A bittersweet sadness stirred deep inside him. The message of need was being telegraphed straight to his loins, encompassing on its way every fiber of his being, the essence of his masculinity, the whole damned package.

"Here's a first edition," Carla said suddenly.

"Umm?" Jonas asked, trying to push his id deeper into his subconscious.

"Washington Irving. *The Alhambra.* In reasonably good condition."

"Valuable, I'd think."

To his surprise she said, "I honestly don't know that much about value, per se, at least when it comes to market pricing. Most librarians don't. That's why, when old books are donated to the library, we call in an expert before doing anything with them ourselves.

"I've dealt with a few such donations both in California and in Bedloe Falls," she went on. "Some rare books that really were quite valuable showed up in a couple of instances, and with the approval of the board of trustees, we sold them. It's too great a responsibility to house extremely rare books in a small public library. Also, the libraries needed money for a lot of practical things the town budgets couldn't be stretched to include."

"Well," Jonas said, before he thought, "Fred can take care of the evaluating. I consider him as expert as anyone I know."

Before Carla could frame a retort, he added hastily, "Unless you'd prefer someone else, of course."

He saw a smile hover around her mouth. It made him yearn to touch his lips to hers, to see how the smile felt. She said, "No, Fred will be fine. Matter of fact, I'd like to meet him."

Jonas thought about Fred, who was a couple of years younger than he was—thirty-four, to be precise. Fred was anything but a bookworm type, despite his love of books and his expertise in his chosen field. Fred, a bachelor, was a very attractive guy who played a mean game of tennis and an equally mean game of Scrabble. And he had a quirky sort of one-sided smile that seemed to drive women crazy.

Jonas felt a sudden, absolutely ridiculous pang of jealousy.

It was Carla who called the next break. In the midafternoon, she said, "Let's go down and get a cup of tea, or maybe a glass of wine."

They opted for wine and shared some Chablis while sitting at the kitchen table. Jewel had gone out earlier to do some shopping. Jonas became acutely conscious that he and Carla were alone in the house. He thought about taking her to bed with him. The thought staggered him.

Suddenly he had to know more about her. "Just how long ago did your father die, Carla?" he asked her.

Her thoughts evidently had been miles away. She looked startled, but she answered easily enough. "Two years ago," she said.

"Jewel's a very attractive woman," Jonas observed. "Do you suppose maybe one day she'll remarry?"

"I hope so," Carla said sincerely. "Jewel was deeply in love with my father, but I think she's much too young and attractive to go on forever with a—a ghost."

"What about you?" Jonas dared to ask, and immediately questioned his decision.

"Are you asking me how long ago my husband died?"

"Well—yes."

"Brian died six years ago. I'm sure I've already told you that, Jonas."

She spoke matter-of-factly. Jonas could read nothing in either her expression or her tone of voice.

"If I'm...probing too much," he said carefully, "just tell me so, Carla. But...I wish I knew what happened. I mean...was it an accident?"

He spoke as if his words were walking across a thin skim of ice under which there lay very deep, dark, frigid waters.

"Brian had leukemia, Jonas," Carla said quietly, giving no indication that tears might follow, as he'd begun to fear. "I knew that when I married him. We met in college. He was a terrific person. He did everything in his power not to let his illness stop him. I admired him tremendously, from the very beginning. Then, I fell deeply in love with him."

Despite himself, Jonas winced.

"Brian was in remission for a long time. He'd been in remission for a while before I married him, and, fortunately, that state lingered until, finally, the disease took over again. We'd been married two years when he died."

"Rough," Jonas said compassionately. The word was wrung out of him.

"Yes, it was rough," Carla agreed in that same level tone, which he couldn't quite figure out. Had she really come to grips with her husband's early death to the point of adjusting all that well? Or was this merely a brave facade he was seeing?

"Brian had the best care anyone could possibly have," she went on, when Jonas, by now, would as soon have had her call a halt. "Nothing was spared. Not because of anything *I* could do. Brian's parents are very wealthy people. They saw to it that nothing was overlooked. I think till the last second they prayed that Brian could suddenly pioneer a new cure...."

"And you?" Again, the words were wrung out of Jonas.

"I knew Brian was going to die," Carla said with only the slightest quaver to her voice. "Brian knew he was going to die. We made the very, very best of the time we had. He instilled in me his wish that once he was gone, I'd go on. He—he made me promise him that. It took a while for me to begin to live up to the promise. For a while I just wanted to be by myself. I had to get my grief out of my system. Everyone has to do that. But then I went back to school, went on to get my graduate degree and found a library job in Santa Monica."

"Did you live with Brian's parents all that time?" Jonas asked her.

"No. We never lived with Brian's parents. We moved in together before we got married, we had a little apartment near the college campus. Frankly, I think Brian's parents, for a long time, considered me a fortune hunter. But they discovered I didn't want anything from them. I was the beneficiary of Brian's insurance, which was more than enough. That's what enabled me to go back to school.

"One thing," Carla concluded. "I learned a valuable lesson. Money can make the way easier, can buy a lot of things. But it loses total power when it comes to getting what matters most."

Jonas picked up his wineglass and drained it. He felt as if he were hearing her words repeated over and over. They rang in his head.

Was she trying to tell him she didn't give a damn about his money, whatever he might think?

She didn't need to. He already was sure of that.

And he, too, had learned long ago that when it came to having what one wanted most of all, money was powerless. "Let's take the wine back up to the attic with us," Carla said recklessly. "My throat gets dry up there. There's so much dust around."

"It's a good attic," Jonas said. "A great attic. A movie-scene attic. There *should* be a lot of dust around. Nevertheless, you're right," he added, picking up the wine bottle. "No reason why we should let our throats get dry."

In the attic again, they began going through the books and—though Carla acknowledged it could be her imagination—she felt a kind of change in atmosphere between them. An easiness, a camaraderie, that hadn't been there before.

She hoped she hadn't sounded cold when she spoke about Brian to Jonas. She was anything but cold where her memories of Brian were concerned. But he was not a ghost, the way she suspected her father was still a ghost to Jewel. Brian would have so hated to be a ghost. He would never have wished to haunt her. He would have wanted her to go on and do things, make a good life for herself. Which is what she'd been trying to do...and not entirely failing, but not entirely succeeding, either, she conceded.

She was beginning to realize, more and more, that no one was meant to lead a really solitary life. Not until, anyway, they were content to rely on memories, to take nostalgia trips that brought quiet satisfactions.

She was twenty-eight years old...and beginning to see she had a long way to go.

She looked across at Jonas. He was absorbed in a book. He had a tendency to stop, every now and then, and get lost in one of the books he'd picked up.

She asked, "What is it?"

"A volume of poems for children called, *The Gentlest Giant*," he said. "Lots of famous poems in it, as well as ones I've never heard of. They're delightful, though."

"I remember it," Carla said with a smile. "I used to love it when I was little. I think it must have belonged to my grandmother."

"Maybe even your great-grandmother," Jonas said.

He put the book aside and confessed, "I get side-tracked."

"So I've noticed," Carla teased. "Which is great, except that if you keep on getting sidetracked, we're never going to get through with this job."

"Yeah, I know," Jonas said lazily. "Think we could go for another glass of Chablis?"

"I've had two," Carla said sedately. "One more's my cutoff point."

He poured, handed a wineglass to her, kept one for himself.

"To books," he toasted gravely.

"To books," she agreed.

"To friendship?" he suggested.

"To friendship," she agreed, and drank again.

Jonas wanted to go a step further, but, for the moment, he let that suffice.

Chapter Ten

When Jonas appeared to help with the books on Wednesday morning, he invited Jewel and Carla to have dinner with him at the country club that night.

"I've been potlucking and potlucking," he told her. "Now it's your turn."

"I'd love to," Jewel said promptly, "but I'm on a committee making Christmas ornaments for the Hospital Aid bazaar, and the bazaar's this coming Saturday. So I'll have to pass. You and Carla go, though, by all means."

Carla supposed that the Christmas decorations committee was legitimate enough but wondered just how active Jewel had been on it till now. Jewel's matchmaking was showing again, but if Carla refused Jonas's dinner invitation, it would make it all the more obvious.

That, anyway, was her rationale for accepting the invitation.

She and Jonas started out around seven, but they had barely turned the corner when he asked, "Do you necessarily want to go to the country club?"

"No, not necessarily," she answered. "Why. Don't you?"

"Not necessarily," he said, and grinned. "I always get treated like the Wainwright-Davenport scion because my grandfather founded the place," he admitted, "so usually I go there only when I need to take out business associates."

"Don't you like being treated like the Wainwright-Davenport scion?"

"Don't you know me well enough yet, Carla, to be able to answer that question for yourself?"

"Sometimes I think I know you, and sometimes I think I don't know you," Carla said.

That was true. Sometimes Jonas was the sort of man she knew *wouldn't* like being feted as the Wainwright-Davenport scion. However, at other times—when he was being assertive, aggressive and all the other things a good executive was supposed to be—she could imagine that he would love having the red carpet rolled out for him.

"Like Greek food?" he asked abruptly.

"Yes," she said, "as a matter of fact, I do."

"Good," he said with approval. "I'm always pleased when I find something we agree on. There's a good little Greek restaurant over in Watertown, which isn't all that far."

Carla was watching him closely as he spoke. His profile was turned to her. She visually sketched each line of that profile, from the rather high forehead to the straight nose, the full mouth and the determined chin. The small mental exercise made her wish, not for the first time, that Jonas had never heard of her grandfather's books and that they weren't in such different social realms, that their personalities weren't so absolutely opposite.

It occurred to her she actually didn't know all that much about Jonas's background, except that he had been a loner as a child, had inherited a family business and also a big old mansion up on a hill overlooking the Silver River, which he was presently renovating.

Was he really going to stay in Wainwright and live on his hilltop in solitude? Or, was there someone—

She blocked the vision.

The vision returned, though, once they were sitting opposite each other in a booth at the Greek restaurant, which was indeed small and very unpretentious. In fact, she wondered how Jonas had ever found it.

He'd ordered ouzo and some dolmas for appetizers, and as they were waiting to be served, Carla said, "What made you decide to come back to Wainwright to live— that is, if you *have* decided to come back to Wainwright to live?"

Jonas chuckled. "Which question am I supposed to answer first?"

"Both."

"Okay. I decided to make Wainwright my primary residence—even though I haven't been around the town much since I was a teenager—because I want a home," he said simply. "A real home. I've never had a real home. Except, to a certain extent, in Wainwright, when my grandmother was alive and I used to visit her summers and on school vacations. I think I already told you I moved from house to penthouse to house when I was growing up."

Jonas toyed with a fork as he continued soberly, "The pharmaceutical firm had already expanded, moved elsewhere, by the time my father took over the business. That was when I was ten or so, and my uncle—my father's brother-in-law, and the last of the Wainwright line and the head of the firm at the time—got himself shot in a freak hunting accident. Later, when my father died, I took over."

"Yes..." Carla prodded, not quite getting the point.

"Well, I also had other aspirations, Carla."

He waited while their waiter put their drinks and appetizers on the table, then said, "It all came back that night in the motel."

"What do you mean?"

"You told me I should have been a doctor, and it was kind of like a punch right in the gut. I hadn't realized I'd still feel that way. It's been a long time since I've thought about devoting my life to medicine."

"You mean you did want to be a doctor?"

"Yes."

"Well, then, why in the world didn't you?" Carla asked. "You certainly could have afforded to go to medical school. You could probably have *bought* a medical school if you'd wanted to."

"Ouch," Jonas said, and reached for his glass of ouzo.

Carla hadn't realized how gauche her statement would sound until she made it. Now she said, "I'm sorry."

Jonas was staring at the ouzo. The normally clear, licorice-flavored drink was cloudy, having been mixed with water and poured on the rocks. "What are you sorry about?" he asked without looking at Carla.

"I suppose sometimes being so rich must get tiresome," she said slowly.

"For one thing, I'm not that rich," Jonas said. "People around Wainwright seem to automatically assume I must be in the super-billionaire class, which isn't so. But even if I *could* have afforded to buy a medical school, I wouldn't have been able to."

Carla wished he'd look at her. She wanted to meet his eyes. She wanted to at least *show* a little more empathy than she'd just expressed.

Jonas kept staring at the ouzo. "I was just out of college and, matter of fact, I had just been accepted by Harvard's school of medicine when my father dropped dead while honeymooning with his fifth wife."

Bitterness laced every word.

"I had to give up my own career plans because I was the last of the line and there was no one else left to take over the family business. My Grandmother Wainwright was still alive. She was the one woman in my life I've ever been deeply fond of. I couldn't let her down. She died three years ago, at age eighty-two. Since then, I've gradually spread the load onto other shoulders, where the business is concerned. I'm still in control, but I don't have to put in ten-hour days, six days a week any longer."

She was the one woman in my life I've ever been deeply fond of....

Carla couldn't resist the question. "What about your mother?"

"What about her?"

"You said..."

"Oh. You're wondering if I was so unnatural as to dislike my own mother, is that it? Well, I never really knew her, Carla, any more than you ever knew your mother. I was four when she died. I think you said you were three when your mother died. I have a very vague memory of mine. Maybe if she had lived, my father wouldn't have set forth on his much-publicized marrying sprees." He shrugged. "Who knows?"

* * *

Jonas kept the conversation impersonal all through the rest of the dinner. He'd been a lot of places, done a lot of things, had a terrific sense of humor and didn't object to telling tales in which the joke had been on him, Carla discovered.

Once they were in his car and heading back to Wainwright, though, he fell silent. The snow had held off, and the moon was flirting with the dark clouds that still dominated the sky.

After a long, blank period, Carla decided she had to straighten out a couple of matters with him, and she said tentatively, "Jonas..."

He'd switched on the car radio, and the station was playing vintage Beatles. Jonas turned the volume down and asked, "Yes?"

"Jonas, I didn't mean to pry, back there in the restaurant. I—I just wanted to know more about you, that's all."

"I'm flattered," he said, but she didn't like the dry way he said it.

"Don't be sarcastic," she said.

"I'm not being sarcastic."

"The thing is," Carla said, "I know how curious people are in small towns, and I know how gossip travels. And naturally there has been a lot of gossip about you since your return."

"Has there really?"

"I'm sure you know the answer to that. People are conjecturing all kinds of things."

"A prodigal son returning?" Jonas suggested.

"Jonas, you can't blame people for being curious. After all, Wainwright was *named* after your mother's family. I expect when you've been living here six months, they'll probably want to elect you mayor or persuade you to run for the state assembly or maybe even congress."

"The hell you say."

"I am serious, Jonas."

"Carla?"

"Yes?"

"How do you know there's been so much talk about me?"

"Jewel told me," Carla said, and then stopped short, horrified. She'd never thought of herself as a blabbermouth, but Jonas did have a way of getting things out of her.

"What did Jewel tell you?" Jonas persisted.

"Oh, please," she protested.

"Okay, I think I can fill in the picture," Jonas said, the dry note even more pronounced. "Bachelor. Wealthy. Relatively young. Etcetera. God, I hate stupid gossip."

Carla shrank down in the corner of the seat and wished she could make herself invisible.

"Knowing Jewel as I've already come to know her, I doubt she added any fuel to the fire," Jonas conceded. "But I can see where she might have done a little bit of thinking, and don't imagine I'm flattering myself when I say that." The question shot out. "Jewel wants you to get married again, doesn't she?"

Invisibility seemed even more desirable.

"Carla," Jonas advised, "stop trying to slink down to the floor. I'm not trying to embarrass the hell out of you, I'm just trying to clarify a couple of things. I don't blame Jewel for thinking you should get married again. *I* think you should get married again."

"Why," Carla shot back, her embarrassment fading in the wake of the annoyance Jonas could so easily arouse in her. "So I'd have someone to take care of me?"

"That's one reason, yes. It's not so terrible to have someone around to look after you, Carla. You might find that out if you ever stopped writing a new Declaration of Independence each morning when you wake up. However…there are other reasons why I think you should get married again, and, no, I am not going to spell them out for you. I just want to warn you about something."

"Warn me?" What was *this* going to be about?

"Be very, very careful, Carla, before you ever agree to marry anyone," Jonas said seriously. "You're a wonderful person, but you're also very vulnerable. You had one marriage that, though it had a sad ending, was happy while it lasted. I'd hate to see you plunge into something that might be miserable for you, so think long and carefully before you ever say yes, will you? I'd also hate to see you hurt."

Carla, astonished, was still trying to recover from Jonas's advice when he pulled into her driveway. Did he have to lecture her as if she were a child? It was nice to know he cared, but he was so bossy. And obviously he didn't care on a very personal, intimate level.

The walk was dry, no treacherous ice patches around. Noting that, Jonas said, "I've observed that each day your knee seems to be better. You're back to about a hundred percent now, aren't you?"

"Yes."

His face was partly obscured by shadows. Carla wished she could see it more clearly. He didn't get out and come around to open her door for her. Instead, he leaned over and kissed her full on the mouth, letting his lips linger just long enough so *both* her knees began to feel equally weak.

Then he reached across her to pull down the door handle and promised, "I'll be around first thing in the morning."

Carla and Jonas finished going through the last carton of books about five o'clock on Friday afternoon. "Okay, before we get down to the nitty gritty of what's missing and what isn't," Jonas said promptly, "I think we should celebrate. Champagne?"

"We don't have any," Carla told him.

"Ah, but we do," he corrected her. "I anticipated this might happen today, so I raided the wine cellar I'm building up out at the house, and there's been a bottle of Dom Perignon chilling in your fridge all day."

Carla had a vague idea of what a bottle of Dom Perignon cost. She shook her head at him and chided, "Jonas, Jonas."

"Come on," he urged.

He was in a hurry because he knew that if he stayed around in this attic with her much longer—now that there were no more cartons of books to be gone through—he was going to make love to her. He had better than average powers of resistance, he thought without conceit— resistance was a quality he'd worked on most of his life— but there was a limit to anyone's fortitude, and he'd been at the brink of his limit all week.

Carla was wearing an old yellow sweater, faded jeans, her hair was tied back in a ponytail with a length of yellow ribbon, and there were dirt smudges on her chin and cheeks. She looked infinitely desirable to Jonas.

She followed him down the attic stairs. They went out to the kitchen, and he retrieved the champagne from the fridge while Carla got out a couple of tulip-shaped glasses.

The Hospital Aid bazaar was tomorrow. Jewel was helping decorate the Masonic Hall where the bazaar was to be held. Again, Jonas and Carla were alone in the house, and that knowledge was getting to Jonas.

It was a hell of a time to get down to business, but with Carla at his side and a glass of Dom Perignon in his hand, he knew it was going to have to be either business or sex. And he had a gut instinct that the time was still not right to approach Carla on a really intense level. She'd responded to him, he knew she was attracted to him, but she was still . . . Carla.

Furthermore, he'd been honest when he'd urged her not to say yes easily to anyone, and he hadn't meant yes to marriage alone. Carla, at this stage of her life, would give so much of herself if the two of them were to start in on *that* kind of a relationship that she could well be left with nothing to retrieve. And, above all else, he didn't want to be the one to hurt her. He wanted to protect her.

"Let's go over Miss Daniels's list," he said brusquely. "I'll read out what's missing, you note the titles down. Then we'll compare her list with Skip Heggerty's list. . . ."

Was it his imagination, or did Carla really look slightly crestfallen? Jonas asked himself. Regardless, they settled in at the kitchen table once again, Carla produced a legal pad and a couple of pens, and they started to work.

The list of volumes that had been on Miss Daniels's list but were not in the cartons grew as they progressed. None of the missing titles appeared on Skip Heggerty's list, so if the auctioneer had moved any of the books in the course of his inventory, they still were not accounted for.

By the time Jewel got back from her bazaar-decorating session, Carla and Jonas had finished the bottle of Dom and were glaring at each other across the table.

"I still say this doesn't *prove* anything," Carla was insisting.

Jewel, divesting herself of a fur-lined car coat, asked cheerfully, "What seems to be the problem, kids?"

"Jonas is about to set out to *arrest* the Heggertys, and I'm saying there's still no proof they stole the books," Carla reported.

Jonas scowled. "I don't know just what the hell kind of proof you need to be convinced," he accused. "Carla, it's plainer than the nose on your face—"

"You are jumping to conclusions, Jonas," Carla shot back.

Jewel sat down at the table and surveyed the champagne bottle. "You brats," she complained. "You drank the whole thing."

"There's another," Jonas said absently, and went and got it.

Carla watched him fill three glasses this time with the sparkling pale gold liquid, and she informed him, "Getting me drunk is not going to make me change my mind, Jonas."

"Oh, for God's sake," Jonas said disgustedly. "Why would I want to get you drunk?" A smile crinkled his face. "You'd be a mess with a hangover," he chuckled.

"Jonas, don't change the subject," Carla commanded. She added, a shade less imperiously, "I admit this looks . . . bad. Because all the missing volumes are valuable ones. Even so . . ."

"Would you care to fill me in?" Jewel suggested.

Jonas took the initiative. "Carla and I have checked and double-checked Miss Daniels's list," he reported. "There are thirty-eight valuable books that are not present and accounted for. I admit there are even more valuable books which are present and accounted for. Even so,

I consider the discrepancy significant and suspicious. Carla is trying to disagree with me." Jonas spoke patiently, as if making the point that there was nothing unusual about Carla attempting to disagree with him.

"What do you think happened to the books, Carla?" Jewel asked.

"I'm just saying, as I've said all along, that Grandpa could have loaned the books to people who didn't return them. Years ago they wouldn't have had the value they have today. Or he could have given some of them away. You knew Grandpa, Jewel. You know how generous he was. Or the books could have been lost. Or they simply could be somewhere else around the house."

"Do you really think?" Jewel asked bluntly.

"I don't know," Carla admitted.

"Carla, I'll tell you one thing," Jewel decided. "I very much doubt your grandfather loaned out any of the more valuable books in his collection, I'd bet my bottom dollar he didn't give any of them away, and I don't think they were lost. Your grandfather, I agree, was the most generous of men, but he cared a lot about his books, and he always had them earmarked for you. He knew you shared his love of books. He'd instilled some of that love in you, after all. Also, he was sharp. And—it hasn't been that long since he died. Not quite seven years. The books I imagine you're talking about were probably pretty valuable long before then. Your grandfather would either have known their value or suspected one day they'd be worth a lot. That's probably why he asked Martha Daniels to list all the books for him, years ago."

"Well," Carla persisted, "the books must be... somewhere."

"Of course, they're somewhere," Jonas snapped. "I'm sure the Heggertys have found a safe niche for them until they're ready to dispose of them."

Carla gritted her teeth. "Are you as suspicious about everything as you are about the Heggertys?" she challenged.

"Suspicious enough," Jonas growled. He stood and said abruptly, "Well, I guess I'd better be shoving off."

"Jonas," Jewel chided, "there's three-quarters of a bottle of Dom Perignon yet to be consumed. We can't let that kind of liquid gold go to waste. Also, I have the makings of a great supper."

"Thanks, Jewel," Jonas said with an uncomfortable glance in Carla's direction, "but I need to make a couple of phone calls...."

"Use the phone in the study," Jewel invited.

Jonas shrugged. "Okay."

He didn't look at Carla as he accepted Jewel's suggestion. Her attitude was galling him. She was without a doubt the most stubborn woman he'd ever known, he decided. The most stubborn person he'd ever known. You could include both sexes in that estimate.

He wanted to shake her, he wanted to kiss her, he wanted to inject some sense into her, he wanted to make love to her....

He turned his back on her and shuffled off to the study where he placed a call to Fred, in Utica.

When he came back to the kitchen, Jewel was alone, fussing over a variety of pots and pans.

Jonas raised an inquiring eyebrow, and Jewel said, "Carla went upstairs for a moment. Jonas, don't be too hard on her."

"I'm being hard on her?" Jonas demanded bitterly. "Jewel, for God's sake, she's being impossible."

"Carla's not a child," Jewel said by way of answer. "In fact, she has a spine of steel. She proved that in the way she dealt with Brian's illness and his death. By then, Brian's family had reversed their first conclusion that Carla had married their son for money, knowing that he had an illness that would inevitably be fatal. They quickly learned that Carla wanted no financial help from them and, unfortunately, they had already distanced themselves from her to the extent the gap couldn't be bridged. It would have been wonderful if they could have managed a genuine rapport—Brian's parents and Carla. But, it just wasn't there. Nevertheless, they offered Carla anything in the world she might want. She politely but firmly refused them and set about building up her own life again.

"She was so young, Jonas. She had to grow up very fast, and, believe me, she did grow up. Carla is very much her own woman."

"Tell me about it," Jonas grumbled.

"She values her independence...."

"Tell me about that, too."

"She's also intensely loyal, Jonas. I know that Carla looks soft and cuddly and vulnerable—I find myself wanting to protect her when she doesn't either want or need my protection—but that's an illusion. Carla's a strong, secure and sophisticated young woman, despite those outward appearances. I'd say she's naive about only one thing. Which might be lumped, I guess, under the general heading, 'friendship.' It's her small-town background. She's a staunch friend. Friendship is a commitment to her. I think she could accept that William Heggerty might be involved in some chicanery, but she finds it very, very difficult to think that Skip would treat her in such a fashion. So difficult, she's trying to block out what you're saying to her."

"Ever think of turning psychologist, Jewel?" Jonas asked with a feeble attempt at a smile.

Jewel laughed. "Me? No, that would never do for me. I've never especially liked probing into other people's pasts and secrets. I just happen to know Carla very well, that's all."

They both heard Carla's footsteps on the stairs. Jewel said hastily, "You will stay for supper, won't you, Jonas?"

"Sure," Jonas said. "I need to tell Carla that Fred's agreed to come up here Sunday and go over the lists, take a look at the best of the books, anyway, and give her some idea of their value.

"That is, if," Jonas concluded carefully, "Carla doesn't object to my having made the arrangement without previous consultation and her consent."

Jewel smiled. "Don't overdo it, Jonas," she advised.

Jonas polished off the last of the Dom Perignon and carried the empty bottle over to the sink. He was wishing he knew where lines should be drawn with Carla. When was it wise to offer to help her and when would it be better to simply butt out?

He doubted even Jewel knew the answer to that one.

Chapter Eleven

Carla had done some thinking while she was upstairs. The more she thought about it, the more she could understand Jonas's impatience with her and his annoyance at her seeming failure to admit the Heggertys might be dishonest.

Despite her reluctance to accept what Jonas was saying, logic—plus a deep gut feeling—was beginning to convince her he was right. And the only fair thing to do was to admit that to him.

Once downstairs again, though, the atmosphere she walked into kept her from telling Jonas the odds certainly were in favor of his being right and her being wrong.

He was opening up a couple of cans for Jewel, and he looked so...unapproachable. Through the meal that followed, he was polite but distant. Carla began to wonder why he'd stayed around to take potluck with them in the first place.

"I meant to tell you, Carla, that I've talked to my partner, Fred Morris, and he's going to come up Sunday to give us—you, that is—an idea of the value of the books," Jonas finally said over dessert. "If, that is," he added, his face a mask, "that's agreeable to you."

It wasn't like Jonas to be so conciliatory. Yet even when he was being conciliatory he gave the impression that he'd already taken charge—as, indeed, he already had.

Just to be ornery, Carla wanted to tell him that Sunday wouldn't be a good time for a book appraisal. But she knew that would be plain foolishness. There'd be other ways in which she'd see that Jonas got his come-uppance, she thought direly. Just now she did need an expert to give her a better idea of the books' value than she had herself.

"That would be fine," she said.

Jonas, who had been prepared to have her squelch the plan he'd made with Fred, had a ready answer he had to quickly toss on the discard heap. Rallying, he said, "Okay, Fred plans to be here around noon. We can all go to the country club for lunch, if you like, and then come back here and start in on the books."

"That would be a waste of time," Carla said. "Can't we just have some sandwiches here while we go over the lists?"

"You will win Fred's heart with that suggestion," Jonas said, with a slight smile. "All he's going to be interested in is plunging right into that book list."

That was not the entire truth, he admitted to himself. His partner had an appreciative eye. If he was half the man Jonas thought he was, he was also going to be interested in Carla.

Jonas had a vision of a funny-looking green monster with a suggestive leer and a rather obscene wink, and the fact of what was happening to him hit him with the force of a well-tossed brick. He was falling in love with Carla. He was absolutely bewitched by this stubborn, impossible, beautiful, pigheaded librarian, God help him.

Jonas was so shocked by his discovery he didn't even hear Jewel, who evidently must have asked him if he wanted another piece of chocolate pie. And he must have nodded, because a second piece of pie suddenly appeared at his place.

Jewel shooed Carla and Jonas out of the kitchen while she put the china and the cutlery in the dishwasher. Jonas stopped short of going into the living room with Carla. He literally couldn't trust himself to be alone with her right now. He was afraid he might suddenly blurt out an impassioned declaration, and he couldn't risk her possible ridicule. He needed to get used to his sudden discovery before he could bring himself to the point of chancing one of their usual verbal sparring sessions.

"Carla," he said, as she was about to step over the living-room threshold.

She turned. The light caught her hair, burnished its copper with gold glints. "Yes?" she asked.

Jonas caught a whiff of the light perfume she used, and it went to his head considerably faster than the Dom Perignon had. He said uncomfortably, "Look, I want to run along but..."

He was remembering that he'd taken over something else in her life, without her knowing it. He'd called the garage in Tompkinsville where Jenny had been resting for over a week, now, before coming over to Carla's house this morning. The head mechanic had told him frankly that the old car wasn't worth the money it would cost to put it on the road again.

Jonas had nearly made the obvious decision to junk the car, then had stopped himself just in time. Jenny was more than just a car to Carla, he knew that. Also, dead or alive, Jenny was *her* car, not his.

He'd told the mechanic he'd bring Mrs. Logan over as soon as possible, so she could make her own decision. But, once at the house, he'd stalled about relaying that to Carla.

Now he was realizing that tomorrow was the logical time to go to Tompkinsville. They could clear up the matter of Jenny's fate, then concentrate on the books and what to do about the Heggertys and the auction.

Carla, watching Jonas, began to feel sure there was something on his mind he didn't want to tell her. After waiting while he stared rather vacantly at the wall behind her head, she asked, "What is it, Jonas?"

"I talked to the mechanic over in Tompkinsville this morning about Jenny," Jonas said.

"Oh, is she ready?" Carla asked eagerly.

"Well," Jonas said vaguely, "they've run into a few problems. I think you and I should take a run over there so the mechanic can explain what's to be done and you can decide if it's worth putting what might be a considerable amount of money into Jenny."

"I'll put as much money into Jenny as it'll take to fix her up," Carla said promptly.

That was what Jonas had been afraid to hear.

"Umm," he said, which—he hoped—might be taken as either agreement or disagreement. Then went on quickly, "How about going over to Tompkinsville tomorrow?"

"You and me?" Carla asked.

"Well, that's what I *did* have in mind," Jonas admitted.

"It would be an imposition," Carla stated. "There's no reason for you to drive me to Tompkinsville."

"Then how do you plan to get there?" Jonas asked logically.

"I'm sure Jewel can find time to take me. I could borrow her car and drive over myself, except, obviously, another pair of hands will be needed to bring Jenny back here."

Jonas didn't say anything to that. He took another approach. "Why don't you want me to drive you to Tompkinsville?"

She seemed genuinely surprised. "It isn't that I don't *want* you to drive me over there."

"Then exactly what is it, Carla?"

"You have better things to do than chauffeuring me around, Jonas." Carla made it a statement instead of a question.

"Not tomorrow," Jonas said. "That's why I'm suggesting tomorrow. Next week I have to spend some time in New York on business." While she digested *that*, he pointed out, "Jewel couldn't drive you over, anyway. Tomorrow's her bazaar."

Carla had forgotten all about Jewel's bazaar. To her own chagrin, she also admitted that she hadn't been giving Jenny much thought this last week. Her time and attention had been so occupied by the books and Jonas Davenport—no, make that Jonas Davenport and the books, if the priorities were to be straight—she hadn't been able to think of anything else.

Now, she discovered, both Jewel's bazaar and Jenny were being eclipsed by Jonas's announcement that he was going to have to go to New York next week.

It was foolish to feel so bereft because a man had to get back to his business, she told herself. Though Jonas had increasingly delegated authority in the pharmaceutical firm, he still held the reins. Obviously, he'd been slackening those reins because of his interest in old books and—more specifically—his curiosity about the contents of her grandfather's library. Now it was time to tighten up again.

Curiosity about the contents of her grandfather's library? It suddenly occurred to Carla that somewhere along the line Miss Daniels had turned her list of the library contents over to Jonas. When he'd come to Bedloe Falls to make his offer to buy the collection before the auction, Jonas had known very well what to expect. He'd known, at least, what volumes were *supposed* to be in those cartons up in the Hendricks' attic. He'd been wary of the Heggertys because they'd sold his partner rare books of "suspicious origin." Still, the collection contents had come as no surprise to him at all.

"Carla," Jonas said, puncturing her thought processes, "will you kindly tell me what it is *now*?"

"What do you mean?" she hedged.

"In case no one's ever mentioned it to you, you have a very expressive face. That face has just run through a gamut of an amazing number of expressions, denoting an equally amazing number of emotions. Right now, you look like you could poison me. May I ask why?"

Carla turned away from him because she was sure there was still another expression playing across her face and she didn't want Jonas to do any more diagnosing. She was feeling... unhinged. Betrayed. Tears were welling deep inside her, and she knew it would be easy for them to surface. She told herself it was crazy of her never to have realized before that Jonas actually had known all about the books all along. The facts—thanks to Miss Daniels's list—had been right there before her. Jonas hadn't attempted to camouflage anything. Nevertheless . . .

Bitterness took over. "Why didn't you tell me you weren't offering to buy a pig in a poke?" she demanded.

Jonas's brows knitted. "What the hell are you talking about?"

"You knew damned well, Jonas, what was in Grandpa's library, or what was supposed to be," Carla accused.

"So?"

"So? How can you simply say 'So?'" she fumed.

"Look," Jonas said, "I don't know what you're getting at. We were talking about going to Tompkinsville, I was telling you Jewel couldn't very well drive you over there tomorrow because she has her Hospital Aid bazaar. I was pointing out I couldn't go with you next week because I have to be in New York. Then, all of a sudden, you drifted off into space, and right now I'd hate to put a dagger in your hand."

"Don't be so dramatic."

"*Me* dramatic? Have you ever looked in the mirror, lady?"

"The last thing in the world I am is dramatic."

"Carla," Jonas said patiently, "sometimes I don't think you know yourself very well. I think you've conjured up an image you think fits, but it doesn't. You picture yourself as a sedate librarian type. You see yourself fitting right into the groove that's already been carved out by that gray dragon over in Bedloe Falls—what's her name? Miss Needles?''

"Miss Bobbins."

"I knew it was something to do with a sewing machine. Look, Carla..."

Carla kept her head averted.

"Carla," Jonas said, "look at me. Okay, damn it, don't look at me."

Before Carla knew what he was about to do, Jonas clasped her shoulders and swung her around to face him. Then he drew her close to him, pillowing her head against the thick black wool sweater he was wearing. Despite the thickness of the wool, she could hear his heartbeat thudding.

She felt strong fingers at the nape of her neck. Felt her head being tilted back, firmly but gently. Felt Jonas's lips on hers and swiftly came to learn that her resistance had never been much lower. They clung and kissed, and Carla stood on tiptoe, throwing her arms around his neck and drawing him even closer. She plunged her hands into the thickness of his dark hair and let her fingers rove in little concentric circles as the kiss deepened.

She felt Jonas's breath coming faster. Her respiration rate wasn't exactly normal, either. Desire twisted, and she wanted Jonas with a fierceness, an urgency, that made her feel as if a camp fire had suddenly been lit inside her.

She forgot that any minute now Jewel would finish with the kitchen chores and would be coming along to join them.

Jonas didn't. He was burning up, but he forced himself to disengage Carla gently. Carefully he propped her on her own two feet. He looked down at her flushed and lovely face. At some point she'd slipped her glasses off and put them on a small hall table. Her drenched violet eyes held a sort of foggy expression that Jonas doubted had much to do with her eyesight. She looked dazed, staggered in fact . . . and Jonas loved it.

It took a large chunk of his willpower to say, "I'll pick you up at nine tomorrow morning, and we'll head over to Tompkinsville, okay?"

He sealed off Carla's answer with a quick but—he hoped—effective kiss, and got away before she managed to recover.

Saturday was bright and beautiful. Jewel left the house early to head for the Masonic Hall and the last-minute bazaar preparations. Carla sat at the kitchen table once Jewel was gone, sipping coffee and wondering if she should call Jonas and point out that she'd never agreed to go to Tompkinsville with him today. She soon reached the obvious conclusion that to do that would merely mean putting on an exhibit of childish, needlessly perverse behavior.

Jonas was doing her a favor. Maybe sometime she'd be in the position of doing him a favor.

She smiled wryly at *that* thought. What kind of favor could she ever do for Jonas Wainwright Davenport? She thought about the Christmas catalogs that offered ridiculously expensive gifts for "the man who has everything." The description fitted Jonas. What could she possibly ever do for him? What could she possibly ever give him? She was ready when the sleek burgundy car pulled up in her driveway, and she went out to meet him.

Jonas, watching her come down the steps, thought it was as well she'd come out of the house instead of waiting for him inside. He was sure Jewel must already be at her bazaar, and he didn't think he could trust himself to be alone with Carla this morning. His wanting for her hadn't ceased, once he'd made his abrupt exit last night. He'd dreamed about her last night, and the wanting had come back all over again once he'd awakened.

She got into his warm car, and her glasses promptly fogged. He watched her take them off and rub them dry with a handkerchief, and the simple gesture had an out-of-proportion sentimental effect on him. Even Carla's less-than-perfect eyesight was endearing to him. He slanted a loving look in her direction.

Carla, concentrating on polishing her glasses, didn't see it. By the time the glasses were back in place again, Jonas had gotten a grip on himself, and they were on their way.

Though the predicted storm had gone off somewhere else, the weather had been so cold that everything was still thickly frosted with snow, made dazzling by the sun's touch. The whole winter world sparkled, and Carla said, "We should have a sleigh, and there should be an orchestra playing 'Jingle Bells' in the background."

"One sleigh, two horses, plus orchestra coming up," Jonas answered promptly.

"And a partridge in a pear tree to you, too," Carla quipped, and favored him with a smile he found more dazzling than the sunlight.

Jonas didn't think he'd ever seen her in as carefree a mood as she was in this morning, and he wondered what had happened.

He wished she'd stay this way, at least for a little while. He began to relax, something he hadn't done too much of when with Carla. They'd gotten off on a wrong foot initially, and there'd been a sparring contest between them most of the time since. About the only times there hadn't been tension between them—and resulting bickering—were the too few times they'd been in each other's arms.

The beautiful snow-covered countryside, Carla's radiance, and just being here with her right now mellowed him. The mellowness engendered a kind of nostalgic mood.

"Have you ever wondered how it would have been to live in the days when people really did get around with horses and sleighs this time of year?" he asked her.

"Oh, romantically, once in a while, I guess," she said. Amusement laced her voice. "Jonas," she teased, "don't tell me you wish you'd been a Victorian gentleman?"

"Not exactly," he said. "But sometimes I think life was a lot simpler and happier when there wasn't so much tension and competition and you couldn't span continents in the course of a few hours."

"You would have been bored to death if you'd lived any time but now," Carla said.

"What makes you so sure of that?"

She shrugged. "Oh, I don't know. You seem like the epitome of the modern man to me, that's all."

Jonas glanced at her. She looked comfortable and happy. He had no wish to rock the boat. On the other hand, he needed to know why she thought that of him, if finding out might lead to yet another difference of opinion.

"I'm not sure I find that flattering," he said carefully.

"I didn't intend it to be flattering," Carla told him. "I only intended it to be factual."

"Must you always be so great for facts?" Jonas asked. "Isn't there ever room for a little fantasy in your life, Carla?"

"How can you ask me that when you already know the answer?" Carla rejoined softly. "You're a book lover, so am I. Need I say more?"

"No," he said. "No. In its way that does say it all. Except..."

"Except?"

"Except that you baffle me, lady," Jonas said with a smile. "You could give lessons in how to keep a guy guessing."

Carla was surprised. It had never occurred to her she might be able to give Jonas Davenport lessons about anything. He seemed so absolutely sure of himself.

Was some of that ultra-poise, ultra-confidence, a veneer?

Maybe, maybe not. She nearly chuckled aloud at the concept of Jonas masking a quaking inner self. It seemed highly unlikely. Then, sobering, she reminded herself that there was more than one Jonas. He was a man with many facets, each of them fascinating, some of them formidable, some of them intensely lovable...

She looked at his hands, resting on the steering wheel. He wasn't wearing gloves. He'd mentioned once that he hated driving with gloves on.

His hands were like the rest of him—strong, capable, she doubted if Jonas ever fumbled, whereas she fumbled so often.

But those capable hands could be gentle, inexpressibly tender. And they were also, in their way, tip-offs to the intensity of emotion and deep passion Jonas usually controlled—with the same expertise with which he controlled most things—but which she'd seen flare on a couple of occasions.

Last night she'd seen that passion flare, she'd seen the wanting in his eyes as he'd released her outside the living-room door. Knowing that his desire matched hers had given her a moment of heady triumph, even while the knowledge frightened her. A couple of steps farther along that particular emotional road, and Jonas would soon have possessed her.

She could only imagine what being possessed by Jonas would be like. But she had the gut feeling that being made love to by him would be like being spun out into the far reaches of fantasy, then spiraling into the very vortex of ecstasy. Afterward, one could never possibly be the same....

Carla stiffened her willpower. She couldn't risk reaching Utopia for just one season of her life, only to spend the rest of her years in an emotional desert.

Jonas broke in on her thoughts to ask, "Want to stop for coffee?"

"Not especially," Carla said. "Unless you really do."

"No, that's okay. We'll get some lunch on the way back. Or, we might catch lunch at Jewel's bazaar."

Carla stared at him. Was Jonas Davenport, the man who had been keeping a low profile ever since coming back to Wainwright, actually suggesting they go to the Hospital Aid bazaar together?

If they made an appearance at noon, she thought wryly, by two o'clock it would be all over town that Carla Logan was going out with Jonas Davenport, and the gossips would take it from there. Human nature, she supposed. The combination of a young widow and the area's most desirable, wealthy, handsome bachelor would prove irresistible to wagging tongues.

"I don't think we should go to the bazaar together." She was actually thinking of Jonas more than of herself.

She saw Jonas frown. "Now exactly what am I to read into *that*?" he demanded.

"Jonas," Carla said, "I know you value your privacy."

"So?"

"Well, one aspect of your privacy would be shot to pieces if you and I were to show up at the bazaar together."

"Are you saying we'd become an item, as the gossip columns put it?" Jonas asked, a quirky little smile replacing the frown.

"It's not funny, Jonas. People would talk."

"Does the idea of people talking about us bother you that much, Carla?"

"I don't especially like being talked about," she admitted honestly. "And I know you detest being talked about."

"Who told you so?"

"The life-style you've set for yourself, stuff I've read about you, stuff I've heard about you . . ."

"There are exceptions to every rule, Carla."

"Are you saying you don't *mind* the idea of starting the gossip mill grinding?"

"About you and me?"

"Yes."

"No," Jonas said, to her astonishment, "I don't mind at all."

Carla looked at him and saw that the quirky smile had grown into a full-sized grin. "I told you, Jonas," she said, "it's not funny. Though you seem blissfully unaware of it, your reappearance in Wainwright is the most exciting thing that's happened in town in a long time. It's natural for people to wonder about you and to conjecture and . . . yes, and to gossip."

"Do tell."

"I don't like gossip," Carla stated.

"Well, on that we agree," he said amiably.

It was her turn to frown. "I don't know what to make of you," she admitted. "The other night when you took me out to dinner and didn't want to go to the country club, I thought maybe the real reason was that you didn't want us to be seen together..."

Jonas's smile faded. "Are you serious?"

"Yes."

"You couldn't be more wrong. I told you I don't like having the red carpet rolled out every time I show up there, and that's the truth and the whole truth. I was thinking about myself, not about you. Can you really believe that I wouldn't take you to the Wainwright Country Club because I don't want our names linked?"

Carla didn't answer him.

"Damn it, Carla," Jonas said, his voice deadly calm, "I think that reeks of an inferiority complex on your part, or else I don't even like to think about your opinion of me. Maybe the real problem is that you don't want your name linked with mine."

She still didn't answer.

Heat crept into Jonas's voice. "Will you have dinner with me at the country club tonight?" he asked her.

"No," she said, so softly he had to strain to hear her.

"Will you have brunch with me at the country club tomorrow? I think I already mentioned maybe you and Jewel and Fred and I might go there together. Ah...I can see you might accept that suggestion, because then it wouldn't be just the two of us. Right?"

"Please," she protested.

"Please nothing," Jonas said roughly. "This is something we have to get straight. It's important. Look...*will* you go to the damned bazaar with me on the way home?''

"Yes—no—maybe. I don't know," Carla said miserably. And she was vastly relieved when they crossed the town line into Tompkinsville at that very moment.

Chapter Twelve

The mechanic at the garage in Tompkinsville reminded Carla of her grandfather, though her grandfather had never gone around in grease-stained overalls.

He was probably in his late fifties or early sixties, a tall, rangy, gray-haired man with kind hazel eyes and a gentle, understated manner. She had immediate confidence in him, which was fortunate. If anyone else had told her that Jenny was beyond help, she doubted she would have believed them.

But there was understanding and even—she thought—sympathy in this man's eyes as he said, "You really would be throwing good money away, Mrs. Logan. We could put in a rebuilt engine, but there'd still be so much to be done. In the end, in order to make this car really fit for the road, about all you'd have left of the original is the chassis, and you know yourself *that's* not in the greatest of shape. You need a paint job and—"

"Yes," Carla said hastily. "Yes, I know. But . . ."

She stood, ankle-deep in snow—but this time she'd worn high winter boots—staring at Jenny, who'd been dragged to the back of the lot once her hopeless condition was diagnosed. She'd been covered with a tarp to protect her sorry exterior in the event of another snowstorm.

You couldn't throw your arms around a car, you couldn't hug a hood, but Carla felt a wrenching affinity to her old heap because she and Jenny had shared so much. She'd bought Jenny right after Brian's death, when she'd moved to her little apartment in Santa Monica, and Jenny had been an aging lady even then. But Jenny had carried her faithfully back and forth to college and then back and forth to work. Sometimes, still so very lonely without Brian, she'd actually talked to the car. Remembering, she wondered ruefully what a psychiatrist would make of *that*! Worse, there'd been moments when she'd even felt Jenny was hearing her, and she'd been grateful.

She'd needed something solid at that time of her life, and Jenny had become that something solid. They'd trekked across the country together, not without problems. She'd had to stop once in Colorado and once in Illinois for repairs. But they'd been relatively minor repairs.

Jenny had moved to Bedloe Falls with her, had made the number of safaris back and forth to Wainwright to see Jewel, without further mishaps. Until the night of the blizzard when she'd had to push Jenny to the maximum of her capacity in her effort to get to Wainwright ahead of Jonas Davenport.

Carla stared at him resentfully. He caught her stare and correctly interpreted what she was thinking. "Look," he said, "regardless of that last drive through the blizzard, Jenny was on her way out, Carla."

"If I hadn't pushed her so hard, this wouldn't have happened," Carla muttered.

"That's not so, and you know it," Jonas said sharply. He was still irked at her assumption that he'd tampered with the car, and he hadn't been able to entirely wash his anger out of his system while watching the mechanic patiently go over Jenny's condition with her.

Now, in his opinion, Carla was carrying sentiment about an old car a shade too far.

"Carla," he said impatiently, "I'd say Mr. Baldwin's laid it all out for you. Obviously you could buy another used car in good working condition for less than you'd spend trying to have this one fixed up. It's a hopeless case," Jonas added and immediately wished he hadn't.

Carla favored him with an icy stare. "I realize, Jonas, that you've never felt like this about anything," she said. She turned to the mechanic. "Mr. Baldwin, can you tell me exactly how much it would cost to put my car into good running condition?"

The mechanic sighed. "Why don't we go into the office, Mrs. Logan, and let me run up some figures?" he suggested unhappily.

The office was small, cluttered, overheated and smelled of gasoline fumes. Carla began to feel slightly ill, and her spirits plummeted when she was finally presented with an approximate tally of the cost of repairs.

"Could run into more," Mr. Baldwin warned. "Depends on the labor costs. Might take more time than I figured, which would run it up."

Carla stared at the figures. She noticed that Jonas, sitting ramrod straight on a nearby chair, was trying to peer across so he could see the total and quickly turned the estimate upside down.

She wouldn't have believed it could cost this much to fix a single old car. Jenny needed absolutely everything. As the mechanic had pointed out, with the job done, only the chassis would be left. And the one thing she'd been thinking of doing for Jenny was to give her a new paint job.

"Mr. Baldwin, may I see your copy of the estimate, please?" Jonas said imperiously.

The mechanic obliged before Carla could tell him she didn't want Jonas to see the estimate. Jonas surveyed the figures and came to his own quick decision.

It was never any problem for Jonas to come to quick decisions, whether or not they involved him personally, Carla thought resentfully.

"You're quite right, Mr. Baldwin," Jonas said coolly. "This would be a ridiculous expenditure, and, as you've indicated, the labor costs would probably run higher than you've estimated because of the amount of work involved."

"I'm afraid so," the mechanic admitted.

"Could you dispose of the car?" Jonas asked.

"There's a junkyard over in Enderstown," Mr. Baldwin acknowledged. "We do business with them. They'd tow the car over there without a charge, sell it for parts. Might give Mrs. Logan twenty or thirty dollars, but that's about all, I'd venture to say."

"That's not important," Jonas was saying brusquely. Carla saw him pull out a checkbook. "Let me settle with you for your time and trouble, and we'll appreciate it if you'll handle the junkyard detail. If there's any money to be derived from the sale, why don't you donate it to some project for youth here in town?"

"Fine," Mr. Baldwin said, letting his relief show.

Carla was speechless. Rage surged, and it took real effort to keep her voice level as she said, "Thank you, Jonas, but I'll write my own check. How much is it, Mr. Baldwin?"

Mr. Baldwin gave her the figure. She made out a check, her hand shaking only slightly as she signed her name. The mechanic followed them out to Jonas's beautiful burgundy car.

"Nice," he approved.

"Thanks," Jonas said.

Carla choked out her own thanks for the mechanic's time and trouble. Jonas got behind the wheel. They started off.

For the first few hundred feet they didn't say anything. Then Carla let out all her feelings in a pent-up, "I honestly think I hate you, Jonas. You are the most overbearing, arrogant, egotistical . . ."

Jonas pulled into the parking lot of a lumberyard on the outskirts of town and ground the car to a stop. He turned and faced her, his chin set, his features stony.

"Go on," he invited. "Say it all."

"There isn't much else to say. I've just described your most manifest characteristics."

"Carla, look," he said, "I do understand how you feel about Jenny. You apparently think I'm incapable of caring for anyone or anything, but I *do* understand how you feel. A mechanic who's been in the business as long as Mr. Baldwin has doesn't advise you to give up where fixing a car's concerned, unless he's dishonest. Maybe," Jonas said deliberately, "your problem is that you find it easier to deal with dishonest people. Like the Heggertys."

"You still don't *know* that the Heggertys are dishonest," Carla fumed. "You make your own assumptions, Jonas, then you consider them to be the gospel truth. If you're asking me if I admire that kind of conceit, no, I don't."

"I wasn't asking you, Carla."

"All right. Then I'm telling you. I also don't admire people who go around making nasty allegations with no facts to back them up."

"I'm sorry," Jonas said.

"What?"

"Sorry that you're so blind about some things," he qualified. "Or, shall we say, just plain stubborn? Why is it you can't let anyone help you, Carla? Especially me? Is it pride or the need to prove yourself or just what is it? I..."

Jonas temporarily ran out of words. Carla listened and didn't attempt to answer the questions he'd posed. What could she say to him? *When the chips are down, you intimidate me, Jonas.*

That would be too big an admission.

"Sweetheart..." he said gently.

The honeyed term of endearment was new, coming from Jonas.

"Carla," he amended, "we're acting like a couple of kids, do you know that? Squabbling when there shouldn't be anything to squabble about?"

After a moment, he continued, "Look, if you want me to, I'll go back to the garage, get the damned car fixed, and I'll..."

"Don't you *dare* offer to pay the bill," Carla threatened.

"I wasn't about to," Jonas said quietly. "I was only going to say I'll accept your decision and won't nag you about it in the future. Okay?"

Once again, Carla felt ashamed. She tried to convince herself he made her feel ashamed too often, tried to resent that, but it didn't wash. When she felt ashamed of herself after dealing with Jonas, she deserved to feel ashamed.

Her thoughts began tumbling all over each other. "Jonas..." she began.

"What?"

"I'm sorry. I was wrong. You were right."

Jonas wasn't faking his amazement. "Am I hearing you?" he demanded.

"Yes. Okay, I don't like having people take over and tell me what to do, you already know that. But, in this instance, you were right. I was upset about...well, about losing Jenny, that's all. I know that must seem ridiculous to you. I *do* realize that Jenny is...a car. But sometimes objects can be special in your life. Jenny's been special in my life...."

"I already knew that," Jonas reminded her.

"Yes, I know you did. I'm just trying to make the point that it was hard for me to let go of her. It was like severing a real cord with the past...."

"Sometimes we need to sever cords, Carla."

"Yes, I know that, too."

"Do you want to go back to the garage anyway?"

"No."

"You're sure?"

"Yes."

Jonas nodded and started up the car again.

He was quiet on the drive back to Wainwright. He asked, once, if she'd like to stop somewhere for lunch, and she confessed she really wasn't hungry. But if he wanted to get something to eat, she'd be happy to go along with him.

This acquiescence was made in a rather small voice. Carla felt small. Once again she felt like scrunching into the corner of the car seat, even wished she could make herself invisible for a little while so she could think without being so tremendously aware of Jonas's presence.

His sympathy and understanding were throwing her a curve, not for the first time, either. Every time Jonas was like this, he melted her. It was a lot easier to keep a stiff spine with him when he was being overbearing and dictatorial.

Overbearing and dictatorial. It occurred to Carla that a lot of the time the adjectives she chose were stronger than Jonas deserved.

As they neared Wainwright, he asked suddenly, "Would you mind if we stop by my house?"

The question was so unexpected Carla couldn't come up with a quick answer. So he explained, "I promised Jewel I'd dig out a couple of so-called attic treasures for the bazaar. Seems they ran short in that department. I got out a few things last night, and I meant to put them in the car this morning, but I forgot.

"Anyway," he concluded, "I'd like you to see the house and to get your opinion about what I'm doing with it."

The Wainwright house had always been the most impressive house in town. The property encompassed several acres and still fell into the classification of a private estate.

From the main road, Jonas drove up a winding driveway to the landrise atop which the house stood, overlooking the Silver River, which was shallow along here.

The water glinted over broad, flat rocks, reflecting the clear, metallic color that had given the river its name.

The house had been built in the early years of the century, and the Wainwright who'd built it had favored simple, clean architectural lines. There was no Victorian gingerbread in the design. The three-storied house was painted white; its shutters and wide front door matched the red brick of the several chimneys in color. *Gracious* was the word that came to Carla's mind to describe Jonas's house, as they pulled up in front of that front door.

She'd been aware of the Wainwright house ever since she could remember. It was a landmark around town. But this was the closest she'd ever been to it, and she felt a sense of unreality as she climbed out of the car.

She watched Jonas fumble in his pants pocket for a key—as one would fumble for the key to any old house—watched him turn the key in the lock. The door swung open smoothly, and he stood back to hold it open for her.

She stepped into an entrance of exquisite proportions. A central staircase curved to an upper landing. The prisms of a magnificent chandelier reflected the rainbow's spectrum.

Jonas said, "All the woodwork has been done over. Fortunately, everything was good and solid to begin with. All that was needed after all these years was refinishing. I thought of carpeting the stairs in red or maybe deep blue. What do you think?"

"Red," she said impulsively. "A deep crimson. It would give such warmth, emphasize the chandelier all the more."

"Come in here," Jonas invited. They stepped into a drawing room—at least Carla was sure the room was meant to be a drawing room. Right now there was a concert grand piano in it and nothing else.

"Do you play?" he asked her.

"Not really," she said with a smile. She'd been the prototypical reluctant pupil in those years when her father had insisted she take piano lessons. Later, she wished she'd paid more attention, practiced more.

"I've promised myself I'm going to take lessons once I've really settled in here," Jonas said, to her surprise. "I balked when I was a kid..."

"So did I."

He chuckled. "Maybe we should take lessons together."

He moved on into a more intimate room where there were a few pieces of sheet-covered furniture in the center of the floor. "The family sitting room," he said. "Now, come look."

They stepped into a large room with a central fireplace. The beautiful wood-paneled walls were lined with bookcases. "This is to be my retreat," Jonas announced. "Sometimes I just like to stand in the doorway and picture the way it'll be before much longer. Most of the actual work has been done. I think I can start stacking the shelves any day now."

"Where are all your books?"

"Everything's stored in the garage out back," Jonas said. "It used to be a carriage house, back in those horse-and-sleigh days we were talking about. It's a good, solid, dry building—fortunately."

Beyond the family room there was a solarium with a river view. "My grandmother used to grow all sorts of plants in here," Jonas said.

He led her back to the central hall, showed her the formal dining room and, to one side of it, a smaller room, which he said always had been called the breakfast room. Carla saw that a bed had been set up against one wall, and there was a desk—upon which there was a telephone—and a single chair.

"My present place of abode," Jonas explained. "Week after next, once I'm back from New York, I'll get my room upstairs settled. Want to go upstairs? There really isn't much to see except a lot of empty rooms and some pretty countryside views. Maybe when I get around to placing furniture you'll help me decide what should go where?" he added hopefully. "I picked the colors myself, entirely to my own taste. I don't know what a professional decorator would think of them."

Carla had already taken note of his color choices and liked all of them. She could begin to visualize the way this house was going to look when it was finished. A mansion, to be sure. But also a beautiful, comfortable home.

Jonas led her on into the kitchen, which had been completely remodeled so that the appliances were as contemporary as appliances could be. Yet the wainscoting and wallpaper gave the room a distinctly individual charm and an old-fashioned quaintness.

Jonas, whatever else could be said about him, was not a carbon copy. He was expressing his own unique style in this family house soon to become his home. He *was* unique, Carla acknowledged, and with the acknowledgment came a sweet sadness. From the beginning she'd recognized the separation of their two worlds. And that hadn't changed. But for a few moments, she let herself imagine that they were both walking along the same path in life. She let herself fantasize about sharing this house with Jonas.

It was a dangerous exercise.

Jonas had put the "treasures" for Jewel in a fairly large carton that stood on the kitchen counter. Indicating the carton, he said, "I went out to the carriage house this morning and dug around for some stuff. If I'd had more time, I'm sure I could have come up with a lot more. So far, I haven't bought anything new, incidentally—for the house, I mean. I'm going to bring in the old family stuff and see how it works. There are some good pieces, as well as some rather dull ones. Some things'll have to be reupholstered or refinished, of course. But once I have the whole picture, then I can decide what to add or subtract. Carla?''

Carla had been toying with her fantasy again. She'd heard what he'd said. Still she looked at him, knowing a kind of blankness clouded her expression.

"Something wrong?" he asked.

"No," she said quickly. "No."

"You looked so far away." Jonas came closer. "Look," he asked her, "will you stop by the bazaar with me?"

"If you're sure you're not going to mind the tongues wagging," Carla said reluctantly.

"I'm not going to mind. Just to fortify us, though, how about pausing for a glass of wine? I do have a pretty decent wine cellar laid in. May I tempt you?"

"Yes," Carla said. *You always do,* she thought.

There were no chairs in the kitchen. Jonas poured wine for the two of them, then carried the glasses back into the breakfast room he was now using as his sanctum sanctorum. He let Carla take the single chair, he sat down on the edge of the bed and raised his glass.

"Welcome to my home," he said. "You're the first person to have come into it, aside from the workmen. I'd like to say..."

He hesitated, and she asked, "What would you like to say, Jonas?"

"Well," he said, "I'd like to paraphrase that old Spanish motto, *mi casa es su casa*. I'd like you to know that if you ever need a place of refuge you can consider this a retreat from everything that's going on out there in the world—" he nodded toward the window "—for as long as you might want it. I want you to be sure of your welcome here. I want you to know you'll always be safe here. And..."

He broke off. "I didn't intend to make a speech," he said rather sheepishly.

He'd spoken simply, with a sincerity Carla couldn't quibble with. There'd been none of the autocrat in what he'd just said to her. Rather, there had been warmth and friendship, and as his words echoed, she felt a lump start growing in her throat.

Tears filled her eyes. Jonas saw the tears and said quickly, "Sweetheart, what is it?"

She shook her head.

He got to his feet and crossed the distance between them in a couple of steps. He leaned over her, placing his hands on her arms as he asked urgently, "Why are you crying, Carla? Tell me!"

"Because I think you meant what you just said," Carla said unsteadily, the tears escaping and beginning to dribble down her cheeks.

"I wouldn't say something like that if I didn't mean it," Jonas said quietly. He paused, then confessed, "I've never said anything like it to anyone else before."

He drew her toward him as he spoke. One hand reached up to brush the tears away. The other began to slowly caress her hair, his palm rubbing over its silkiness, his strong, warm fingers gently massaging her scalp.

"You're so damn tense," he said, moving on to feel her shoulders and the tautness of her neck. "You're all wired up, sweetheart. I wish to God you could relax more of the time when you're around me. I seem to have the damnedest effect on you. Certainly, you have the damnedest effect on me ... but it's quite a different kind of an effect."

He stared at her. "Carla," he said simply, "Oh, God, Carla. I want you so much. So much."

He took her glasses off as he spoke and gently set them on the desk. He straightened, and gradually drew her up so that she was standing beside him, the top of her head coming barely to his shoulder. "Maybe we'd better get out of here and go to the bazaar," he said huskily. "Or I'll take you home, if that's what you want."

Carla pushed away from him, looked up at him and forgot about everything *except* him. "That's not what I want," she managed in little more than a whisper.

He looked baffled. He was holding her shoulders, and his grasp tightened. "Then what *do* you want?" he asked her.

Carla blocked out the past, blocked out the future and concentrated on the present. She let herself believe that right now she and Jonas were the only two people in the entire world. That nothing else mattered. That, for now, they belonged together.

"I want what you want, Jonas," she told him.

Above all else, Jonas wanted this time to be very special for Carla. His personal needs were becoming fierce in their demand, but he was determined to keep them at bay until he'd first conveyed to her—with his lips, with his fingers—all he wanted to convey.

He undressed her slowly, carefully, letting his hands play across her body as he removed her sweater, then her skirt. Then he had to fight harder than ever for self-control as she lay before him, clad only in a deep blue satin wisp of a bra and matching satin briefs.

Her skin was like rich cream in both color and texture. Was it as soft as it looked? Jonas touched it, caressed it and found out.

She'd had her hair tied back with a ribbon. Jonas released the ribbon, and coppery, silken tendrils fell free to curl softly around her shoulders.

Her lips were parted slightly, there was a dreamy look in her violet eyes, and, leaning over her, Jonas wanted to make what was about to happen between them better than the best dream she'd ever had.

With his own clothes still on—right now masquerading as a suit of armor, he thought whimsically—he lay down alongside her and started to touch her, just to touch her, all over. Carla, at first, was taut—this, in itself, telegraphing that it was a long time since she'd made love. Then, slowly, she began to relax. Jonas's hands moved farther, his touch deepened. He invaded Carla with his fingers, and she moaned. And suddenly she was reaching for him, drawing him to her and the source of her passion, as long-suppressed instincts began to smoulder and then to ignite.

She moaned again, and Jonas couldn't hold on any longer. He yielded himself to her searching hands, watched her fumble as she feverishly tried to get his clothes off. Finally he couldn't wait any longer; he helped her, until they were together, skin touching skin, Carla's hands playing over him even as his played over her. Until finally the ultimate second came when there was *no* doubt about what Carla wanted, and Jonas gave her himself.

The afternoon waned, the sky darkened, the moon came to replace the sun. Jonas went out to the kitchen and got more wine out of the fridge, and they lay side by side, a thick quilt pulled over them, and sipped the chilled, delicious wine. They didn't have to say very much to communicate fully.

Jonas looked through the curtainless window and saw the stars pinning themselves to night's dark fabric, and he let his love for Carla possess him without reservations.

She stirred at his side, and he put his arm around her and pulled her a little closer.

"Know what?" she said.

"What?"

"I'm afraid we missed Jewel's bazaar."

Chapter Thirteen

Jonas called early Sunday morning to say that Fred would be arriving in Wainwright around noon. He thought it might be wise if they had brunch at the country club after all, though Jewel had offered to fix something at home.

"I don't want Jewel slaving over a hot stove for us after a heavy day at the bazaar," he said.

Carla doubted that was his real motive. Rather, she suspected that Jonas was trying to prove he was not going to shy away from local gossip by avoiding being seen in public with her.

That amused her, but she decided to go along with him. She put on a violet wool dress that was the most becoming thing she owned, made up carefully and at last dispensed with her glasses in favor of the contacts. Taking a long look at her reflection in the mirror, she felt a surge of rare self-confidence and smiled. There were times when it was a good idea to gild the lily.

They'd come home last night to find Jewel in the living room, her "aching feet," as she described them, propped up on a hassock.

"You two chickened out," she accused them.

"We got tied up," Jonas said before Carla could say anything. "Jewel, I'm sorry about not getting my attic treasures to you. They're in the trunk of the car, I'll bring them in now if you want."

"So I can hold my own bazaar?" Jewel teased. "No, that's okay, Jonas. Bring them in, stash the box in the hall closet for me, will you? Maybe at the Hospital Aid meeting next month we can auction the things among the membership. Tell them they're old Wainwright family heirlooms."

Jonas shook his head over that, but he went and got his treasures for her. Only as he was carrying them into the house did it dawn on him that if Carla went ahead and held her auction, Jewel would have to be "stashing" these things elsewhere. Soon this house would be empty. He didn't want to burden her with looking after his things.

Jonas left after assuring Jewel there'd been plenty of room in his own hall closet for this box of treasures, and that he could easily bring them back when she needed them. Jewel and Carla went to bed early, Jewel frankly saying she was bushed.

Carla was glad to be alone. Her mind was whirling around and around, and she marveled that Jewel, so very perceptive, hadn't noticed just by her voice and attitude that something pretty overwhelming had been happening to her.

It was as well the Hospital Aid bazaar had temporarily worn Jewel out!

Fred Morris wasn't as good-looking as his friend Jonas, but he still was very attractive. Tall, sturdily built, with sandy hair, green eyes and rugged features, he looked more like a football player than a rare-book dealer.

Since Sunday brunch at the country club was a major social diversion in Wainwright, especially in the wintertime, the dining room was crowded. But the red carpet definitely was laid out for Jonas. He and his party were ushered deferentially to a choice table for four, and, after they'd been seated, Fred laughed. "Jonas sure gets enough attention," he noted.

"And just thrives on it," Jonas gritted.

"Yes, I can see that," Fred teased.

Carla, about to glance at the menu, laughed. Then something impelled her to look up...and she found herself staring at Skip Heggerty.

Skip was also with a foursome, and Carla suspected that the pretty brunette to his right must be his wife.

When she saw Skip shove back his chair, she muttered under her breath, "Trouble."

"What's that?" Jonas asked quickly.

"Skip Heggerty," she said. "He's on his way over here."

"Damn," Jonas muttered. "It never occurred to me we might meet up with him here. I don't like the idea of his seeing you with Fred..."

He broke off as Skip neared their table.

"Well, Carla," Skip greeted her, "I'm glad to see you recovered so quickly from your injured knee."

Carla bypassed that and simply said, "Skip," trying to make her rendition of his name sound as if she were glad to see him.

She introduced Jonas and Jewel and was about to introduce Fred when Fred spoke up.

"Mr. Heggerty and I have met," Fred said. "We've done some business together over the past couple of years." Carla held her breath when Fred plunged on to say, "Matter of fact, I've been intending to contact you, Mr. Heggerty. I've been wondering if you've come across any more rare books since we last met. If so, I might be interested."

"Nothing at the moment," Skip said blandly, and turned back to Carla.

"We need to talk," he stated. "How about lunch tomorrow?"

"Skip, I really can't," Carla said quickly. "My knee *is* a lot better, but I've just begun to be able to get around again, and I've a tremendous lot to do between now and the auction next Saturday."

"I need to talk to you before the auction, Carla," Skip said tersely. He added, a shade more graciously, "I'll give you a call tomorrow."

Nodding to the others, he moved away.

Carla, once he was out of earshot, murmured, "Whew. If I'd realized we might run into him here, I'd have remembered to limp."

Jonas had to smile at that, but the smile was soon overridden by his worry. This was his first meeting with Skip Heggerty and, based on gut feelings that weren't, admittedly, always reliable, he hadn't liked him any more than he'd expected to.

There was a quality about Skip Heggerty he couldn't define precisely, a brashness, a certain furtiveness of expression, that confirmed Jonas's opinion—which he admitted was prejudiced—that the auctioneer was not someone he'd be able to trust.

"Skip looks a lot more like his father than he used to," Carla said. "Not exactly, of course. Mr. Heggerty, as I remember him, is bigger, heavier."

"I'd say the two of them are pretty much birds of a feather," Fred put in. "I've often wished I'd done a little investigating before buying those books they brought in. But naturally they weren't about to sit around very long and wait for me to check my grapevine while I pretended to be trying to make up my mind about the prices they were asking. Top dollar," Fred added, "but I have to admit the books were worth the price. Whatever else you may say about the Heggertys, Jonas, they're knowledgeable."

"I don't want to discuss anything about them right now," Jonas muttered. "I don't want Skip to catch a word of what we're saying." He picked up his menu. "Shall we order, people?"

The brunch was delicious... but not enjoyable. The four of them were too aware of the auctioneer's presence to be able to relax. Carla was glad when Jonas signed the check. Then, as she stood up, he said swiftly, "Now don't hobble on your way out of here, Carla. That would really look phony."

Carla did not dignify his suggestion with a reply. She walked out of the dining room with her head held high, and was so intent on being aloof she stumbled going down the clubhouse steps and might have fallen if Jonas hadn't gripped her arm.

"Really trying to wreck that knee again?" he growled in her ear. "Look, you don't have to oblige Heggerty *that* much."

"I don't want to oblige him at all."

To her astonishment, Jonas said in a tone so soft only she could hear, "I love you."

Even last night he hadn't come out with those three simple words. She stood rooted to the spot, staring at him while he ignored her and opened the car door for Jewel. On the way back to the house, they were all so quiet Fred laughed and commented, "You'd think from the way we're acting that Heggerty had the car bugged."

Back at the house, Jonas produced a bottle of brandy he'd brought from his wine cellar, and they settled around the fireplace in the living room. Carla produced the lists—both Martha Daniels's list and the one the Heggertys had given her—and turned them over to Fred. He scanned them, whistling softly every now and then.

Finished, he said, "Okay." He reached for the attaché case he'd propped by the side of his chair, took out a lined pad and slipped a slender gold fountain pen out of his breast pocket.

"Take it slow, Carla, and read me the missing titles one by one," he instructed. "As we go along, I'm going to try to put down some kind of a valuation for each book. I can't be precise because, as you well know, condition is a big factor. Do you remember anything about the condition of the books in your grandfather's library?"

"Well," Carla said, "judging by all the volumes we've been through upstairs, I'd say most of them are in surprisingly good condition, wouldn't you, Jonas?"

Jonas nodded.

"What I was thinking about was the condition of the missing volumes," Fred admitted. "But, I guess that'd be too much to ask."

"In my case, yes," Carla admitted. "It's been too long since I last saw any of those books. I was young at the time...and not a librarian," she added with a smile. "A book I liked was a friend. I really didn't care if it was dog-eared or not."

She happened to glance at Jonas as she said that and noticed a tender but brooding expression in his eyes. The hint of tenderness, though, reminded her again of last night. It was proving very difficult for her to be around Jonas while discounting last night. Not *discounting* it, she amended. But today there was the need to get back to business where the books were concerned. Which, maybe, was a good thing. When she thought about last night she felt so vulnerable it was scary....

Fred, she saw, was writing something at the top of the pad of paper he was holding. Finished, he looked up and said, "Okay, Carla. Start with the first missing title."

Carla forced herself to concentrate on Miss Daniels's list. The valuation process became time consuming because Fred not only gave each title a great deal of his thought but, frequently, reached into his attaché case to produce one of several reference books to further guide him.

After a while, Jonas and Jewel got up and went into the kitchen. In the silent periods when Fred was either thinking or consulting a reference, Carla could hear their voices. Jonas's, of course, was in the lower register, and he seemed to be doing most of the talking. She wished she had the kind of extrasensory perception that would enable her to zero in on what he was saying because she had a strong feeling it concerned her.

Finally she and Fred finished with Miss Daniels's list. Fred stood, stretched and favored her with a grin. "I feel like I need to get out and run around the block," he admitted.

"Why don't you?" Carla invited.

"I'm not dressed for it. Besides, I want to get up to your attic and look over some of your books myself. Jonas said he put what you felt were the rarer volumes into separate cartons..."

Carla hadn't been aware of that.

"I'd like to see those first," Fred allowed.

Jonas appeared and offered to escort Fred to the attic. "No need for you to come unless you want to," he told Carla.

She accepted that and let him go alone with his friend. Then she wished she'd accompanied them. Again, she felt sure that *she* was going to be talked about, and she wished she knew what was going to be said.

She got up and started roaming around the room, picking up first one object then another, fingering it, then setting it down again. There was a small, exquisitely fashioned marble statuette of Aphrodite on an end table, and she could visualize it in Jonas's finished drawing room. An aurene powder jar in an exquisite shade of peacock blue, would also look good in his drawing room, while the ruby glass collection would be glorious in the niche she'd noticed in his entrance hall, especially if he did carpet the curving staircase in red....

"Carla, please. Sit down, will you, and try to relax?" Jewel said. "I've never seen you so fidgety."

Carla sat down, but she couldn't relax. There was a whole, high-ceilinged floor separating the living room from the attic, so no sounds came from above. Still, she strained her ears.

Finally Jewel said abruptly, "I'm sorry Jonas is going to have to be in New York most of next week."

Carla waited.

"Skip Heggerty made me uncomfortable, there at the country club," Jewel admitted. "There's something about him..." She sighed. "I wish you'd never gotten involved with the Heggertys."

"So do I," Carla admitted. "But it's too late now to backtrack."

"No," Jewel said, "it *isn't* too late. Jonas and I were talking about that and..."

"And what, Jewel?"

"Nothing," Jewel evaded.

"Come on, now," Carla chided. "What else did you and Jonas talk about?"

"He wishes he could present you with some concrete evidence that the Heggertys are not the people who should be handling your auction for you, that's all," Jewel said. "He's sure he can, given a little time. But he's also sure there's no way you'll call off the auction now if he asks you to."

"He thinks I'm that stubborn?"

"That's not what he said," Jewel said quickly.

"But that's what he meant, isn't it?"

"He doesn't want you to make a serious mistake, that's all."

"No. I know. He wants to protect me," Carla said bitterly. "He wants to handle all this for me."

As she spoke, she was acknowledging that there were actually twin Jonases. She'd become able to pull his personality pieces together into two distinct profiles.

There was the wonderful man, the wonderful lover with whom she'd been last night and with whom she could happily spend the rest of her life. Tender, compassionate, caring, passionate, *that* Jonas was all any woman could ever want in a man.

Then there was Jonas Wainwright Davenport, autocrat, executive, dominating force, *do-gooder*. A man she couldn't live with happily for twenty-four hours.

Was one of the other the *real* Jonas? She didn't think so. *Both* were the real Jonas...more's the pity.

Fred and Jonas came back downstairs, Fred reporting that, even without the missing volumes, Carla's library was worth a lot of money.

"Don't do anything quickly with those books," he advised. And added, "I hope you'll reconsider letting them go at auction—or making a side sale to the Heggertys—until I can do some checking."

"I'll remember that," Carla promised rather evasively. "Thank you, Fred." She added quickly, "I really appreciate your coming up here and doing what you've done."

That was true. She honestly was grateful to Fred, despite Jonas's fine hand in all of this. Fred had, after all, given up a perfectly good Sunday to her and her books. She favored him with her most dazzling smile.

A short while later Fred said he'd have to be starting back to Utica, and Jonas prepared to leave, too, since Fred had parked his car at the Wainwright house and the two men had driven over to Carla's together.

In parting, Fred held Carla's hand a fair bit longer than necessary and said he'd be in touch. Jonas scowled. Carla bid both of them a pleasant goodbye and felt weary and wrung out once she'd closed the door on them.

Jewel suggested retiring early for the night, and Carla was more than willing to agree.

When the telephone rang at nine-thirty Monday morning, Carla was sure it was Skip Heggerty calling. She geared herself to pick up the receiver and say, "Hello."

"Mrs. Logan?" a masculine voice that certainly didn't belong to Skip answered.

"Yes?"

"Brad Shapiro," the lawyer said. "I'm sorry to be so last minute about this, but do you suppose you could meet with me in my office this morning? I would have put this to Jonas, but I checked his house. There are some workmen there, but Jonas has already left for New York."

He went without saying goodbye.

That was the first thought that thudded through Carla's mind. She tried to tell herself she was overreacting. Jonas *had* said goodbye yesterday—at least he'd said a usual goodbye when he'd left the house with Fred—and he'd mentioned several times he'd be in New York on business this week.

She just hadn't expected him to go so *soon*.

She said to Brad, "I'd be glad to meet with you."

Carla arrived at the lawyer's office an hour later. He procured coffee for both of them, then sat back in his swivel chair and seemed at a momentary loss for words.

Finally he confessed, "I don't know exactly how to get into this with you, Mrs. Logan." He gave her an apologetic half smile as he spoke.

"Jonas," he went on, "tells me you're determined to do business with the Heggertys—or will be, unless we can really prove they've been up to some chicanery."

Jonas again.

"I am not being obdurate, Mr. Shapiro," Carla said rather stiffly. "It's just that I don't like to condemn people without some very good reason—proof—for the condemnation."

"I appreciate that," the lawyer conceded. "And, believe me, normally I wouldn't touch this. This case, I mean. The situation puts me in the position of making allegations, when it should be the client who should be making those allegations, and I should then try to prove or disprove their validity."

"So," Carla asked, "why are you touching this case, then?"

"Jonas asked me to," Brad said simply.

Carla stared at him. "My God," she blurted, "are you that willing to go against your principles because of Jonas Davenport?"

She put aside her coffee cup, stood up. "I won't be needing your services anymore, Mr. Shapiro," she stated. "If you'll just send me a bill..."

To her surprise, Brad grinned. "Sit down, will you, Carla?" he suggested. "And let's get on a Brad-Carla footing, shall we? I think less overt formality will make this easier for both of us.

"I don't know your feelings about Jonas Davenport," he added, "but he and I have gone a few routes together, and I admire him very much. He cares. Maybe that's the way I can sum up why I'm willing to stick my neck out for him where the Heggertys are concerned. He cares about people, about what happens to them, and he's the fairest person I've ever met. As I say, I don't know how you feel about him, but I know how I feel about him. And if he wants me to go to bat for you, then I'm willing to do so. It's as simple as that. If Jonas didn't think what we're doing here was the way to go, he wouldn't have gotten me into this."

Carla sat down and slowly shook her head. "Well," she said finally.

"Yes, I guess that was quite a speech, wasn't it?" Brad agreed. "We need to know where we stand, though. Also, I'm fully aware that this is your case we're dealing with, not Jonas's. He made that abundantly clear to me, in case you wonder.''

"You mean that Jonas said if I wanted you to back off, you should back off?''

"Yes. So now the question becomes—do you want me to back off, Carla? In other words, do you want me to escort you to the door and say, 'Goodbye, it's been nice meeting you,' and then you can go along and let the Heggertys auction off most of what you own Saturday. Is that what you want?''

Carla said slowly, "I'm not sure I know what I want, Brad. Initially, this was all to be so simple. I talked my stepmother into putting our house up for sale—she owns half of it—because I want to give her the chance to move back to New York, where I think she could lead a life she's more geared to. Most of the things in the house would have to be sold because neither Jewel nor I would have any place for them. So, because I'd known the Heggertys a long time ago, I turned to them. If Jonas hadn't appeared on the scene, the auction would have been fait accompli over a week ago.''

"Do you wish that had happened, Carla?''

"How can I?" Carla asked honestly. "I'd be an idiot if I didn't see that there's something fishy about how the books came to be missing. There are too many of them for this to just be chance,'' she went on, expressing for the first time what she'd been trying to avoid facing up to. "Grandpa might have loaned out or given away a few of his books over the years but not that many. I know that. I didn't want to admit it to Jonas, that's all.''

"Why?''

"I guess you could call it a matter of pride.''

"I think you need to learn a few things about Jonas,'' Brad said unexpectedly. "But that's not the issue right now. What is your feeling about the missing books, Carla?''

"Either they're elsewhere in the house and we'll come across them; or else they were stolen at some point; or else—'' these words came painfully ''—the Heggertys removed them when they were listing the collection titles for me.''

"Is there a chance the books could be elsewhere in your house?''

"Yes. They could even be elsewhere in the attic. The cartons containing the books all appeared to be together, in one area, but that doesn't mean there couldn't be some more cartons among all the other paraphernalia in the attic. There's years of family living stored up there.''

"I can imagine.''

Brad leaned forward. "Is it likely that a number of rare books could have been stolen out of your attic without any of the cartons having been disturbed?'' he asked. "What I mean to say is, if a thief had operated up there, and the attic's as crammed as you say, wouldn't he have left some traces? Somehow I can't buy the idea that someone went up there and managed to remove forty-odd volumes from a collection of several hundred volumes without leaving any trace of his presence.''

"We don't go up to the attic that often, Brad.''

"But you've been up there, going over the books with Jonas,'' he pointed out.

Yes, she had indeed been up in her attic going over the books with Jonas. Their first kiss had happened in that attic. Remembering the kiss, remembering Jonas, Carla felt a sharp pang of loss. Today, being here in Brad's office without Jonas present, it was like he'd already gone out of her life. Or a hint of what it would be like when he did go out of her life.

She didn't want him out of her life!

Brad, she remembered, had asked if she thought there was a chance the rare books had been stolen. Thinking about that, she said, "I agree it's very unlikely any ordinary thief could have ransacked the attic and taken the choicest books without leaving any clues. For one thing, there are a lot of other things around that would have been a lot easier to steal. For another thing, picking out specific books of value would require a fair amount of knowledge...."

"Right," Brad agreed. "My sentiments exactly."

He sat back, regarded her and said, "Carla, right now I'm going to counsel you... as your attorney."

She smiled faintly. "Does that mean you really are taking on my impossible case?"

"I was ready to take on your case as soon as Jonas voiced his suspicions about the Heggertys. You are not the first person to come up against the Heggertys' way of doing business. The thing is, they're smart... or maybe I should say sly. They know their clients. But some clients are beginning to get suspicious."

She nodded.

"Most, however, are not up on current market values. Maybe, like yourself, they've known the Heggerty family for a long time. It never occurs to them they could be victimized. Also, you see, Skip and his father—to all extents and purposes—actually run two businesses. I'd venture to say they keep two, if not three, sets of books."

"What are you saying?"

"I'm saying that a lot, even most, of what the Heggertys do is strictly legal. Aboveboard. But for that, they would have been closed down a long time ago. I'll tell you his, in strict confidence. Other, bona fide auctioneers in his entire area of New York State have approached me, heir aim being to close down the Heggertys' operation, because they have a very good idea of what is going on.

"Skip and his father buy and sell, as well as auction. I don't imagine they've ever given top dollar for what they've bought from anyone, but that's the seller's problem. More important, from our point of view, is that they conduct a lot of honest auctions. Then, every now and then something like your auction comes up.

"The Heggertys size up the clients. Sometimes they make offers for a few things which they know are valuable, but are reasonably certain their client considers just something else to get rid of. Sometimes there's the more distinct opportunity to simply remove some choice items from the auction and later cash in on them, after an interval of time has elapsed. If the client misses something at the time of the auction, the object can easily be rediscovered. If the client—probably already pressured by a lot of other details involved in a move or a death in the family—doesn't get wise, then the Heggertys are home free."

"I see," Carla said, and she did. But she didn't like what she was seeing.

"The problem is, Carla, we have to prove something concrete about the Heggertys if they're to be caught up with," Brad said. "Thus far, some items of furniture, china, glass and so on have shown up in other locales. But they've been sufficiently unidentifiable, though antique, so it's been impossible to prove they're things the Heggertys withheld from various auctions.

"Fred Morris feels certain the Heggertys didn't come by the books he bought from them honestly. The problem there is that it's extremely doubtful the Heggertys would now approach Fred with any of your books since as Jonas told me, Skip Heggerty saw you together at the country club yesterday. So we'll have to keep checking farther afield. Also . . ."

"Yes?"

"Well, I've heard rumors that the Heggertys, for all their chicanery, have made a few bad investments and also, Skip has developed a fondness for gambling over the years. He hits Atlantic City pretty regularly, Vegas every now and then. Old William doesn't like it, but there's not much he can do about it. Skip's become pretty much his own man. The result, though, is that right now the Heggertys are evidently hard up for cash.

"That may mean some of your books may show up for sale sooner than they would otherwise. They may take a chance and get rid of some things even before the auction is held, which brings me to my final point. Again, you have to stall them, Carla. Don't break off with them entirely, let them think you are still going to hold the auction. But, definitely, not this coming Saturday."

Chapter Fourteen

Carla stopped for a light lunch at a little coffee shop in the center of town, then browsed through a few of the shops on her way back to the public lot in which she'd parked Jewel's car. She'd borrowed the car since this was Jewel's volunteer day at the hospital and she had alternate transportation.

The shops were beautifully decorated for Christmas. Carols played softly in some of them. There was even a scent of pine in the air. Carla thought about Christmas. It was less than ten days off, and she hadn't even bought any cards yet. Nor had she done any shopping. She wanted to get a few gifts for various friends—all of which had to be mailed—plus something very special for Jewel.

And for Jonas? What could she possibly give Jonas Davenport?

Jonas or no Jonas, you'd better start catching up, she warned herself, *or it will be too late*.

It came to her that her admonition did not apply to Christmas alone. There were a lot of big decisions looming on her horizon. Very big ones. The first of which was the auction.

Thinking about the auction, the books, made her think of Martha Daniels, who had alerted Jonas to the possibility the Heggertys might be up to something in the first place, and she made the impulsive decision to pay that lady a visit.

The Wainwright Library, endowed by Jonas's grandfather, was a couple of blocks off Main Street, edging one of the town's best residential districts. It was an imposing brick-and-stone structure that looked as if it had been built to stand through the ages.

As she pulled into a parking space, though, Carla saw that something had been added. A new wing soared from the side and back of the old building, as sleekly contemporary in design as the original structure was classical, yet the architect's cleverness had created a marriage that was a delight to the eye, rather than an anachronism.

Clever architect Carla silently applauded as she took time to fully appraise the united structure before seeking out Miss Daniels.

She found it hard to believe she hadn't visited the library on any of her short, sporadic visits to see Jewel. The problem, of course, was that the visits had been exactly that, short and sporadic. And though, as a librarian herself, she was always interested in taking a look at other library facilities, she just hadn't gotten around to doing so right here in her hometown.

She hadn't even been aware that the library had expanded. Those plans must have been made and finalized and the construction completed while she was in California. Matter of fact, she couldn't remember *when* she'd last visited the Wainwright Library. It was just enough off the beaten track so that one had to make a point of going to it—something hundreds and hundreds of local residents did with regularity.

Carla confessed all of this to Miss Daniels once she and the librarian were seated together in a spacious corner office in the old building. The office looked out on a small patio, snow covered now, but undoubtedly a lovely little retreat at other times of the year.

"Well," Miss Daniels said, "I'm glad you're here now, and once we've talked a little, I'll show you around, if you like. We're quite proud of the addition. Some of the townspeople were horrified when they first saw the architect's renderings. They seemed to think we were plunging haphazardly into the twenty-second century, and they didn't like what they saw. But I'm glad to say now that the finished product's been around a while, the consensus is very favorable."

"It should be," Carla said.

"We have Mr. Wainwright to thank for much of that," Miss Daniels said, and when Carla looked blank added, "Jonas, that is."

"Jonas?"

"He made a significant financial contribution to the library building fund, which is what put us over the top so we could get exactly what we wanted," Miss Daniels said. "State and town funds weren't quite enough. We needed that extra cushion, and I'll always be thankful to Jonas for giving it to us.

"Then," Miss Daniels went on, "Jonas helped us find the right architect. Craig Claymore, the man who designed the addition and coordinated the two buildings so they're amazingly harmonious—don't you think?—is a friend of Jonas's. Usually he doesn't spend time on minor projects like small-town libraries because he's so much in demand for much, much bigger projects. But Jonas got him interested...."

Jonas again.

"How long ago was all this?" Carla asked.

"Since Jonas entered our library picture? About three years ago," Miss Daniels said. "Jonas had started coming up to his house for an occasional vacation—he's told me it was the one place he could get away from a lot of routine pressures—and you know what a book lover he is. He stopped in at the library one day and saw how cramped for space we were, and I told him the trustees were organizing a building committee, but, frankly, they weren't getting very far. Jonas asked if I'd mind if he helped. Believe me, I didn't mind at all, I was delighted. After that, he started coming back to Wainwright more regularly. He had his finger right on the library's pulse from the beginning of the project right to completion. But... Jonas is a remarkably diplomatic man."

"He is?" Carla asked weakly.

Miss Daniels laughed. "I used to love having him drop in at a trustees' meeting—as you know, they're open to the public, but, at least here, it's seldom any of the public attends."

"That holds true in Bedloe Falls," Carla admitted. "I imagine it does most places."

"Well, Jonas would drop in and just sit there quietly, listening and observing, then ask if he could make a suggestion. I don't think I've ever seen anyone with more finesse. By the time he was through, the trustees would think that what he'd suggested was their own idea, and they'd take a unanimous, affirmative vote, which was unusual enough in itself. Jonas just sat back. He never claimed any of the credit. I think he simply wanted to see us get the kind of library we needed in a minimum length of time. Without him, the whole thing could have dragged on for years.''

Miss Daniels stood up slowly and winced. "Arthritis,'' she said. "Old bones. Well, my dear, would you like me to show you around?''

Carla and Miss Daniels spent the better part of an hour going through the library. By the time they returned to the librarian's office, Carla was frankly impressed. The library was comfortable, and not only functional but totally up-to-date. Among other innovations, Wainwright's computerized library catalog was tied in with major metropolitan systems for quick access to reference material. "We really keep up,'' Miss Daniels said proudly as she showed Carla some of the latest in their equipment.

Settling down in her chair again, she laughed. "I like to think I'm pretty much computer literate, but I admit I don't fully understand all the inner workings. However, we have a couple of bright young women who are *right* with it.''

"Did Jonas hire them?" Carla asked innocently.

"Jonas suggested we insert blind ads in area papers as well as professional publications so that we could weed out candidates without hurting feelings—in cases where the applicants were local," Miss Daniels said. "You know the way it is in a small town. Some young girls who had taken computer courses at the high school thought they were qualified, when they really weren't. We're giving them opportunities to learn so if they are sufficiently interested, we may very well be able to find positions for them at a future time. Meanwhile, thanks to our funding, we were able to offer a good enough pay scale to recruit the kind of people we needed.''

Miss Daniels paused. "My, I am babbling on," she observed mildly.

"I find it all extremely interesting," Carla said. She was enough of a dedicated librarian herself to always be interested in library progress. She also was trying to put together a few more fragments of the complex dual character of Jonas Wainwright Davenport. Pieces she wished would fit, but so far wouldn't.

She stuck to professionalism. "We need expansion at Bedloe Falls," she began, "but so far our trustees insist we have adequate space. We just don't seem to be able to get them to see the whole picture...."

For the next half hour or so, Carla and Miss Daniels devoted themselves to libraries and the difficulties of dealing with lay people—in other words, the trustees—who weren't as versed in library science as the two women were. And, for a little while, Jonas was almost, but not quite, forgotten.

With one thing and another, a major part of Monday slipped by. It was late afternoon when Carla pulled into her own driveway, saw lights on in the house and realized guiltily that Jewel had gotten home ahead of her.

She hoped Jewel hadn't wanted her car.

"I don't want to go *anywhere*, these days," Jewel announced. "It's getting colder and colder out. I just had the news on. We missed that second snowstorm last week—it went off in another direction—but there's another one heading this way, and this time I don't think we're going to be so lucky."

"Want me to go to the store and stock up on some stuff in case we do get hit?" Carla asked.

"No need," Jewel said. "I have a freezer and fridge full of food, and they do an excellent job around here getting everything plowed out, anyway. No, the thought of a snowstorm, even a blizzard, doesn't daunt me especially. There's something more imminent on the horizon.''

Carla was brewing some tea. She paused to ask, "What?"

"Skip Heggerty," Jewel said tersely.

Carla looked at her stepmother and saw that Jewel's lovely face was set in tight lines. Jewel, in fact, looked worried.

"I forgot all about Skip," Carla confessed, as indeed she had for a few hours there. "I know he wanted to touch base..."

"I got home thirty minutes ago, and he's already called three times since then," Jewel reported. "He's becoming increasingly irate each time he's failed to connect with you. He said you were supposed to meet with him this morning. He said he came over here several times today, and he claims he's lost count of how many times he's phoned. Carla...he sounded so *menacing*."

Carla, trying to make light of it, said, "Look, Jonas has been giving you a lot of grim ideas about Skip. I admit I didn't like his attitude when I told him I wanted to postpone the auction. Even so, he's no one to be afraid of, Jewel."

"I'm not so sure about that," Jewel said darkly.

"Jewel, come on," Carla protested. "I know the way Jonas has gone on about this...."

"Why do you blame everything on Jonas?" Jewel cut in sharply. "All Jonas has been doing is to try to help you. You seem to have this idea that he wants to run your life, and I wonder if you've ever paused to think *why* he'd want to do that...if, in fact, he did. Jonas is an influential person with a lot of connections. I should think you might be glad to have him on your side.''

Carla tried to smile. "You'd think we were about to get into a classic battle between the good guys and the bad guys," she said, still trying to shake Jewel out of her mood.

"Well, maybe that's exactly what is going to happen," Jewel predicted. "And, believe me, the bad guys don't always wear black hats and the good guys white hats, anymore, but it's not that difficult to distinguish between them if you just *look*. You seem to refuse to look, Carla.''

Carla sighed wearily. There was no reason why there should be *sides* taken in any of this, no reason why she should be feeling that there were sides being taken, and she seemed to be standing all alone while everyone else— her stepmother, her lawyer, the town librarian—were all on Jonas's side.

"I wish Jonas hadn't left town just now," Jewel admitted.

"Oh, come on, Jewel," Carla protested. "Don't you think I can stand up and fight for myself if the chips start to fly?''

"As well as most people could," Jewel said. "Maybe even a shade better. But you're not used to dealing with people like the Heggertys. They fight by different rules.''

"So you think that Jonas should rush in on his white charger, his armor gleaming, and help me out?''

Jewel sat back and gave her stepdaughter a long, level look. Then she asked, "Why do you resent him so much, Carla?''

"Resent Jonas?" Carla asked, her voice cracking slightly.

"I don't think we're really talking about anyone else, are we? Yes, why do you resent Jonas so much?"

"Because he's so damned overbearing, some of the time, anyway," Carla snapped. "Because he takes over, he arranges everything. Even when you don't think he had a finger in a specific pie, you find out he did. Brad Shapiro's agreed to look out for my legal interests only because Jonas is a friend of his. The Wainwright Library, magnificent example of how the old and the new can be blended to perfection, came about because Jonas knew a world-famous architect who normally wouldn't even glance at such a small-time project but leaped into it because of Jonas. Martha Daniels obviously worships the ground he walks on, which is why she tipped him off about Grandpa's books.

"You can see his friend Fred also considers Jonas an oracle. I'm sure the workmen who are doing over his house think he's the best person they've ever dealt with. And his employees probably idolize him. Shall I go on?"

"And what about you, Carla?" Jewel asked. "How do you feel about Jonas?"

It was Carla's turn to sit back, but she didn't look at Jewel. Instead, she stared at a painting she'd been looking at all her life, but she couldn't possibly have said what she was seeing.

"I feel all mixed up about Jonas," she finally conceded. "Love-hate, you might call it. No, that's not right. Fear mixed with admiration comes closer."

"You *fear* Jonas?"

"Not in the sense I think he'd ever do me any harm," Carla said. "I know he wouldn't. I'm sure he honestly thinks that everything he does is for the best. But sometimes...being around Jonas makes me run scared. Sometimes I think that if I were around Jonas too much

I'd lose my identity. His own personality is so strong, I think he'd totally swamp mine..."

Before Jewel could think of an answer to that, the telephone rang.

Skip Heggerty said, "I suppose your stepmother told you I've been trying to get ahold of you all day."

"Yes," Carla said, "and I'm sorry, Skip. I didn't think we had a firm date for today."

"I told you I had to talk to you," Skip reminded her.

"Yes, I know. But there were some things I had to do."

"Such as stay out of your house so you wouldn't have to face up to me?" Skip asked nastily.

"I'm not trying to avoid you, Skip." She wasn't, damn it! He was the last person in the world she wanted to see, but she still wasn't trying to avoid him. The inevitable was the inevitable. She'd learned to accept *that* a long time ago. And certainly a confrontation between Skip and herself was inevitable.

Skip, unexpectedly, gave her a reprieve. "I'm tied up tonight," he said, "so it'll have to be in the morning. I'll be at your house by nine."

He hung up before she could respond, and Carla stared angrily at the phone receiver. "Damn him," she muttered.

"What does he want?" Jewel asked nervously.

"He's *demanding* to see me first thing in the morning," Carla said, still scowling at the phone receiver. "He didn't ask me if he could meet with me, he *told* me, and I don't like that."

"I don't like it at all," Jewel agreed, her dislike stemming from basic concern for Carla. "Perhaps you should phone Mr. Shapiro and ask him to be present when Skip talks to you."

"Jewel, I can't ask a lawyer to come out here and fritter away his whole morning because of Skip Heggerty," Carla said. "He told me he'd be here by nine at the latest, but he just might prefer to keep me waiting a while, hoping I'll then be all the edgier. Who knows?"

She turned her back on the phone and faced Jewel. "Stop looking like that," she urged. "Jewel, Skip is hardly going to do away with me in broad daylight just because I've made him change some plans."

She was trying to make a joke, trying to ease some of the tension lines from Jewel's face. But the joke fell flat.

Later, despite repeated assurances to Jewel that she could handle Skip Heggerty—after all, she'd known him most of her life, hadn't she?—Carla began to have misgivings of her own. Certainly she was not afraid of Skip. Rather, she wanted to handle him the right way. Her way. Which, she was becoming increasingly certain, was not going to be his way.

She was also becoming increasingly certain that never, never, was she going to let Skip and his father conduct an auction for her.

Carla was dressed and downstairs, ready and waiting for Skip Heggerty before eight the next morning.

She let her first cup of coffee get cold as she waited, trying to read the paper only to discover that she couldn't even concentrate on the headlines.

Carla tossed the cold coffee down the sink and poured herself a second cup. This time the coffee tasted so bitter she quickly thrust it aside.

The clock struck nine without Skip appearing. Carla waited a few more minutes, then dialed Brad's office. She was alone in the kitchen as she dialed. Jewel was still sleeping. Carla, waking once or twice during the night, had seen Jewel's light on and knew that Jewel must have been lying awake. She wished she wasn't causing so much grief for someone she cared about as much as she did her stepmother.

Her heart sank when Brad's secretary told her he'd already gone to court. "He'll be phoning in later, though," the secretary added. "Would you like him to get in touch with you?"

"No," Carla said. "If there's anything to report, I'll call him."

By the time the clock struck ten, she was becoming really annoyed. She was beginning to catch on to another angle of Skip's mode of operation and felt certain he was playing cat and mouse with her. He was letting her worry until he was ready to pounce.

Well, the hell with him! she thought angrily. If she'd had any doubts about the Heggertys, Skip was confirming them by his present actions. Jonas was right. She still hated to *admit* Jonas was right, but Skip was making his own case. And, in her eyes, swiftly losing it.

She was staring out the kitchen window at the backyard, watching heavy, dark clouds pushing away the pale gray sky, when someone said, "Hello," and, startled, she turned to face Skip.

Only then did it suddenly occur to her he had a key to the house. She'd given him an extra key so he could get in and out when he needed to, in the interest of the impending auction.

Yesterday he could have been here in the house when neither she nor Jewel were around. The thought struck and appalled her.

She said coldly, "You might have rung the bell, Skip."

When had Skip's smile stopped reaching all the way to his eyes? Carla tried to remember exact details about the boy she'd once had such a crush on and tried to relate that boy to the man standing in front of her, surveying her with a brash expression she didn't like. Tried and failed. Time had blurred the edges of her image of Skip, maybe because he'd really never been all that important to her in the first place.

Now Skip shrugged and said, "Thought I'd save you the trouble of coming to the door, Carla. How's the leg, by the way?"

"What?"

"Your bum leg? It looked to me like you were doing pretty good on it, out at the country club Sunday. I'd have said if there was an orchestra playing, you and Davenport would have been out on the floor dancing together. I didn't know you knew him, Carla."

"I met him only recently, Skip."

"When?" he asked bluntly.

Why did she feel the need to hedge about when and how she'd met Jonas?

"A few weeks ago," she fibbed.

"Davenport wants to buy your granddad's books, doesn't he?" Skip asked suddenly.

"Why would you think that?"

Carla heard her own question. If it sounded feeble to her, how was it going to sound to Skip?

"Where's your stepmother?" Skip asked suddenly.

"Out," Carla said automatically. Now, why had she said that? Because she didn't want Jewel in on this, that's why. She suspected Jewel, unable to sleep, had finally taken one of the relatively mild sleeping pills the doctor had prescribed for her right after Carla's father died. Because Jewel seldom took so much as an aspirin, the pills had more of an effect on her than they did on most people.

Carla hoped this time around the effect would linger until she could get rid of Skip.

They were both still standing, facing each other across the width of the kitchen. Skip, Carla thought, looked like an impatient tiger. Not a lion. A tiger. He was built compactly. Despite his slight beer belly, he was muscular, and, she didn't doubt, strong. Certainly a lot stronger than she was.

Now, why was she thinking of anything like that?

Skip had straight dark hair and dark eyes. He took after his mother in coloring. She supposed a lot of people might consider him handsome. Once, she had, herself. But no longer.

She thought of Jonas, contrasted him to Skip and felt her heart turn over. Skip Heggerty wasn't worthy of being in the same universe with Jonas.

It occurred to her maybe she'd been idiotic to tell Skip that Jewel was out, which would only lead him to the conclusion that the two of them were alone in the house. Uneasiness stirred, but she squelched it by sheer force of will. She was damned if she was going to let Skip Heggerty get the best of her, and with a sudden surge of renewed strength she started to map out a campaign.

"I just made a fresh pot of coffee," she said, which happened to be the truth. She'd been thinking of trying for a third cup to see if it would taste any better than the first two had when Skip had walked in on her. She asked, as if this were any normal social encounter, "Would you care for a cup?"

"Thanks," Skip said, and walked across to the kitchen table, pulled out a chair and sat down.

Carla poured coffee for both of them, carried the cups across to the table, watched the contents sloshing and realized her hands were trembling, though so slightly she doubted Skip would notice.

She was right. Skip was watching her, not her hands. He was watching the way she moved, and his silent scrutiny made her uncomfortable. She quickly sat down, passed cream and sugar across the table to him and tried to start this game playing by her rules.

"What made you think Jonas Davenport's interested in my grandfather's books?" she asked.

"Stands to reason," Skip said, stirring sugar into his coffee. "He's in business with that friend of his who was with you at the country club Sunday."

"Fred? You sold some books to him, didn't you?"

"Yeah, Dad and I sold some books to him," Skip allowed. "A few things that have been around the house for as long as I can remember. Dad had no use for them, neither did I. And I doubt Gwen would have wanted them up in Alaska, so we got rid of them."

Was Skip explaining a shade too much? Which, in itself, could be a sign of guilt.

"I realize Jonas Davenport's interested in books," Carla conceded. "He asked to see a list of titles. I let him look at the one you made up for me."

"Oh?" Skip asked casually enough, but the expression in his eyes was wary.

"I don't know how interested he is, now he's seen the list, but he did mention he plans to attend the auction. So it wouldn't surprise me too much if he bid on a few of the books."

Skip grinned. "So," he said, "his money's as good as anyone's. Matter of fact, I guess a lot of people around here would tell you it's even better."

Carla let that pass and made a direct attack. "Was it the books you wanted to talk to me about this morning, Skip?" she asked.

"Among other things. Naturally, I wondered what Fred Morris was doing up here Sunday."

"He was here visiting Jonas," Carla said promptly. "As you mentioned yourself, they are friends."

"Are you telling me nothing came up about your grandfather's books?" Skip asked skeptically.

"Yes, they were mentioned. Fred was interested in the books. Maybe he'll also come and bid on them—when the auction is held."

"When the auction is held? According to my calendar, the auction's going off four days from now. Just about this time, my father should be pounding the gavel."

Carla girded herself for battle. "I want to talk to you about that, Skip," she said, sounding far calmer than she felt. "That's why I'm glad you were able to come over this morning." She tried to speak as if the meeting had been her idea. "I think we should postpone the auction."

Skip leaned forward. "Exactly what the hell are you saying, Carla?"

"I remember when I was a child people around here used to speak about getting on with things 'once winter's back was broken.' I know I told you that I thought we could benefit by a pre-Christmas auction," Carla said carefully, "but the more I've thought about that, the more I've concluded I was wrong."

"Why?"

"Because we have a lot of valuable things to auction off, Skip. And I think most of them go beyond the average Christmas present, if you know what I'm saying."

"I think I know what you're saying, Carla . . . but I don't think it's what I'm hearing," Skip informed her.

His dark eyes were raking her face as he spoke, and Carla didn't like the ugly light in them. Jewel was right, she had to admit. Skip Heggerty could be menacing. Right now it would be easy to shrink away from him, to feel genuinely afraid of him.

Instead, Carla stiffened her spine. "I want to postpone the auction until spring, Skip," she said.

Skip pushed aside his coffee cup and stood, leaning over the table toward her, anger making his face as dark as the hovering clouds outside.

"I don't know what the hell your game is, Carla, but I'm not playing it," he snarled. "Dad and I went along with you the first time around because we thought you had a bum knee and couldn't get around and needed some time to get your act together. We're not about to repeat that mistake. You've got a contract with us, we let you get away with not honoring that contract once, but it's not going to happen again. This time I *will* get a court order, and I can assure you if you try to lock us out we'll break your doors down."

Carla faced him, her face expressionless. "No wonder every legitimate auctioneer in this part of the country is trying to close you down, Skip," she said.

"Just what the hell is that supposed to mean?"

"Just what I said. They're on to you, Skip, a lot of people are on to you. The other auctioneers. The antique dealers you've been selling to have begun to wonder where your things have been coming from, and they don't want to get in any deeper with you than they already have. Then there are the people who thought you were doing them favors by giving them pittances for their family possessions, only to discover later that you and your father had victimized them. And other people from whom you've actually stolen in the course of preparing for an auction. Need I go on?''

To Carla's astonishment, Skip smiled. But it was a smile laced with malice. ''You always were a cheeky little brat,'' he said. ''But this time around you've overstepped. I suggest you get it fixed in your head that you're not going to put anything over on Dad and me. I can imagine where you're getting your ideas . . . and your information . . . but let me tell you Jonas Davenport doesn't know what the hell he's talking about. My father and I have been in business for a long time around here, Carla. People know us. They trust us. Who do you think they're going to believe?''

''I'd like to think they'll believe the facts when they're faced with them, Skip,'' Carla said, tilting her chin up at him and staring him right in the eye.

''Look, I'm warning you,'' Skip said tightly. ''Don't fool around with us. Forget about the garbage Davenport's been feeding you. He thinks now he's decided to move back in town he's become the patron saint of Wainwright. I advise you to forget about patron saints, Carla. Jonas Davenport won't be able to do a damned thing to save your hide if you step out of line again with Dad and me.''

Carla actually managed to smile. She said softly, ''One hair of Jonas Davenport's head is worth more than you and your father put together, Skip. In fact, I'm doing him a serious injustice to make even that much of a comparison between you two and him.

''As for your threatening me . . . I don't appreciate it, and you don't frighten me, Skip. I don't know what you and your father do to people who don't play your game, and I should imagine there must have been a few of them along the way. Do you beat them up and leave them in some dark alley, maybe? Is that your style? Or do you have other methods? I really don't care. Try to use any of them on me, and I think that's all that'll be needed to put both you and your father behind bars."

Skip glared at her, and muttered, "Bitch." His voice stronger, he added, "You're not going to get away with this."

"I wouldn't bet on that, Heggerty," Jonas Davenport said, stepping into the kitchen with both Jewel and Brad right behind him.

Chapter Fifteen

I'm sorry, Brad," Carla said unhappily.

"Sorry about what, Carla?" Brad asked her.

"Well, you told me to keep the Heggertys thinking I planned to have them hold the auction, and I couldn't hold to that. Skip knew very well I was going to back out. Unless he could scare me enough to convince me I had to go along with his father and him."

"And he certainly failed to do that," Brad said admiringly.

Jonas hadn't said anything, so far. He'd escorted Skip Heggerty to the door, then come back to join the others in the living room. He was sitting on a straight-backed chair, leaning forward, his hands clasped. Carla could read absolutely nothing from his expression. He'd never been more inscrutable.

"That'll teach me not ever to take another sleeping pill," Jewel said. "I thought that if I could get even a few hours' rest, my head would be clearer. Carla, when I think of you down here alone with that man..."

"I don't think there was ever anything to worry about," Carla said, and she meant it. Skip was a bully, she'd found that out, and it had taken courage to call his bluff. But despite his implied threats and his demeanor, she felt sure he would have had the basic common sense not to try to use physical force on her in her own home.

"Jonas, aren't you going to tell Carla about the latest development?" Brad said.

"What latest development?" Carla asked.

"Fred called me in New York last night," Jonas said, sounding almost reluctant about having to speak at all. "He'd put out feelers through the whole rare-book-business network, and yesterday he came up with pay dirt. The three-volume set of *The Adventurer* turned up in Philadelphia last Friday."

"In *Philadelphia*?"

Jonas nodded. "Evidently Skip was making one of his frequent visits to Atlantic City to consort with Lady Luck, and he went via Philadelphia. He made a deal for *The Adventurer*, asking a price that was pretty outrageous, rare though the books are. The dealer knew that the word was out to look for those books. He paid Skip's price, told him he'd be interested in further purchases and so got one of Skip's business cards out of him. Once he contacted Fred, the whole thing fell into place. I think we're going to be coming across more and more of the merchandise the Heggertys have been disposing of illegally. Meantime, *The Adventurer* volumes are, you might say, Exhibit A, and they're being held as evidence. When everything's been resolved, they'll be returned to you, Carla. The dealer involved was aware the purchase was not bona fide when he made it. His money will be re-funded."

Carla listened to Jonas and wished he'd *look* at her.

"Is that why you came back to Wainwright so soon?" she asked him. "Because *The Adventurer* had shown up?"

He shook his head. "No."

"He came back to Wainwright late last night because I called him up after you'd gone to bed, Carla," Jewel said. "Now go ahead and be furious if you want to be. I thought you needed protection with Skip Heggerty coming here today, and I doubted I could give it to you myself."

"Don't try to protect *me*, Jewel," Jonas advised with a wry smile. "The fact is, Carla, I gave Jewel my private number in New York and asked her to contact me if Skip started getting heavy-handed with you because...well...because I thought maybe you might need me.

"Obviously, you didn't," he concluded. "You handled him extremely well yourself."

Carla tried to assess the underlying meaning of Jonas's flat statement and couldn't. Was he relieved because she'd been able to deal with Skip? Was he disappointed? She couldn't tell.

"I think I'd better get back to the office and do a little paperwork," Brad said. "While I'm at it, I'm going to see that there's a court order issued which will instruct the Heggertys to cease and desist from doing business of any kind until certain facts have been determined. We'll take it from there.

"This won't be over in a minute," he warned Carla. "But I think the Heggertys will have the sense not to try to cause you any trouble. Skip's somewhat hotheaded, but the old man's a sly fox. He knows when to draw in his horns, and he's going to keep a tight rein on that son of his, unless I'm much mistaken.'' Brad broke off, then said, "Jonas, walk out to my car with me, will you? There are a couple of other things—not to do with the Heggertys—I want to talk with you about."

With the men gone, Carla and Jewel met each other's eyes, and Jewel said, "Don't start telling me I shouldn't have called him, Carla."

"I'm not going to."

"I knew you'd probably resent it," Jewel went on, as if Carla hadn't spoken at all, "but I felt it was the thing to do. Jonas is the only person I know whom I'm sure has your interests at heart as much as I do. I felt you needed him, I felt he should be here."

"He did have business in New York, Jewel," Carla put in. "Probably very important business you dragged him away from."

"I did what he asked me to do," Jewel said. "You were more important than the business, whatever it was—and I'm not denying his business was probably quite important. But I think Jonas has a better sense of priorities than most people. Maybe that's why he's been so successful. And you were his priority."

Carla frowned. "I wish you'd stop that, Jewel," she admonished.

"Stop what?"

"Giving me such an important place in Jonas Davenport's life," Carla said. "I know you're always thinking of me, and it isn't that I don't appreciate it. But even you should realize, Jewel, that Jonas is a very special kind of person, and . . . well, I'm just not in the same orbit."

Jewel let her annoyance show. "I don't know why you so consistently try to underestimate yourself, Carla," she said. "I only know that you do. However, in this case I also know what you're thinking, and you're wrong. I am not trying to matchmake between you and Jonas. Oh, I know I teased you about visiting more often now that we had a highly eligible bachelor in town, but I was only teasing. Or, maybe, indulging in a little wishful thinking," Jewel admitted. "Once you got to know Jonas, I shut that off. I admit that I, personally, think he's an absolutely fantastic man, but I am not, I repeat, I am *not* trying to matchmake. Obviously you don't share my opinion of him, and that's your business. But..."

Jewel broke off, and the consternation on her face clued in Carla to the fact that the subject of their conversation must just have come back into the room.

She turned, then wished she hadn't. For she met Jonas's eyes and was reminded of a storm-tossed sea. An Arctic sea. They were very cold, an icy blue, yet at the same time they were tormented.

"I just wanted to say goodbye," Jonas said. "I want to attempt to get back to New York before the snow starts. Brad and I paused to listen to a weather report on the radio in his car. It looks like we're in for a minor blizzard, anyway."

"If we're really in for a severe storm," Jewel said, "should you leave, Jonas? Why not wait till morning?"

"I'd just as soon get under way," Jonas said. He shrugged. "I'm used to driving in bad weather."

"Well," Jewel said, "I think I'm going to get out and do a little shopping before the snow starts. It might be wise to put in a few provisions."

Carla looked at her stepmother suspiciously. When she'd offered to go stock up supplies against a possible blizzard, Jewel had assured her they had plenty of everything on hand.

Jewel swept out of the room, and a couple of minutes later they heard the front door close. Jonas, Carla saw, looked absolutely miserable.

"Don't go, Jonas," she said impulsively.

He looked at her, his bewilderment showing. "What did you say?" he asked her.

"I said, don't go."

When he didn't answer, she asked, "Must you be back in New York tonight?"

He smiled wryly. "I'm to be one of several guest speakers at a rather important banquet," he admitted. "But it's not vital. I'm sure they could get a substitute."

"Then let them get a substitute," she urged. "There's no point in your starting out on a drive like that if the weather's going to turn bad."

"You did," he reminded her.

"Oh, come on," she protested. "If you're talking about my starting out from Bedloe Falls, I didn't even know it was going to snow. People coming into the library had been talking about it, but most of the time the weather never turns out the way people say it's going to. Anyway..."

"Anyway what?"

Carla drew a long breath. "I'm glad I started out on that drive," she admitted. "I'm glad you followed me. I'm glad it all happened exactly as it happened."

"That's a rather profound change," Jonas commented dryly. He looked skeptical, and she couldn't blame him. She suddenly knew she had much to make up for.

"I think we got to know each other a lot faster under those circumstances than people usually do," she began.

"Was that good?"

"I think so," she said and saw his start of surprise.

"Well," Jonas said, crossing the room and sitting down in an easy chair, "I'm glad to hear that. I admit it's not what I expected to hear, but I'm the first to admit you're unpredictable, to say the least. In fact, much of the time I wonder if I know you at all, Carla."

"I'm not that complicated, Jonas," she protested.

"Ha!" he snorted. "There was never a woman born who wasn't complicated, and you hold your own with the best of them."

"Jonas, could we please not squabble?" Carla pleaded.

The snort converted into a derisive laugh. "Aren't you the one who initiates most of the squabbles, Carla?" he demanded.

"Not necessarily."

"A lot of the time?"

"Maybe a lot of the time. But only because I haven't been willing to go along with what you've wanted every step of the way."

Jonas surveyed her moodily. "How do you know what I've wanted every step of the way?" he asked.

"You've made it plain enough, most of the time."

"I don't think I've made it plain at all about what matters most to me. Except . . ." He hesitated.

"Go on," she urged.

"Well, except the other night at my house."

Silence descended, and it had the quality of a misty twilight veil. Into it, Jonas said heavily, "I hope you don't regret the other night."

"Do you think I do?"

"I'd like to hear that you don't."

It was Carla's turn to sit down. She faced him, and because he was staring into space at the moment, she was able to observe him closely. He looked tired, for one hing. Fatigue was etching shadows on his handsome ace, and she discovered she wanted to kiss the shadows away.

She repressed that particular impulse and said, "I went nto the town library yesterday...for the first time since was a teenager."

Jonas swerved his eyes, let them scan her face. But he only said, "Oh?"

"Miss Daniels gave me the grand tour. It's a beautiful library, and I understand the people of Wainwright have you to thank for it."

"No," Jonas said.

"Why do you say no? Miss Daniels thinks so."

"Miss Daniels gives me too much credit. The library was a community effort."

"You don't even attempt to hog a portion of all the credit that might be due you—for so many things—do you, Jonas?" Carla asked him.

"I've never been especially interested in hogging credit, Carla. I like to see things get done, preferably done well. I like to see issues resolved. If I can lend a helping hand, that's fine. But I neither expect nor want any laurels."

"Mmm, yes, I can see that," Carla mused.

Jonas frowned. "Carla," he asked her, "just exactly what are you getting at?"

"I guess I'm redefining a few things about you," Carla admitted.

"What?"

"Don't sound so astonished. All I'm doing is replacing what might have been considered negatives with what definitely may be considered positives."

Jonas leaned back and closed his eyes. "You are not making sense," he said, both looking and sounding very tired.

"Jonas," Carla said, "I've been wondering what could get you for Christmas."

"Get me for *Christmas*?" he echoed disbelievingly.

"Yes. It's not that far away."

"I know that Christmas is not that far away, Carla."

"Well...when I thought about getting you something for Christmas, I at first put you in that man-who-has-everything category."

"That was a hell of a fallacy," Jonas muttered bitterly.

"What *do* you want for Christmas, Jonas?"

He looked away. "Something there's no chance in the world of my getting," he said bleakly.

She hazarded a guess. "Grandpa's library?"

Jonas sat bolt upright. "Just what the hell do you take me for, Carla?" he demanded. "I withdrew my offer for your books, and as far as I'm concerned, that was final. What you do with your grandfather's library is your own business, and I don't like the idea you evidently have such a low opinion of me you think I've been angling for those books all this time."

"I don't think that," Carla said quietly.

"Then why make such a crack?"

"I didn't mean it to be a crack. I asked if you'd like my grandfather's books for Christmas because that's what I'm giving you."

Jonas looked at Carla as if he'd become convinced she'd suddenly taken leave of her mind.

"I honestly don't understand this," he said after a moment, "and I'm not going to try to, to tell you the truth."

"There's nothing very complicated about it," Carla told him. "I want you to have my grandfather's books because I think you're the one person I know, aside from myself, who would appreciate them."

Jonas shook his head. "I'm not hearing this," he commented to the room at large.

"I guess maybe I should have waited till Christmas to tell you," Carla said, "but Grandpa's library isn't exactly something you could wrap up with a big red satin bow, and, anyway, I wanted you to know now."

Jonas stared at her. "You're serious, aren't you?" he finally asked.

"Yes," she nodded.

"I am...overwhelmed," Jonas said, a strange huskiness creeping into his voice. "No one in my entire life has ever offered me a gift even remotely approaching the one you're offering, Carla, and I doubt anyone ever will again. I feel tremendously appreciative...even though, of course, I will have to refuse your gift."

"Why?" Carla asked bluntly.

"That's pretty obvious, don't you think?" Jonas asked. "You have a tremendously valuable collection of books. I couldn't possibly take them as a gift from you."

"But you'd buy them?"

"I would have bought them," Jonas corrected.

"There are some things that can't be bought, Jonas," Carla said rather darkly.

His mouth twisted. "Don't you think I know that?"

Looking at him, Carla became suddenly and sharply aware of how many things had been lacking in Jonas's life that *couldn't* be bought, and she knew that he did indeed know—far more than most people—what true value was.

"What *do* you want for Christmas, Jonas?" she asked softly.

He looked at her as if he were in actual pain. "Please," he protested, "get off this Christmas bit, will you?"

"I'd like to know."

"Well, I'm not about to tell you."

Carla took an enormous chance. "Does what you want for Christmas involve me?" she asked him.

He groaned. "Oh, God," he pleaded, "will you lay off? No, I can see you're not going to lay off. Yes, what I want for Christmas involves you. What I want for Christmas *is* you, damn it!"

Outside, it began to snow. Fleecy white flakes drifted earthward. Carla was snuggled in Jonas's lap, her head against his shoulder.

They hadn't gotten much beyond his last statement. She'd gone to him impulsively, fitting herself into his embrace, initiating a kiss that went on to become another kiss and yet another kiss. But she was still aware of his tenseness.

She reached up to explore the tendons in his neck, the muscles in his shoulder, with gently probing fingers. He was as taut as she'd thought he was, and she asked, "Are you worried about not getting back to New York tonight?"

"New York?" Jonas queried, as if he'd never heard of the place. "What does getting back to New York have to do with anything? That does remind me, though, I should at least make a phone call."

He gently pushed her away from him. Carla stood, feeling at a loss. There was so much she wanted to say to Jonas. But the words weren't coming, nor was his attitude helping.

Despite his blurting out that it was she he wanted for Christmas, he seemed so remote.

Carla followed him to the kitchen, and as he made his call, she stood at the window looking out at the snow that was coming down faster and faster. As he hung up the receiver, she turned to him to say, "Jewel has been gone an awfully long time. I'm worried about her."

At that instant, the phone rang.

Jonas asked politely, "Do you want me to answer it?"

"Please."

She heard him say, "Jewel? We were just beginning to wonder about you." He continued after a pause, "Yes, that sounds like a smart idea. But if you want me to come and get you, I don't think it'd be any problem. My car's gotten used to cold-weather traveling." Another pause, and Jonas said, "No, you're right. I'll tell her."

There was a strange expression on his face as he hung up the receiver again. "Jewel says her car came to a halt right in front of her friend Mary Grogan's house," he reported. "She said she thinks she's run out of gas. She doesn't think there's any more than that to it, but she's not sure. This wouldn't be the case of another Jenny, would it?"

"No," Carla said. "Jewel's car is in very good shape."

"Well, anyway...it seems Mary Grogan has convinced Jewel that since the snow's coming down pretty hard the sensible thing would be to stay and spend the night with her. Evidently Mary has plenty of room. So, Jewel's agreed to that."

"Mmm," Carla said.

Jonas eyed her narrowly. "It's a setup, isn't it," he said.

"A setup?"

"I heard you accuse Jewel of trying to play matchmaker and her deny it. But, right now she *is* trying to play matchmaker, isn't she? I'd venture to say she has a full tank of gas and there isn't a damn thing wrong with her car. She's just trying to bring the two of us together. Do you think I'm right?"

Carla's cheeks flamed. She'd never been more embarrassed.

Jonas said, "I knew Jewel was an ally, but I didn't realize she was *that* much on my side. I'm flattered. Very flattered. But that doesn't mean we need to go along with her, Carla. What I'm saying is, if you want me to, I'll cut out to my place."

"Is that what you want to do, Jonas?"

"I'm asking what you want me to do, Carla," Jonas said patiently.

Carla said, "I want you to stay here."

Jonas shook his head. "You are the most baffling person I've ever known."

"I think I need to maybe straighten out both you...and myself," Carla said, knowing she was thinking out loud but, in this instance, letting her thoughts take over. "Jonas, there's something you have to understand."

"And what would that be?"

"You can be...pretty formidable," Carla said. "But I'm beginning to see that what I considered arrogance and aggressiveness is actually a form of unusual executive ability."

"Let me think about that," Jonas suggested. "Or maybe I should simply come out and ask, is that supposed to be a compliment?"

"Yes. You're accustomed to handling things, you know how to handle things and you handle them very well. When you see someone floundering, as at times you've seen me floundering, it's instinctive for you to take over, and you have only the best of motivations. Except, knowing that doesn't always help."

"Yes, I've rather gotten that impression."

"Jonas, sometimes I feel like I couldn't be me if I became very much involved with you because you *are* so strong. Other times, I feel like if I were with you, I'd be more me than ever. Does that make sense?"

"No," Jonas said.

Carla stared at him helplessly. "Well, I can't blame you," she said finally. "I know what I mean, but I can't expect you to know what I mean."

"Maybe I do know what you mean, Carla," he said gently. "I've thought that you were independent to the point of blockheadedness, just for the sake of asserting yourself. Now I can see that you worked for that independence, worked for the right to stand up for yourself, because you *are* so small and cuddly and sometimes look so vulnerable the people close to you want to take care of you.

"But," he went on, seeing a glint in Carla's violet eyes that threatened to erupt into annoyance, if not full-fledged anger, "I learned today that you're extremely capable of standing up for yourself and your rights. I was eavesdropping, as were Jewel and Brad, most of the time when you were out in the kitchen with Skip Heggerty. I was all prepared to rescue you with a grandstand performance, but there wasn't any need for me to rush in and save you. You handled Skip very well all by yourself. Which, I admit, was something of an ego blow, but I'm trying to deal with it."

He smiled ruefully as he spoke, and Carla's love for him overflowed. She said suddenly, "Jonas, there's something you should know."

"What now?" Jonas asked with a sigh.

"You're all I want for Christmas, too."

* * *

They met in the middle of the kitchen, but they didn't stay there. Jonas put on a show of superior strength that Carla had no intention of resisting. He swooped her into his arms and stalked up the stairs with her.

She directed him to her room, and when he'd lowered her onto the big old four-poster bed, he paused to look around and said, "This is where you spent your nights during all those growing-up years?"

"Uh-huh," Carla said.

"Have many men ever invaded these premises?"

"I should refuse to answer that," she said, "except I really wouldn't have any valid grounds. Not, of course, that I haven't had men in my room. Grandpa, way back, as well as my father."

Jonas sank down on the bed next to her, stretched out alongside her and reached out an encircling arm. For a long time they lay side by side, closer than close, while patches of windblown snow curtained the windowpanes.

Then, slowly, he undressed her, and she undressed him, and they made love. Unhurried love, at first, that picked up in tempo and kept pace with the storm outside. And, as the snow kept falling, they drifted off into their own united world again and again, as the night passed.

At some point in the dark, pre-dawn hours, Jonas said, "Martha Daniels wants to retire in another year or so."

"So?" Carla asked.

"Well, I figure that would give you just about enough time to catalog our joint libraries."

"Until what?"

"Until you take over as the Wainwright librarian, of course," Jonas said.

"I see."

"As far as this house is concerned," Jonas said, "whether you keep it or not is up to you, of course. If you think Jewel really wants to move back to New York, we can fix up an apartment for her in our place she can always call her own."

"Oh," Carla said innocently, "are you saying I'm going to be moving in with you?"

"Where the hell did you think you'd be living?" Jonas asked her. "I don't much believe in separate establishments for husbands and wives, but you, of course, may have another opinion."

She chuckled. "I don't always disagree, Jonas."

"I'm sure there'll be more than enough room for your things and my things," Jonas went on. "It is an awfully big house. There've been moments when I've thought I was an idiot to even consider living in it, but now..."

"Umm?"

"I think it's going to be just right," Jonas said, and he went on to tell Carla about all the things he was planning for both of them. His plans included children, and both of them taking piano lessons again and traveling to all the far corners of the world, and...and...and...

Carla listened and smiled into the snowy night. Jonas was being Jonas. Jonas was taking command.

But, knowing him as she now knew him, she loved it.

* * * * *

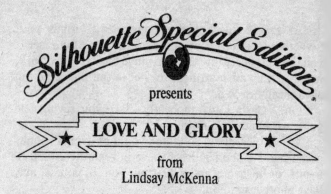

Silhouette Special Edition

presents

★ LOVE AND GLORY ★

from
Lindsay McKenna

Introducing a gripping new series celebrating our men—and women—in uniform. Meet the Trayherns, a military family as proud and colorful as the American flag, a family fighting the shadow of dishonor, a family determined to triumph—with **LOVE AND GLORY!**

June: A QUESTION OF HONOR (SE #529) leads the fast-paced excitement. When Coast Guard officer Noah Trayhern offers Kit Anderson a safe house, he unwittingly endangers his own guarded emotions.

July: NO SURRENDER (SE #535) Navy pilot Alyssa Trayhern's assignment with arrogant jet jockey Clay Cantrell threatens her career—and her heart—with a crash landing!

August: RETURN OF A HERO (SE #541) Strike up the band to welcome home a man whose top-secret reappearance will make headline news . . . with a delicate, daring woman by his side.

Silhouette Romance®

LONG, TALL TEXANS

Diana Palmer brings you the second Award of Excellence title

SUTTON'S WAY

In Diana Palmer's bestselling Long, Tall Texans trilogy, you had a mesmerizing glimpse of Quinn Sutton—a mean, lean Wyoming wildcat of a man, with a disposition to match.

Now, in September, Quinn's back with a story of his own. Set in the Wyoming wilderness, he learns a few things about women from snowbound beauty Amanda Callaway—and a lot more about love.

He's a Texan at heart . . . who soon has a Wyoming wedding in mind!

The Award of Excellence is given to one specially selected title per month. Spend September discovering *Sutton's Way* #670 . . . only in Silhouette Romance.

RS670-1R

Silhouette Intimate Moments®

NORA ROBERTS
brings you the first
Award of Excellence title
Gabriel's Angel
coming in August from
Silhouette Intimate Moments

They were on a collision course with love....

Laura Malone was alone, scared—and pregnant. She was running for the sake of her child. Gabriel Bradley had his own problems. He had neither the need nor the inclination to get involved in someone else's.

But Laura was like no other woman... and she needed him. Soon Gabe was willing to risk all for the heaven of her arms.

The Award of Excellence is given to one specially selected title per month. Look for the second Award of Excellence title, coming out in September from Silhouette Romance—**SUTTON'S WAY** by **Diana Palmer**

Im 300-1

Go Wild With Desire....

THIS SEPTEMBER
Silhouette Desire
Fires Your Imagination With
A HOT NEW LOOK!

Slip between
the striking new covers
to find six sensuous
contemporary love stories
every month from

DNCS-1